# THE
# DRINKER
# OF HORIZONS

# THE DRINKER OF HORIZONS

## SANDS OF THE EMPEROR: A MOZAMBICAN TRILOGY

*Book Three*

# MIA COUTO

*Translated from
the Portuguese by David Brookshaw*

Farrar, Straus and Giroux    New York

Farrar, Straus and Giroux
120 Broadway, New York 10271

Copyright © 2017 by Editorial Caminho
Translation copyright © 2023 by David Brookshaw
All rights reserved
Printed in the United States of America
Originally published in Portuguese in 2017 by Editorial Caminho, Portugal, as *O Bebedor
de Horizontes*
English translation published in the United States by Farrar, Straus and Giroux
First American edition, 2023

Library of Congress Cataloging-in-Publication Data
Names: Couto, Mia, 1955– author. | Brookshaw, David, translator.
Title: The drinker of horizons : a novel / Mia Couto ; translated from the Portuguese
by David Brookshaw.
Other titles: Bebedor de horizontes. English
Description: First American edition. | New York : Farrar, Straus and Giroux, 2023. |
Series: Sands of the emperor : a Mozambican trilogy ; book three | "Originally
published in Portuguese in 2017 by Editorial Caminho, Portugal, as O Bebedor de
Horizontes"—Title page verso.
Identifiers: LCCN 2022053688 | ISBN 9780374605537 (hardcover)
Subjects: LCSH: Mozambique—Fiction. | LCGFT: Novels.
Classification: LCC PQ9939.C68 B3613 2023 | DDC 869.3/42—dc23/eng/20221122
LC record available at https://lccn.loc.gov/2022053688

Designed by Abby Kagan

Our books may be purchased in bulk for promotional, educational, or business use. Please
contact your local bookseller or the Macmillan Corporate and Premium Sales
Department at 1-800-221-7945, extension 5442, or by email at
MacmillanSpecialMarkets@macmillan.com.

www.fsgbooks.com
www.twitter.com/fsgbooks • www.facebook.com/fsgbooks

1   3   5   7   9   10   8   6   4   2

Me?—I drink the horizon . . .

—CECÍLIA MEIRELES, *Absolute Sea*

In times of terror we choose monsters to protect us.

—EXCERPT FROM A LETTER BY ÁLVARO ANDREA

# CONTENTS

# CONTENTS

# INTRODUCTORY NOTE

Summary of the Previous Volumes, *Woman of the Ashes* and *The Sword and the Spear*

At the end of the nineteenth century, Portugal is facing resistance from the State of Gaza, which dominates all of southern Mozambique. The Portuguese Crown, already having to deal with the British Ultimatum, can no longer afford to delay a military offensive against Ngungunyane, the emperor of Gaza, whom the Portuguese call Gungunhana. The challenge is clear: either Portugal can prove that it effectively rules its African territories, or it will lose them to other colonial powers.

In December 1895, a small group of Portuguese soldiers, under the command of Captain Mouzinho de Albuquerque, storm the royal kraal of Chaimite and capture Ngungunyane. Along with the king of Gaza, his son Godido is also detained, as well as the king's uncle and counselor, Mulungo, and his cook, Ngó. The Portuguese authorize the emperor to choose seven of his more than three hundred wives to accompany him. Elsewhere, along the banks of the River Limpopo, they also capture the Mfumo chief, Nwamatibjane Zixaxa, who is sent into exile along with the prisoners from the court of Gaza. Zixaxa is deported, accompanied by three of his wives.

Included among the prisoners is a young black woman, Imani Nsambe, who studied at a Catholic mission and is a translator for the Portuguese authorities. She is pregnant by a Portuguese sergeant named Germano de Melo. It is Imani who narrates the tragic events surrounding the downfall of the kingdom of Gaza.

In this final volume of the trilogy, the African prisoners board a corvette at Zimakaze, which sets off in the direction of the military post at Languene. There, they will make a brief stop before leaving for the estuary of the Limpopo, from where they will begin the sea voyage that will take them to their distant, permanent place of exile.

# THE
# DRINKER
# OF HORIZONS

# 1

## THE WOMAN WHO SPOKE TO RIVERS

*The blind man was the only one saved from the fire. Because he was the
only one who couldn't see the fear.*

—ZIXAXA

*Ask that white man if he wants me to speak to the river.*
These are the words of Queen Dabondi. I don't dare translate
them for Captain Mouzinho de Albuquerque. Nor would he have
heeded such a strange interference, busy as he has been issuing orders to his men, who are splashing around in a shallow stretch of the
Limpopo. The corvette in which we are traveling ran aground on a
sandbank and the Portuguese soldiers have been trying to refloat
the vessel for hours. Some of the more resolute ones, their bodies
half submerged, are pushing the sides of the boat. This is a rare
sight: Whites slaving away under a burning sun while blacks sit and
wait in the comfort of some shade. Mouzinho orders his soldiers to
get back on deck, for the waters are infested with crocodiles.

It isn't the delay that concerns Mouzinho. Ever since we left Zimakaze, the journey has proceeded swiftly and without any stops.
What the captain fears are the dangers of the surrounding bush,
where, even though we cannot see a living soul, we can hear voices
and see shadows moving around furtively. Before long, there will
be an ambush to free the prisoners traveling on his boat.

Queen Dabondi is one of these prisoners. She is even tenser than the captain over this stop. It is she who suddenly raises her arms ordering everyone to be quiet. A shiver runs through the whole of the vessel's crew: As if born from the ground, a crowd of men, women, and children emerges on the riverbank. Mouzinho orders his men to prepare their weapons. An icy silence falls over everything and even the rumble of the river itself ceases.

*Can I speak to the waters?* Dabondi asks again. Then she addresses me: *Have you told that white man I speak the language of rivers?*

A word from her and the River Limpopo would come and lick her hand like a docile puppy. Mouzinho mutters under his breath: *Shut that woman up!* The tension is unbearable. All of a sudden, Queen Dabondi leaps off the boat and heads toward the growing silent multitude on the riverbank.

All eyes are focused on the queen as she crosses the flat waters of the river. Dabondi's feet touch neither water nor earth. In truth, the queen isn't walking. She is executing a dance. The swaying of her hips makes her copper anklets tinkle.

When she reaches the bank, the queen addresses in animated fashion the crowd surrounding her. We cannot hear anything, but we can see that she is pointing insistently toward us. Suddenly, the crowd rushes headlong in the direction of the boat. The terrified Portuguese raise their guns to their shoulders. But there's no time. Hundreds of men and women have already waded through the shallows and are throwing themselves against the vessel's hull, shoving it with their legs and arms. The boat begins to sway violently, the crew screams, and the horses whinny.

In a trice, the boat is once again afloat. And only when they are sure that everyone is united in peaceful intention, do they all, blacks and whites alike, cheer enthusiastically. They help Dabondi back on board. The queen is out of breath but pleased. I ask her why she helped her jailers.

*Someone is waiting for me at the end of this journey*, she answers.

Two days ago, the unthinkable happened: At Chaimite, Captain Mouzinho captured the emperor Ngungunyane and brought him down to the quay at Zimakaze in chains. He was accompanied by the seven wives he had chosen to travel with him. This choice was his last act of sovereignty. I, Imani Nsambe, was also included in the retinue because the Portuguese had chosen me as a translator. Finally, at Zimakaze, the Mfumo chief, Nwamatibjane Zixaxa, joined the prisoners. This rebel was accompanied by three of his wives.

From Chaimite to Zimakaze, the same scenes of amazement were repeated: The inhabitants of Gaza looked on in disbelief at the emperor Ngungunyane bewailing his fate as he was dragged along. The Portuguese soldiers were so few in number that the spectators' bewilderment in the face of this unusual cortege was all the greater.

It was not just a vanquished emperor that the Portuguese were exhibiting. It was the whole of Africa in procession there, barefoot, crushed, and humiliated. Portugal needed such a display in order to discourage new uprisings on the part of the Africans. But it had an even greater need to impress the other European powers competing to carve up the continent.

Proud but apprehensive, Captain Mouzinho de Albuquerque contemplated the hordes packed together along the route. And time after time, the same thing happened: the mass of people broke out in festive cries.

*Bayeté!* they yelled as one.

The captain asked me to translate their vociferations. He grinned proudly as I whispered to him that the crowd was acclaiming him, the leader of the whites. Moreover, their praise was so fervent, according to Mouzinho himself, that not even his most loyal compatriots could equal it. The captain never imagined that more Africans than Portuguese would salute him as a liberator. This was what he proudly confessed to me. And he added:

*Who knows, maybe the blacks will raise a statue to me with greater haste than my fellow countrymen will back in Lisbon.*

Ever since we resumed our journey, Queen Dabondi has remained close to me. It was she who wiped away the blood of the snipe that had been decapitated by a soldier, splashing me in the process. *You're pregnant*—she said as she cleaned me—*no blood should touch you.*

Now the queen is contemplating the heavens and sees the clouds in disarray. She nudges my arm and warns me of an impending storm. Together we approach the captain of the vessel, an officer in a dark blue uniform. His name is Álvaro Soares Andrea. This tall, well-proportioned man gazes at me distantly. He is a navigator. But his look is that of a shipwrecked sailor.

However, we do not manage to speak to the captain. Godido, Ngungunyane's son, approaches us and orders the queen to return to her proper place next to her king. Dabondi pretends not to hear. Godido persists, now more firmly:

*Go and take your place next to your husband, my queen!*

*Queen?* Dabondi protests. *What kind of queen am I if I have to cook with my mother-in-law's pots?* She stabs her finger accusingly at Godido's chest: *Don't call me that again. I'm a widow. That's what I am.*

Prince Godido returns to the other prisoners. He cannot explain the failure of his mission.

*What's wrong with you?* I ask Dabondi. *Why do you disobey Nkosi?*

*I'm not queen. I'm a* nyamosoro. *I listen to the dead and I speak with rivers.*

The boat slows down. We have reached Languene, the last Portuguese military redoubt on the estuary of the Limpopo. Mouzinho de Albuquerque greets the sailors who await us on the riverbank. As soon as we are moored, I convey Dabondi's concern to Mouzinho: A storm is brewing beyond the estuary of the Limpopo. It does not consist of winds made in the sky, I explain. It is a storm made to order.

*My God, how backward these people are,* the soldier comments, raising his hands to his head. *And black women are worse than the men.*

He does not understand how much this offends me. The Portuguese in which I express myself, fluently and without hesitation, has made Mouzinho no longer able to see my race. I remain silent. I cease to speak in the language of the man who humiliates me.

At last, we disembark at the tiny military post of Languene. It will be a brief stop in order to bring weapons and the injured aboard. The African prisoners are led to some shade. They are given some hardtack and a glass of wine. And there they remain, weakened by fatigue. Dabondi once again leaves the group and comes and sits next to me. She has kept a drop of liquid in the bottom of her glass. She lets a few drops fall onto the burning sand. This is to slake the thirst of those who have died ever since the world was born.

*Do you know how I learned to speak to rivers?* she asks.

It was when she was a teenager, she says. It happened before she was taken as the king's wife. Every morning, she would watch a spider crawling in and out of a hole in the yard of her house. On its legs, it carried drops of dew into the earth. It beavered away like a miner in reverse: taking water from the sky and storing it underground. It had been doing this for so long that a huge subterranean lake had taken shape at the bottom of its lair.

The queen tried to help the creature in its watery excavations. One morning, when there was no dew, she left a cup of water outside its lair. But the spider declined to accept her generous gift, and told her with a smile: *What I'm doing here isn't work, it's merely a conversation.* And it added: *I can see how sad you are, you must be terribly lonely to notice such insignificant creatures as myself.* Then, as a sign of its gratitude, the creature taught her the language of water.

*Now I talk to rivers, both big and small,* Dabondi concludes. *And I call each one by a name that I alone know.*

We are interrupted by Muzamussi, the eldest of the wives. She unceremoniously pulls Dabondi by her wrists and drags her off, over to where the rest of the captives are. Then she shouts to me that Ngungunyane requires my presence. I present myself to him without delay.

I kneel before the king and clap my hands, in accordance with convention. The king wants to know what I and Dabondi were talking about. I have no time to explain. *I can't hear you*, the king says. I raise my voice. He shakes his head: My voice is not the problem. He cannot hear me because I am wearing shoes. *Those shoes of yours have too loud a voice*, says Ngungunyane. *From now on, make sure you are barefoot before you come near me.*

I was to be in no doubt: The ground the emperor treads becomes sacrosanct. My shoes are an offense against this divine state.

8

The queens listen to him and laugh out loud. Their laughter sweeps my shoes away.

Squabbling is not just limited to us Africans. Not a day goes by without the Portuguese military chiefs pointing a finger at one another. And everyone, whether European or African, seeks me out to express their grievances to. I do not know why they confide in me. More than just a translator, I am a bridge. Perhaps I am the spider that dwelled in Dabondi's yard. My legs carry words, and with these I spin a web that joins the different races.

During the course of our march, Mouzinho de Albuquerque had already spoken casually to me. Now he sits down beside me, unmoving, his eyes fixed on Álvaro Andrea.

*That fellow hates me*, Mouzinho declares. *I can tell you that not a single black despises me as much as he does.*

The lackadaisical way the captain places his hat on his knees reveals his desire to talk.

*I know who you are*, he starts by saying. *And you know what we want from you. Translating will only be the visible part of your work.*

He pauses, and strokes his mustache. *The kingdom of Gaƶa lasted for too long*, he says. *And do you know why?* he asks. And he answers his own question: *This man Gungunhana knew everything about us, while we knew nothing about him.*

Those blacks seated over there, with their wrists bound, aren't just mere prisoners, according to Mouzinho. They are the masters of valuable secrets, and it is their confidentialities which I shall deliver to the Portuguese army. That is the real motive for my presence on this journey. I clear my throat, fearful:

*I understand, sir.*

Mouzinho rolls a cigarette. He doesn't light it, but puts it between his lips and lets it hang there. I look at him out of the corner of my eye. He is a handsome man. Bianca had good reason to dream.

*If you'll excuse me now*, I mumble, *I'll go and join my people* . . .

*I'd rather you stuck to the whites*, Mouzinho replies. *It is they who harbor the most serious betrayals.*

# 2

## A HASTILY SCRIBBLED NOTE

*The activity of the Portuguese in the Crown Lands of Southern*
*Mozambique . . . may be summed up as follows: In October and*
*November of each year they range through the villages, and at every*
*hut, they collect the tax, distribute hippo-whip lashes here and there to*
*any Negro who does not show enough respect, take the product of their*
*levy to the military post at Anguane, receive their percentage and then*
*go back to sleep for another eleven months.*

**—EXCERPT FROM EDUARDO NORONHA, IN "A REBELIÃO DOS INDÍGENAS EM LOURENÇO**
**MARQUES" ("THE REBELLION OF THE NATIVES IN LOURENÇO MARQUES"), 1894**

*Chaimite, December 28, 1895*

My dearest Imani,

Don't see this as a letter. It is no more than a hastily scribbled note.
Before long, they will take me to Inhambane. More than anything
else, I want to give you some good news: I am free! I no longer have
the burden of suspicion hanging over me with regard to Santiago
Mata's death. In order to exculpate you, I declared myself responsible.
It was more credible that I should have been the one to fire the shot.

My sacrifice did not cause me greater hardship, for another version of events emerged, which claimed it was suicide. I even thought
that it was my republican friends who were trying to save me. But
no. It was Mouzinho de Albuquerque himself who defended the

theory that it had been suicide. And who was going to doubt the word of the great hero? So I owe that favor to my faithful enemy.

Mouzinho, Mouzinho, Mouzinho! When will this Mouzinho stop occupying my thoughts? I sometimes regret this feeling of dislike I have: It's so easy to hate the success of others! More often than not, though, I am suspicious of Mouzinho's recent euphoria. How can someone so fascinated by death be so concerned about his immortality?

What really matters, dearest Imani, is that in a few hours' time I shall be at the Military Hospital in Inhambane. I shall use my disabled hands to exempt myself from military duties. I am hopeful, or rather I am sure, that they will send me back to Portugal. It's not that I yearn to return. My real desire is to find you again. If all goes well, we shall still see each other in Lourenço Marques.

I am giving this note to Álvaro Andrea, the captain of the corvette you will board at Zimakaze. He is an old friend who shares my republican ideals. Through him, I shall also send you a proper letter, a decent letter in terms of length, with indecent proposals between the lines.

*Your Germano*

# 3

## MUD AND SNOW

You men who raised columns of stone, who gave names to
capes!
You men who were the first to trade with blacks!
Who first sold slaves from new lands!
Who gave the first European spasm to startled black
women!
Who brought gold, beads, scented wood, arrows,
From cliffs exploding with green vegetation!
Men who pillaged quiet African villages,
Who put to flight those races with the roar of cannon fire,
Who massacred, robbed, tortured, gained
The rewards of Novelty from those who, their head bowed
Hurl themselves against the mystery of new seas!
        **—FERNANDO PESSOA, EXCERPT FROM <u>MARITIME ODE</u>**

Never curse a place upon arrival. That is what I was taught. Mouzinho does not follow such a principle. Ever since we got here, he
has done nothing but vilify the post at Languene.

*I'm going to have this wretched place burnt down!* he complains.
*This isn't a barracks, it's a hiding place. These people are so scared of
dying, they do all they can to avoid a fight.*

He rails against what he calls a "pack of political horse-traders."
And he warns of a conspiracy of "double-dealers." He uses these

terms with the same fury as when Ngungunyane calls his enemies "women."

*Imani . . . That is your name, isn't it? My question may seem strange, but I need to ask you: Do you feel you belong to a country, a nation?*

He talks to himself and answers for me. It's true that I lack a sense of belonging. Despite appearances, I am still a native, loyal to my family and to my race. And he reminds me of the curse that afflicts twins. Finding ourselves faced with one of the siblings, we think we recognize the other and we thus end up not knowing either of them. That is how he sees me and all the other Africans: We are all twins. Next time we speak, I will have to remind him of my name.

Mouzinho de Albuquerque's exasperation toward Languene had its explanation. The captain had been at the post two weeks before on his way to the attack on Ngungunyane's court. His intention had been to obtain reinforcements from among the sailors serving on the corvette *Capello*. He had arrived there on Christmas Day and had discovered, with a mixture of horror and commiseration, that the captain of the corvette, Álvaro Andrea, had converted the barracks into a place of Christian celebration. Sheets of zinc had been put to use as tabletops and tree trunks turned into seating. Empty cartridge cases and machine-gun belts decorated a tree in the middle of the compound.

To the captain of the cavalry, this Christmas fantasy seemed pathetic. And it did not reveal any particular Christian devotion, but rather a dangerous weakness. If the military chiefs started opting for pretense, the soldiers would soon ask for even bigger lies. For an accurate simulation of Christmas, they needed cold, snow, and the smells of their homeland. In contrast, there was an overabundance of mosquitoes and fevers, and a fetid stench coming from the marshes. And the soldiers were even eclipsed by their packs, which seemed to swathe their skinny bodies. At one point, one of these scrawny bodies fell to its knees at Mouzinho's feet. It was a young private, with a dopey look, who babbled with difficulty:

*Captain, sir, this post is so pretty it even looks like my churchyard back home. And down there is the River Tagus flowing by. Can I ask for your permission to bathe in these waters, which are those of my childhood?*

Mouzinho looked at him blankly. He asked how old he was. Eighteen, the boy replied, but then shook his head. He wasn't sure. He would ask his parents to confirm this, for they lived very near the Languene post in a village farther along the Tagus. *I can summon them here if you want, Captain.* These were the words of the young soldier. Mouzinho reacted as if the lad hadn't even spoken. He summoned Álvaro Andrea and asked for his sword. With both hands, he drove it into the earth, right next to the astounded soldier. The blade penetrated the soil as if there were no ground at all.

*Does this noxious mud look like snow?* Mouzinho asked.

*Yes, it's snow, black snow. It was white, but it came back from Africa like that.*

The soldier plunged his hands into the earth and his fingers were swallowed up by the slime. At that moment, it seemed to Mouzinho de Albuquerque as if the young soldier were digging his own grave.

*Don't worry about your sword*, Mouzinho told Álvaro Andrea. *I'll see it gets cleaned and Lieutenant Miranda will deliver it to you on your boat.*

All around the post, black auxiliaries were packed together, with their campfires, songs, and dances. Mouzinho even considered ordering them to be quiet. In the end he didn't. The wounded lay at his feet, on stretchers made out of *capulanas*. It was strange, watching lives drain away on such brightly colored fabric. The songs drowned out the groans and prayers of the dying soldiers. Black voices fulfilled what the decorated tree had failed to do: They released him from the absurd idea of celebrating Christmas in the middle of the inferno.

Then Mouzinho asked Álvaro Andrea to address his men and give them a blessing. There were only two bottles of wine fortified with quinine. But that was enough to drink an improvised toast. Álvaro Andrea raised his glass but was lost for words, mortified by the childlike longing in their staring eyes.

Mouzinho ordered the soldiers to make space, sat down on a box of weaponry, and addressed Captain Andrea:

*Here I am sitting on this crate of cartridges, but I don't have enough people to fire them. Choose twenty of your fittest, bravest men.*

Captain Andrea looked to the heavens in search of the best words with which to answer:

*Forgive me for being so forward, but I consider this operation of yours . . .*

He failed to finish the sentence. Mouzinho's reaction was prompt and abrupt:

*I asked you for soldiers, not advice . . .*

The dispute grew in intensity and the soldiers were astonished by the uncontrolled stream of oaths and insults. Álvaro Andrea was peremptory:

*If you want to die, then you can die alone. But you're not getting any of my boys.*

*I understand*, Mouzinho snapped back, *you're one of those who advocate for peace because you're scared of war. You're holed up here because like this you can run away. Here's the truth: You only need these soldiers to protect you from your own cowardice.*

*Rest assured, Captain Mouzinho*, the other argued, *the Nation will call you to account for this reckless pursuit of Gungunhana. You are going into this blindly and without support, sir. That's why I'm telling you, and let me repeat it: You won't get a single man from me.*

All the sailors on the *Capello* silently applauded their captain's sensible stance. Andrea was saving them from certain death. And they used the rest of the wine to give thanks to their wise leader. The blacks gathered up the glasses scattered over the tables and sprinkled the sand with whatever drops were left.

*Do you want to celebrate the Christmas spirit?* Mouzinho asked Andrea. *Well, have some kid goats slaughtered and distribute the meat among the natives.*

All this happened some days ago in this very same place. At the end of his account, Mouzinho puts his hat on again, and its shadow once again masks his words.

*Do you now see why I don't trust that man Andrea?* Mouzinho asks me. And he moves his seat nearer as if, by bringing us closer together, our collusion would seem all the greater. Álvaro Andrea, Mouzinho suggests, had assumed that he would be killed at Chaimite. And there he was, alive and triumphant. Mouzinho was a thorn in his pride. How could he deliver the most precious trophy of all Portugal's colonial wars into that traitor's hands?

Soldiers pass by us on their way to the river to wash their dishes. Mouzinho shakes his head and laments:

*A few days ago, these men saluted their captain's wisdom. Today, they all curse him.*

What before was dignity is now cowardice. Those young men had been excluded from the pantheon of heroes, thanks to Andrea.

A white soldier with a dimwitted air approaches us. The captain introduces our visitor:

*This is the only Portuguese soldier in Africa who has never left his home village. Here is someone who has seen snow in the middle of the inferno.*

The young soldier raises himself on the tips of his toes. Standing clumsily to attention, skinny and straight:

*Private 222, third company, infantry regiment.*

I suddenly cease seeing him. The young Portuguese was standing in front of me, but in his place, my brother Mwanatu appeared. The same caricature of a soldier, the same ill-fitting uniform. And the same remoteness from reality: Mwanatu Nsambe believing himself born a white and this Portuguese taking the burning sands of the tropics for snow. I feel like hugging the soldier. I contain myself when he turns to me and asks, at once distant and curious:

*Are you the black girl who speaks Portuguese? Is it true you speak it better than most of the whites?*

I smile by way of a reply. I hope he will return my smile. But the boy clicks his heels and withdraws, propelled by a strange sense of urgency. Mouzinho watches Private 222 as he marches off and comments:

*That is one very stupid angel, who fell to earth on his head. But it doesn't alter the fact that he's one of those angels whose only function is to remind us that we are living in an inferno.*

The soldiers are like hunters: Their stories have little to do with reality. No one cares about this. In truth, only the dead know exactly what reality is.

João da Purificação, the youngest of the Portuguese soldiers, has already forgotten the first of those realities: his own name. For the last year, all he has been is a number: 222. Did he ever complain? Quite the opposite. For him, there is no name more sublime. Unlike the other soldiers, the former João da Purificação has no glorious feats to tell, with the exception of one or two journeys that only ever existed inside his head. Perhaps that is how journeys always happen: inside our heads. The truth, however, is that 222 has gone mad. Amid the wildest landscape in Africa, the soldier sees a humble homestead in Portugal. In each of the blacks, he recognizes a kinsman from his tiny home village. And there isn't a river in Mozambique that isn't called the Tagus and didn't flow through his childhood.

The soldiers provoke João da Purificação in the hope that he will once again describe his demented journeys. And 222 eventually succumbs to the invitations, happy to be noticed, and proclaims:

*Listen carefully, my brothers: The whole world is no more than the outskirts of our homeland.*

*Have you traveled so much?* the others incite him.

*I have sailed so far that there isn't a patch of sky I haven't seen with these eyes of mine.*

*And what is the firmament like up ahead?* they ask him.

*Up ahead, there's no more sky. It's all earth, it's all Portugal.*

# 4

## THE SERGEANT'S FIRST LETTER

*It is strange what war does to soldiers: It asks them to perfect their aim,
but it only lets them shoot after they have gone blind.*
—SERGEANT GERMANO DE MELO

*Inhambane, December 29, 1895*

My dearest,

I am now in Inhambane and can at last write to you in peace and
quiet. The good news, my love, is that they will soon take me on to
Lourenço Marques, where, if all goes well, we shall meet again. This
hope makes my waiting more joyful. The truth is that I like this little
town which is at once new and familiar to me. For it does no more
than require me to sit on a veranda and await another future. I have
lived in various places, but have only ever had two homes: my childhood one and the little military post at Nkokolani. I remember those
homes as if they were part of my body. And I think to myself: We
stop seeing things that have become too much our own.

Captain Álvaro Andrea, whom you no doubt have already met,
is the person who will deliver this letter to you. As I mentioned in
my last message, this man Andrea is an honest Portuguese whose
acquaintance I made during my republican campaigns. There are
few whites who speak to blacks. When they do so, it is to give orders. But this friend will show you a deference, which is uncommon

but close to his heart and genuinely felt. You will like him. I only hope that it is not too much.

Perhaps you do not know why we Portuguese take so much time before we start talking about ourselves. We do this because of the others, the foreigners. We fear they may see us as small. Our true size does not come from geography but from our way of thinking. And there's nothing like a great enemy—such as in the case of Gungunhana—to distract us from our insignificance. The war against the African king conceals other wars that divide the Portuguese nation. These warring men can be found in Mozambique, wearing the same uniform, monarchists and republicans. They hate each other and would kill each other as easily as each one of them would gun down a rebellious kaffir.

I know you are afraid for me, that you fear my impetuous attachment to political causes. Do not worry. I shall not repeat the daredevilry that earned me my exile in Africa. That punishment is at last over, after having been transformed into the greatest of rewards. What was supposed to be a place of exile was turned into one of affection. It was here, in Africa, that I found love. My only country is you. The only cause I have left to fight for is to return to your arms.

You have escaped, safe and sound, from the most violent of places. But there is one war from which you cannot escape: the conflict between Mouzinho de Albuquerque and Álvaro Andrea. At the moment, you must be in the crossfire. My friend Andrea is secretly preparing a detailed report addressed to the Royal Commissioner, denouncing the way Mouzinho de Albuquerque violated the code of military conduct. Andrea has already revealed to me the title of this explosive document: *Report on the Abuses of the Military Code Committed During the Capture of Gungunhana*. What wouldn't some sectors of the press in Portugal give to gain access to such a report?

I beg you, my love, to help Álvaro conclude his mission. Mouzinho needs to be unmasked with the greatest urgency. That peacock in a uniform needs to learn that there is only one criterion for measuring the greatness of a military commander: the way he treats the vanquished.

The emblematic image of our war in Africa is that of a dandified hussar mounted on his horse. But the military campaigns in Africa were won on the rivers, riding waves, negotiating rapids and narrow channels. No one talks of these battles. Now, there is no one who isn't aware of the deeds of Mouzinho de Albuquerque. And yet Álvaro Andrea also has good claims to glory. His boat, the corvette *Capello*, was part of the so-called Limpopo squadron. For three months, it bombarded the banks of the Limpopo. If the British gave the Portuguese an ultimatum, we also imposed a deadline for the surrender of chiefs loyal to Gungunhana. When they failed to respect our demands, the riverside villages were strafed with artillery and machine-gun fire. And land operations followed. The sailors disembarked and attacked enemy villages.

The campaign on the River Limpopo produced the desired result: Gradually, the local chiefs began to surrender. Not a day went by when they did not present themselves, weakened and submissive. Some of them fell to their knees and mumbled despairingly: *Here we are, we are the king of Portugal's wives.* There was no doubt a mistranslation here. Only you would be able to correct the mistake. The truth is that even Gungunhana sent messengers to negotiate his surrender. By then, the emperor of Gaza had already been vanquished, and had accepted his defeat when he was captured in Chaimite. Mouzinho broke down doors that were already open.

What is certain, my darling, is that life is capricious and we are not satisfied with facts alone. People love a good story. In war, it is not only armies that confront each other. Stories are also in confrontation. And Mouzinho's story is far better than Álvaro Andrea's. It does not matter whether the cavalry officer's story is untrue. His version has heroes in it. And those heroes are us.

The same thing happens with love: Unlike me, Álvaro Andrea does not have a sweetheart to brighten his existence. There is no one waiting for him at the end of his journey. Perhaps you can help him. More than languages, you know how to translate the secrets of the black continent. The whites don't just seek to understand other languages. They want to shed their fear.

*Ever yours,*
*Germano de Melo*

P.S. You will find my handwriting more clumsy than usual. You cannot imagine the storm that is raging here. Only a little while ago, a lightning flash demolished a coconut tree just a few meters from the house. The fruits blazed like lumps of coal.

During the sudden moments of clarity, I see women running down to the river. They shed their clothes as they go, casting aside their loincloths along the paths. The sound of their laughter mingles with the noise of the river water as the darkness hinders my vision once again. Then the women reemerge just as they dive naked into the dark waters. I sit contemplating this and remember it was in a river that we first kissed.

I do not know what else to say. What matters in these letters is not their length. What matters most is that in writing them, your presence is rendered as real as the hands I write with. The ink flows dark and you emerge from the paper in fleeting moments of light.

# 5

## SWALLOWS AND CROCODILES

The rain sensed the young virgin's smell
and with its hot breath invaded the house.

It penetrated the cracks in the door
feigning mist.

And so, in this shapeless form,
the rain seduced the girl and caused her to dream.

In her dreams, the girl saw a cloud hovering.
The cloud knelt down at the door of her house,
so that she could climb up onto its back.

And both the girl and the rain, spent the night on this bed.
That was when the heavens plummeted along with the gods.
And the whole earth was suffused in perfume.

There is a smell of rain, men say.
But they do not know where this perfume is born.
**—DABONDI'S WORDS**

It has been an hour since we left the post at Languene and the corvette *Capello* has made little progress toward the mouth of the Limpopo. Dabondi's omen came true: A storm burst over us, turning
the river into a sheet of waves and foam. Standing in the bows, his

hand shading his eyes, Captain Álvaro Soares Andrea scans the horizon. Swirls of fine dust lash his face darkened by the sun.

The captain's broad shoulders hide the whole ocean. His eyes are narrowed and his gaze inquisitive but sure. And yet this Portuguese navigator hesitates: In the heat of the tropics, nothing is as it seems. How many times, in the harsh African landscape, has the sky surprised him by emerging from the ground? How many times has he felt a gust from the inferno, igniting shapes of ash and fire?

And now, standing at his ship's prow, his hand shading his eyes, the captain senses that the boat is asking him to interrupt the journey. Designed in modern England, the corvette never learned to confront the monsters that cause it to rear up like a deranged colt.

The captain has further reasons to be prudent: Never before has the Portuguese Navy transported such valuable cargo. These prisoners must arrive, safe and sound, at the port of Xai-Xai, where they will be transferred to the *Neves Ferreira*, a much larger vessel. This is the ship that will take them to Lourenço Marques. There, a public ceremony will be arranged in order to display these trophies of war. Finally, the blacks will be taken to Lisbon. When they reach the Portuguese capital, they will be paraded even more ostentatiously.

I am aware of what will happen to the prisoners. But I know nothing of my own fate. Nor do I know what will happen to Germano de Melo. I am moved by one certainty as I caress the curve of my belly: I, Imani Nsambe, am going to be a mother. And Germano is this child's father. We shall meet again somewhere, and we shall be happy.

Behind us lies Zimakaze, where we boarded, and the military post at Languene. The captives left their lives behind on the other side of the river. I am the only one with nowhere to leave my past.

Álvaro Andrea stands at the prow like an irreverent angel, watching God's imperfections. The contour of the coast, impossible to map, is proof that the universe is no more than a rough sketch.

*So what is it that you can see, Captain?* Mouzinho asks.

Andrea takes his time to answer. He contemplates the waves, which blindly break and then disappear into a dark abyss.

*What can I see? I don't know. I see swallows.*

*Swallows?* Mouzinho asks, astonished.

*They say Gungunhana hates those birds as much as he fears the ocean. I've already asked him the reason for his hatred.*

*Let me give you a word of advice, Captain: Don't ask these people anything,* Mouzinho warns. *It's a twofold mistake. First, because they'll lie to you when they answer. And then because by speaking to them, you are giving them an importance that may prove dangerous to us.*

*One of the queens told me that swallows are not birds. They are messengers. We must heed the message they bring us.*

*Nonsense, my dear Andrea. And more nonsensical still is the person who listens to them.*

The journey to Xai-Xai was supposed to take two days. But the sudden storm has hindered the vessel's progress and this has left Mouzinho de Albuquerque on edge. For the cavalry captain, there is no time to lose: Glory awaits him in Lourenço Marques. A choppy estuary is not going to postpone the celebration of his deeds. He is used to issuing orders, and finds it difficult to adopt a solicitous tone of voice. *Keep going, Captain Andrea, this boat was made to ride storms.*

Álvaro Andrea turns to face Mouzinho's haughty gaze and then replies bitterly:

*You, sir, may give your horse orders, but here, I'm the one in command.*

Mouzinho could resolve the argument in one fell swoop by making use of his rank. Apart from being a captain, he is now Military Governor of Gaza. But he prefers to assume a more diplomatic tone. There are prisoners who are eyeing each other, puzzled by the dissension between the white chiefs. Huddled among his baggage, Ngungunyane believes that he is the subject of their altercation. The Portuguese, he fears, are discussing his summary execution.

*Do you know why I captured the Vátua chief so easily?* Mouzinho asks the ship's captain.

At the precise moment of his capture, Mouzinho explains, Ngungunyane's warriors imagined that the platoon facing them was no more than a small detachment of a vast army that surrounded them just over the horizon.

*That's why I'm telling you, my dear Andrea,* Mouzinho concludes, *never place your trust in the horizon.*

There are other reasons why they should make haste: A boat at a standstill in the middle of the estuary may encourage the riverside population to rebel. This is Mouzinho's worry. The blacks who before rejoiced in Ngungunyane's detention may now want their king back. Captain Andrea contests this view: He will remain loyal to the commitments he undertook.

*What commitments?* Mouzinho inquires.

Captain Mouzinho should not forget that long before the capture of Ngungunyane, local chiefs had declared their loyalty to Portugal. They had sworn an oath to him, Álvaro Andrea. He, for his part, had promised them all that, if the emperor were to surrender, there would be no retaliation. The royal family would be respected and the king treated with dignity. These were his commitments.

*The blacks swore an oath?* Mouzinho asks with ill-disguised irony. *Well, I can assure you, my dear Andrea: None of those blacks remembers the oath, just as no white will ever come to know of your moral commitments.*

Andrea accepts the insult without retort. He looks at me as if seeking a translation for his silence. Mouzinho spoke of the horizon. He shouldn't have chosen the topic. After crossing so many oceans, navigators learn to deal with mists and mirages. When it comes to horizons, Captain Andrea is an expert.

With the help of binoculars, Mouzinho starts exploring the riverbank. He is apprehensive: Even if they decide to continue their journey, the vessel would move laboriously through the shallows of the river, and its rear paddle could not match his horse Mike's swift turn of speed, in the event of their having to make a quick getaway. And apart from this, the cannon and machine guns installed on the quarterdeck are cumbersome to manage. Mouzinho doesn't want to picture a deadly storm of arrows falling on the vessel and, worse still, killing the prisoner who has to arrive in Lisbon hale and hearty. It would be an irony of destiny: The enemy he had banked on killing is the same one he now has to protect, at the risk of losing his own life.

*My dear Andrea,* Mouzinho declares, *you probably think I am hellbent on receiving my accolade in Lourenço Marques. But you can be sure: I am in a hurry to get away from these muddy waters because I have just lost one of my men in them. Or don't you remember?*

It was impossible to forget: The voyage had barely got under-way when the soldier, João da Purificação, that boy I had known as 222, was sent to fetch water in order to feed the boiler. As he plunged the bucket into the river, the young fellow fell into the waters and was immediately dragged away by a huge crocodile. Life buoys were thrown into the water from the ship in vain, there were desperate cries, and objects hurled against the monstrous bulk. They expected 222 to put up a desperate struggle, crazily churning the water with his arms. But no. The soldier accepted his terrible fate with the con-tentment of someone returning home. Time after time, his pale face broke the surface, open eyes contemplating us with childlike re-pose. Until 222 spun round slowly and vanished into the murky waters of the Limpopo. Despite repeated efforts, the body was never found. And no one ever recalled him by his number. Only after his death did the soldier gain a right to a name. For me, that name could have been João or Mwanatu. Both died in the water's embrace, buried in the belly of the river.

With all hope of recuperating the body gone, the boat's great paddle began to turn again like a fairground carousel. The water lilies, with their large leaves and extravagant flowers, were hurled into the air as if stirred up by some invisible crocodile. The vessel was a plow and was tearing up the roots of the river itself. The sound of the blades—"feque-feque-feque"—was reflected in the name given to that boat by the local people: *mafekefeke*. The water lilies reminded me of the song my late mother used to sing, which filled the house: . . . *the flowers that grow in the water are made of rain.*

*He committed suicide*, Mouzinho concluded.

For us blacks, that was an unnatural death. The treacherous crocodile belonged to someone and was carrying out a request. What was frightening about the creature wasn't the wild beast in it, but the human.

Dabondi stepped forward and, falling to her knees in front of

Mouzinho, mumbled some monologue in Zulu. For a moment, all that could be heard was a prayer uttered in a language the whites couldn't understand. Mouzinho interrupted her litany. Then he ordered that the queen should be moved away to the prisoners' corner. When the order had been carried out, the Portuguese asked me:

*Was that goddamn woman praying for the unfortunate soldier or giving thanks to the crocodile?*

*That man who died . . .*

*That man didn't die*, Mouzinho corrected me. *He killed himself.*

*That soldier reminds me of my brother who was shot dead by a Portuguese soldier.* No sooner did I speak than I regretted it.

*What was his name?* asked Mouzinho.

*My brother?*

*No. What was the name of the man who killed your brother?*

*Santiago Mata*, I replied. *And it was I who killed Santiago.*

*You're mistaken*, Mouzinho declared. *Santiago chose his fate.*

# 6

## THE SERGEANT'S SECOND LETTER

*My stories are so ancient that whoever listens to them disappears. No
one is frightened by this, for when the next silence occurs, everyone
reappears. That is why I continue to recount my tales in the gentlest
of whispers. I am scared of getting Time entangled, and
so hindering the return of the bewitched.*
—DABONDI'S WORDS

*Inhambane, December 30, 1895*

My dearest,

I wrote the last letter in the glimmer of lightning flashes. As I was
writing, an absurd thought occurred to me: In order to get to know
you, I had to experience a kind of blindness. Now I only see through
your eyes, I only have hands when I am your body. I remember that
stormy night, and I no longer find that thought so absurd. I only wish
the days would go by with the speed of a spark. I would not have to
wait any longer: At the next flash you would once again be in my arms.
In these African tropics, however, time is sluggish and days crawl by
like languid snakes. Without being able to touch you, all I have at my
disposal are two half hands, and once again I suffer the defect resulting
from the shot you so recently fired. In that instant, you opted to sacrifice me in order to save your brother. I do not take offense. Quite the
opposite; that choice reflects the magnitude of your soul.

My previous letter is already with Álvaro Andrea. The messenger assured me he had delivered it to the Languene military post days before you sailed. I cannot imagine the captain did not give it to you immediately. Why don't you answer me, Imani?

In love letters, the greatest happiness is to receive an answer before one has written them. Maybe that is why I started this letter countless times, and each time, I let it fall on the floor. My bare feet wrote the words that were never sent to you. I never pick up these rough drafts. I leave them as orphans on the dusty floor. They are a mat, which I have stitched together for your return. I spend my time treading words just as we tread grapes in my homeland in order that wine may be born.

I reread what I have just written and think to myself: This is all so maudlin, a silly outburst disguised as poetry. The fact is that I have become addicted to these fantasies, like a drunkard clutching an already empty bottle. If all goes well, this letter will not fall to the ground. It will be delivered into Captain Álvaro Andrea's hands the moment he reaches Xai-Xai. It is strange: The first letter was also given to him on a quay, the one at Zimakaze. Each of these missives has been entrusted to a sailor rather than a postman.

It has occurred to me that the captain simply forgot to give you the letter. Knowing him as I do, I can imagine that he is so fired up against Mouzinho that he has become blind to any other obligations. In spite of everything, I can understand what fuels these petty resentments. What is there left for a soldier when the war is over? What survives from a time that one can never forget?

The truth is that those two officers are like chalk and cheese. Mouzinho is a man who is loyal to the monarchy and proud of his pure, timeless Portuguese pedigree. Álvaro Andrea is a republican of Italian origin. His grandfather was a Genoese mariner and his roots are spread between the sea and the land. Mouzinho and Andrea will compete for your complicity in their own private dispute. But you will have no choice. Andrea is a friend. Mouzinho is an ally. Andrea is the commander of the boat. Mouzinho is the commander of the voyage.

The worst thing of all, my love, is that the war in Mozambique is not over. That's why they are taking you as a translator. Their hope is that you will do more than translate. They want you to become a spy in the service of the Portuguese Crown. And that is what haunts me. As you smuggle valuable secrets, you will face serious risks. All this keeps me awake at night. But then, the next day, I come to my senses and decide that you are free of these imagined dangers. After all, only the highest echelons of the Portuguese authorities have been told of your mission. It is very unlikely that anyone will discover your true identity among the Portuguese. None of the prisoners (with the exception of Godido) can speak a word of Portuguese. And even if Godido were to denounce you, who would believe him?

My love, this will be your first voyage across the sea. A year ago, I made the same journey in the opposite direction: from Portugal to Mozambique. It was two long months on a ship. During that time, I learned the following: It isn't just the vessel that is moving across the ocean. It is the souls of the passengers that are in transit and blending together beyond races and nations. I am one of the privileged in this world, one of the few who undertook this other journey. And it wasn't on the sea that I traveled. It was through you that I crossed borders separating me from myself. My eyes are blue so that you may cross me as if I were water.

If it is any consolation, you should consider that your journey hasn't just begun. You have been emigrating from yourself ever since you were a child. Think of the advantages of this involuntary journey: In that other country, which is mine by birth, we shall start a new life together. This is my greatest desire. But I do not want you to experience what I have seen happen to other African women in Portugal. I will not have you humiliated. You will be Imani de Melo. You will be a wife, my wife.

*Germano de Melo*

# 7

## A MANUAL FOR MOTHERS

*Injuries and ruins are not the most serious legacy of war. It is the victors
who are the worst legacy. The victors believe that their victory has
made them masters of the land and consider they have the right
to be its lifelong rulers.*
### —EXTRACT FROM A LETTER BY ÁLVARO ANDREA

I now understand why people along its estuary call the Limpopo
Nambo wa Nhimba, the pregnant river. At this moment, the river
is in labor: its banks are widening, it twists like a serpent, splenetic
in its efforts to expel its waters into the waters of the sea. The corvette rides the swell and there is no part of the deck that has not
been swept by the waves. Ngungunyane's seven wives huddle
tightly around their husband. If they seek comfort, they won't find
it: There isn't a creature in this world more terrified than the king of
Gaza. I take delight in seeing such fear in a man who spread so
much terror among my people.

The river's swollen state reminds me of my own. I have never
felt nausea before. Now all I want is to close my eyes and fall into
some kind of drunken stupor. From afar, Dabondi smiles timidly at
me. She is the only queen who shows me any sign of friendliness.
She creeps furtively over and sits down next to me. The king and
his other wives watch us with suspicion. They are not traveling on

a boat, they are sailing in a coffin. They are already dead as they cross the waters. Only the beautiful Dabondi is alive. I lean forward in order to listen to her hushed tones:

*I want you to do me a favor, sister. Ask the whites to allow Nkosi to wear his crown.*

She conceals in her hands the *chilodjo*, the crown of dark wax which distinguishes the nobility from the lower castes among the VaNguni. The woman is convinced that the emperor would feel relief if he could wear it. She looks around to see if anyone is listening to us. Only then does she speak again:

*I'm the only one in a hurry to leave my homeland. Do you want to know why?* Then she waits for silence to fall once more. Her eyes are full of tears when she announces: *I'm going to see my son!*

At the age of seventeen, her son, João Mangueze, was sent to study in Portugal. "Study" is rather a loose term. For the past two years, he has been working for a locksmith across the river from Lisbon. The Portuguese offered the king of Gaza the chance to have his sons educated in Portuguese institutions. Some were sent to Mozambique Island, others to Portugal. The only one chosen to travel overseas was Mangueze. The emperor told the Portuguese: *See how I trust you, I am delivering into your keeping that which I hold most precious.* The womenfolk were united in opposing his decision. After all, one wife's children were their children too. They shared the same fear: The sea would swallow up the young man whom the Portuguese had baptized "João." Of all the spouses, only Dabondi was happy. She concealed her joy and pretended to oppose it as well. She had secretly been praying that João Mangueze would be taken far away. It would be better for him to be lost at sea than to be poisoned in power struggles.

*It won't be long before everybody sees you are pregnant*, she says, touching my belly.

*Does it show?*

*I knew you were from the start. I'm a* nyamosoro. *I cast cowries. And I've brought the* tintxolo *with me.*

She pushes out her chest to reveal an *mpacatxu*, a necklace made of tiny sticks plaited into a string. This is not a show of vanity. The object proves she was conceived by the gods. She gets to her feet and gives me a *capulana*, which I make a point of refusing. But she is insistent. It won't be long before night falls and it starts to feel cold. The cloth I wear tied around my waist should not be draped around my shoulders because the child inside me will be suffocated. This *capulana* should belong to another woman.

*We shall travel together*, Dabondi affirms. *I shall be the godmother to this child of yours. In exchange, you will be my lady-in-waiting, my slave over there in Portugal.*

*I've never been a slave . . .*

*You'd better make a start*, Dabondi declares. *I've been told that child of yours isn't the bearer of a proper race. You'll need someone to protect you from whites and blacks.*

She allows herself to caress the curve of my abdomen and hazards a guess: It has been three months since I last jumped the moon. According to tradition, I'm in a state of obscurity, my monthly blood having accumulated. It is vital that I should find elsewhere to bleed. She suggests making tiny incisions in my legs so that the blood does not accumulate in my body.

*I have been watching you, my dear*, the queen confesses. *There are things you should learn: For example, when you drink, you should kneel so that the water doesn't fall in a cascade over your child's head.*

Where we come from, girls learn to be no one. Dabondi also eradicated herself. In so doing, she thought she would lose her children without suffering. On the night her son left for Portugal, the queen awoke with her hands stuck together by thick oil. She wondered whether she was still dreaming. But she allowed things to take their course: If it was a dream, then she should experience it from beginning to end. In the darkness, there was a strong metallic smell and she realized she was bleeding abundantly. The hemorrhage originated in her womb: It was João twisting around on his return to the darkness. That son who, everyone said, was leaving to go far away, had really never been born. He had died while still inside her. He was a *ximiku*, one of those who, as people say, returns to the other side. The same name is given to those who have drowned. They die in a boundless womb, without pronouncing the secrets they bore with them.

In the early morning, without being seen by anyone in the village, Dabondi slipped out through the trees. She walked oblivious to whether the ground she trod were real or imagined. With the help of a shovel, Dabondi dug a deep, narrow grave. There, she buried her son, João Mangueze. Later, everyone said she had filled in an empty grave. There was nothing but soil burying soil. Everyone would swear that the young man had not died but that he had left to travel the uncertain byways of the sea, bound for Lisbon.

The allegations and sworn declarations of the others had no effect. All Dabondi wanted to be sure of was whether her breast milk had dried up. That is what women do after a stillbirth. She endlessly squeezed her nipples and not a drop appeared. When she had made sure that she was drier than a stone, she returned home and went to sleep.

The following day, the emperor passed by and did not recognize her. Dabondi had turned into a tree. So that was how the queen resolved something for which there is no solution. To be a mother is a verb with no past tense. That was what the queen said.

*Does the blood on the blade that cut the umbilical cord belong to the mother or the baby?* she asks. Then she adds decisively: *Well, it's that blood of mine that I'm going to find again on this journey.*

One doesn't visit a son, she affirms. One returns to him as if he was forever on the point of being born. She closes her eyes, sways her shoulders, and trills the words of an old song. *Mothers put their hands in the fire and cast the ashes skyward, still burning. It is what they have done since time began. That was how the stars were fashioned. What will befall these lights is what happened to the sun: They will return. They will all return. And they will cause women's hands to glow.*

I interrupt her litany with little conviction: *Your son will return to your arms. Isn't that what the song says?* She looks at me hard. Her fingers knit an emptiness as if, at that moment, she were reading her oracle bones. Something about this woman reminds me of my late mother.

*I envy you*, she confesses in a muted tone. *I am sorry I cannot speak the language of the whites.*

*Don't be sorry, my lady*, I affirm. *That way, you don't hear the insults they direct at us. You don't know how often we are called monkeys.*

*The whites are also ignorant of the ugly names we call them.*

Then her face lights up as she repeats: *I'm going to see my son, that's what matters.* At that point, she asks me to teach her Portuguese. This is the language she will use to address her son.

*João hasn't forgotten how to speak Zulu*, I assure her.

*You don't understand, my dear. I want to speak to my son in a language that none of my relatives can understand.*

To protect himself from the mosquitoes, Captain Mouzinho de Albuquerque has taken refuge on the bridge. He places his right hand on the helm and stands there, as if all humanity were admiring him. Captain Andrea mutters to himself: *He's not to give me orders. It's the sea that gives me my orders. No one else.*

Dabondi takes me by the hand and leads me to Mouzinho. She asks me to help her make herself understood. The captain opens the door a crack and agrees to listen. The queen states her request:

*When I get to Portugal I want to speak to your elder.*

*Elder?* Mouzinho inquires.

*The white folks' elder. I want to thank him for welcoming my son. The king of Portugal is my João's new father. I'm your king's spouse.*

The captain smiles condescendingly. He asks us to leave him alone. And he shuts the door again.

Along the banks of the Limpopo, there are hundreds of tiny, flickering fires. Most of them do not belong to the riverside villages. They are fires lit by people who have set up camp next to the river especially to witness the emperor's deportation. From time to time a malediction can be heard: *Be off with you, you vulture, and never come back!*

Dabondi has gone to join the other queens, leaving me alone with Álvaro Andrea. With his dark greatcoat, the captain is an almost ill-defined shape. The light from the campfires is reflected in the buttons of his uniform.

*Your queen says she speaks to rivers*, the Portuguese affirms. *You who are a translator, do you know what those fires on the riverbank are saying?*

He does not wait for an answer. I look at him from head to foot. That uniform is out of place in the tropical heat. The metal buttons are a source of fascination for the queens. Ngungunyane does not possess such shiny ornaments, no piece of sunlight hangs from his chest. I am the only one who feels sorry for this white man, bathed in sweat, who, if it were not for the solemnity of his uniform, would look like a child lost in the world. The drenched coat almost reaches his feet, which, in contrast to his military rigor, are defenseless. The Portuguese is barefoot. His boots have been taken away to be washed, caked as they were in dark, stinking mud. The queens contemplate this helpless white in amusement, as if, upon seeing him barefoot, they had surprised him naked. Uncle Mulungo remarks out loud: *The zebra has taken off his hooves.* And they all laugh. The elders swore that Europeans were ungulates. As they invariably saw the Portuguese wearing shoes, they assumed the shoes were part of their body.

Wiping his brow bathed in sweat, the Portuguese warns me:

*We've got to talk, my girl. I have a mission for you to carry out that is far more important than commanding a naval launch.*

# 8

## BEFORE THERE WAS A SEA, THERE WAS A BOAT

I threw a stone into the wind
because I took it for a *kuerre-kuerre*.
And the wind ceased blowing.
And slowly the wind turned to dust.
Because I threw a stone
and the wind grew anxious, it turned to dust and flew afar.
Then it blew strong once more
to free itself from the dust.
And the wind overflowed.
The wind that was once a bird.
—SAN NARRATIVE COLLECTED IN CAPE TOWN IN 1870, AND TRANSLATED INTO
A POETIC RENDERING BY THE SOUTH AFRICAN WRITER ANTJIE KROG

Álvaro Soares Andrea believes he learned to sail before the sea was born. For decades he wandered along the African coast and explored rivers that are yet to be named. And there were so many voyages that there aren't enough nights to recount all his adventures. Hence his disdain for the whims of Mouzinho de Albuquerque.

*He who knows of the sea knows of the heavens*, the captain proclaims as he paces up and down the length of his corvette.

He is in high spirits, and hasn't slept a wink the whole night. He was visited by dreams, strange omens. He dreamed he had turned into a black prisoner and that he was traveling in the hold of his own ship. In the same dream, Mouzinho untied his wrists and waved a notebook in his face: *Is this what you've been writing about me, my little son of a bitch?* He nervously stroked the side of his boot with a horsewhip. Then he threw the notebook onto Andrea's lap. He wanted him to read it out loud. Andrea held the pages with trembling hands. He realized it was his handwriting. But then he realized he had written it all in a language he didn't understand. It looked like Zulu, but he wasn't sure. Then he woke up with a start.

*He who knows of the sea knows of the heavens*, Andrea repeats, as if the motto would help him stay awake. He looks again at the dark clouds over the ocean. At last, he submits to the command of the unfathomable forces of nature. He has greater trust in that inner star—which some call intuition—than in maps and compasses, which are of little use in tropical seas.

*Warn the captain that this wind has an ugly name.*

Once again, Dabondi wants to help Andrea overcome his ignorance. And there are many areas in which the Portuguese captain is ignorant. He is unaware, for example, that the wind was once a bird. This is something that we VaChopi know. There are truths we learn from childhood. The wind was a bird that took refuge outside itself when men tried to capture it. It lost its body, and made its nest in the clouds, and travels with them, only pausing when it tires. This is why the wind sings. Because it was once a bird. When I was a little girl, I used to say that the wind "tweetled." And the Portuguese priest, Rudolfo Fernandes, smiled indulgently. Languages are women: they fall in love, get pregnant, and bear children.

*I know this wind*, the queen guarantees. *It's called a* xidzedze.

This *xidẕedẕe* is very different from all the other winds. It howls like an animal and is made to order. Maybe it is the emperor who summoned it.

*The* xidzedze *seiẕes whoever has seiẕed our king*, Dabondi comments.

If the wind commands, the captain obeys: the corvette stops over by the right-hand bank and there, so near the turbulent ocean, it finds a safe harbor. I listen to the anchor being dropped onto the muddy bottom. We shall spend the night in this improvised refuge, in the hope of continuing our journey toward Xai-Xai in the early morning.

*Listen, sisters!* Dabondi urges us. *Can't you hear voices coming from the shore?*

The fury of the sea throws us into mental disarray. This inner turmoil deprives all of us, prisoners and jailers, of sleep. *This darkness isn't the offspring of night*, says Dabondi by way of an explanation as to why we cannot sleep. Then she adds: *This darkness comes from the rocks of Zongoene.*

Beyond the estuary, there are such tall sand dunes that you can see the other side of the ocean from the top of them. At the base of these dunes nestle the rocks of Zongoene. There are no rocks in the entire universe that are so dark or immovable. The roots of these stones burrow deeper than the underground lair where the devil was born.

For centuries, fishermen have come here to pray, pleading for ships to founder and for the waves to wash ashore the riches carried in their holds. A young girl is tied, stark naked, among the rocks while the clamor made by the elders encroaches upon the roar of the breakers: *You, the* psikwembo, *make the sea rage so that the ships may sink and gifts from afar may reach us . . .*

*Listen carefully, my dear*, the queen says, and then asks: *Can you not hear voices coming from the sea?*

All I hear is the noise of the waves and the whistling of the wind. Dabondi, however, is in no doubt: on the shore, there are people clamoring to the gods and praying for a wreck. And there are hands thirsting for a chance to disembowel a ship. And that ship might be the corvette on which we are traveling.

I am alarmed by the queen's foreboding. And I am swept up in a kind of delirium: This is the end of everything, my fifteen years are going to sink ingloriously into the murky waters of the Limpopo. I go and look for Captain Andrea, who is wandering along the deck with a lantern in his hand. He reminds me of a *xipoco*, one of those sleepless phantoms who frighten children. The Portuguese takes time to react to my request:

*Captain, please lend me your lantern.*

*What for?*

*I don't know. I want to see Germano.*

*Germano? For God's sake, Imani!*

*I may be crazy, but let me have a look . . .*

*Don't be long, I can't be without my lantern for long. There are people here who want to harm me.*

Trembling, his hands almost ethereal, the captain passes me that fragile source of light. The wind causes the flashlight to sway, illuminating my body rather than the way forward. At each brush-stroke of light, I become more and more distinguishable, a kind of firefly advancing through the darkness. Maybe that's why the sailors' eyes fasten greedily and lustily upon my body. I seek out

Mouzinho to beg his protection. I shall ask him to protect me from two conflicting aspirations: that of my black brothers who want me dead, and that of the whites who want to rape me.

It is then that Álvaro emerges from the gloom and snatches the lantern from me: *That's enough now,* he declares. *I have more reason to fear the dark.*

It is in his defeat—and not when he is on his throne—that you will see the real emperor. Such was my father's affirmation. And he advised me: Take a look at the king's shoulder blades in order to assess his kingdom's vitality. I look at Ngungunyane and cannot see his body. All I can distinguish is the curve of his subjugation. In contrast, Nwamatibjane Zixaxa still cuts a dignified figure.

*Why don't they all sit together?* Andrea ponders, pointing to the prisoners.

*It's better like this, Captain,* I explain. *There is great bitterness between the two chiefs . . .*

With a subtle gesture, the rebel Zixaxa points toward the dunes of Zongoene. He confirms Dabondi's previous statement: somewhere, beyond the estuary, the spirits are being roused. They are being asked to cause some shipwrecks.

*What's he saying?* the captain asks.

*Tell him I'm talking about the stars,* Zixaxa replies. And he proceeds slowly, giving me time to translate: *The stars are the moon's spouses. That is what they are to us, those of our race. They are overworked spouses, which is why they grow thin. The moon doesn't give them anything to eat.*

The trace of a smile appears on Álvaro Andrea's face. He leans on the deck rail, shakes his head and murmurs:

*I had forgotten it's New Year's Eve tonight.*

I don't bother to translate for Zixaxa. His is another calendar, years are measured in terms of droughts, wars, and famine. The year that is about to begin will never have any name.

Walking around barefoot is a habit that the Portuguese has forgotten, which is why he stumbles off. When his bulk has faded into the gloom, I say to Zixaxa:

*I didn't know that legend about the stars . . .*

*I made it all up just now. Whites love stories. Sometimes I feel sorry for them. I treat them deferentially, and call them "boss," and they believe I really mean it.*

✤

The vessel is at last at rest when we receive a signal from the river-bank. A man is waving a flare and then makes himself known by shouting in Shangaan. He is an *induna*, a representative of the Va-Nguni court. He brings a message from Queen Impebekezane, Ngungunyane's mother. He is supposed to deliver this message in person to the dethroned king. Mouzinho is reluctant to authorize the visit. He asks Álvaro Andrea for his opinion. Surprised at being consulted, the captain declares: *The boat is mine, the prisoner is yours.*

*Queen Impebekezane always helped us,* says Mouzinho. *Let the black come aboard.* And turning to me, he says: *And you, Imani, you know what you've got to do. Afterwards, tell me what they've talked about.*

A dinghy is sent to fetch the *induna* while we listen to voices in Shangaan coming from the riverbank: *Go away, big fat tyrant, who stole our cattle and poultry! So where are they taking you now?* I accompany the emissary to the VaNguni prisoners. As he approaches the emperor, the messenger claps his hands and falls to his knees before uttering the greeting: *Bayete!* At first, Ngungunyane does not recognize the visitor. He raises himself with difficulty, his blanket draped around his back, leaving his ankles exposed. He peers suspiciously at the intruder's face. The emissary identifies himself as the adjutant of General Maguiguane, and he expresses himself in Zulu:

*Don't take any notice of the insults of these river folk. It won't be long before they greet you once more as the nkosi of all the peoples of Gaza.*

*What do you want?* Ngungunyane inquires.

*I bring you news, my king. The commander of your ihimpi, General Maguiguane, is organizing a movement called Ukubuya Nkosi in order to demand your return to Gaza.*

*And what else? Go on, speak! I know your ways only too well: you begin with the good news so as to delay announcing disasters . . .*

*I come to warn you, my king, that your mother, Queen Impebekezane, is the target of serious accusations. And it is because of her, they say, that it hasn't rained for more than two years and that the cattle are dying from some unknown disease. Tell me what you want us to do to save your mother.*

*Don't worry, Nkosi Kakhulo,* Uncle Mulungo replies. The elderly counselor has a clear idea about the future. *The whites,* he says, *are the ones who now rule us.* It is only a matter of time. Soon, the same accusations now leveled against the queen mother will be directed against their new rulers.

*And what else do they say?* the king insists.

The messenger looks down and hesitates. And when he speaks again, his tone turns from reverence to fear:

*Your uncles want to kill Impebekezane. They accuse her of high treason: They say she gave her own son up to the Portuguese.*

Ngungunyane listens as if all this were being said in an unknown language. The emissary waits a long time in the hope that his interlocutor will abandon his lethargy. And as nothing happens he appeals in silence to Uncle Mulungo. But everyone knows that certain silences have an owner. For this reason, the king's counselor pretends not to notice. And everyone waits for the emperor, the owner of all silences, to start talking again:

*For me to be here, the captive of the whites, someone must have betrayed me*, Ngungunyane declares. *Find the culprits and bring them to justice. Start in the family.*

The emissary takes his leave with much bowing and scraping. He backs away without ever turning his back and addresses the king one last time:

*Do you want me to take a message to your mother or to Maguiguane?*

*Tell them to send me Dokotela*, the emperor replies.

He is referring to the Swiss doctor, Georges Liengme, who was his physician in Mandhlakazi. With his head still bowed, the emissary explains:

*The Portuguese expelled the Swiss. Dokotela had to leave for the Transvaal.*

The *induna* returns to the dinghy that had brought him, and we listen to the sound of the oars splashing in the waters. The last of the king's messengers disappears into the gloom. Never again will Ngungunyane receive visitors from his kingdom. His exile has begun even before he has left the land of his birth.

On deck, Mouzinho de Albuquerque awaits my report. I climb up the steps, recalling my father's words: In times of war, every translator is an informer.

✦

It is early morning when Captain Álvaro Andrea offers me a bowl of soup. I refuse the offer gracefully and he helps himself unceremoniously to the meal that was destined for me. He wipes his lips with the back of his hand, and I can scarcely understand him when he speaks to me:

*You mentioned Germano.*

*He's my sweetheart.*

*I know who he is. I have a letter for you from him.*

*So why do you only tell me now?*

*I forgot. I'm a solitary man.*

*I don't understand, Captain.*

*Solitary men aren't aware how forgetful they are. It's possible I may remember things. Perhaps you will help me to remember them.*

The silver buttons on his uniform glimmer but there is a far brighter glint in the eyes that are fixed on me.

*I'm pregnant, Captain,* I declare.

I'm surprised by my own speech. What I have just said is not in self-defense. It is an accusation. For a moment, the captain lowers his head, overcome by shame. But he soon regains his composure and responds, every bit a man, a white, and a soldier:

*You're pregnant but you haven't lost your memory. There are things you're going to tell me. Things you saw during the capture of Gungunhana.*

The captain has in his possession Germano's letter. My first instinct is to react with anger. However, it would be best to proceed just as I always have done: by delaying any dispute, and feigning obedience. I accept that I shall talk, but I set about warning him: Our conversation would breed suspicion among both blacks and whites. It would be better if I wrote these confessions down. All he had to do was to allow me to use the storage area and give me a pen and paper. I don't know, the captain ponders. People lie, he says, mostly without even being aware of it. When they write, they lie even more. But then he agrees. There's no truthful solution to the question of truth. In my case, a lie is almost always an error of translation.

# 9

## THE HANDWRITING OF THE ILLITERATE KING

*Horses are what remain of the dragons of old.*
**—NWAMATIBJANE ZIXAXA**

It is late afternoon, and I am sitting in the ship's storage area. A notebook, a pen, and a pot of ink await me on a table. The captain has closed the door to the compartment, and believes that I shall provide proof to incriminate Mouzinho de Albuquerque in that little cubbyhole. I do not get a chance to start my report because I am suddenly surprised by a visit from Ngungunyane.

*I hate your shoes,* he comments as he enters the compartment. *I hate your ways and cannot abide the way you slip away from me. But you needn't worry,* he adds, *I haven't come to do you any harm.*

Then he snatches the notebook from me. He holds it above the little reading lamp as if he were assessing its weight. *Why do you write so much?* he asks. And then he remarks, his eyes narrowing: *Not even the whites write so much. I've never seen any of them writing after sunset.*

I am looking at the floor and I see his bare feet. They are the roots of a dead tree. I feel his hot breath when he orders me to throw the notebook and all the other papers into the sea.

*What papers,* I ask in the faintest of tones.

He rummages around in my bag and pulls out the letters to

Germano that I have never got as far as sending. I had never realized how many there were. The emperor has to use both hands to collect all of them together. He takes a few steps and then drops the sheets. He does this on purpose. His intention is that I should have to bend over to pick up all that is scattered across the floor. He takes advantage of my vulnerability. His toad-like hands touch my thighs, feel my buttocks, and, after a deep sigh, grip my waist.

I let him abuse me. I want to distract him so as to keep him away from where I have hidden my other bits of writing. Let him keep the letters, but he mustn't touch the notebooks where I have been writing my account of this troubled journey. I hurriedly choose the still incomplete letters and place them in his arms. The emperor shakes his head and murmurs: *You're going to be mine, my eighth wife, my newest witch!*

He steps onto the companionway, his body swaying as if he were rocking a child. With an extravagant gesture, he tosses the letters overboard. The sheets of paper fly momentarily, spinning like blinded gulls. When they flutter down onto the surface of the waves, the whole sea changes color. It becomes as black as night. Ngungunyane is unaware of this change. For him, the ocean always was a darkened blanket.

*It wasn't because of your papers that I came here*, he says. *It was because of my letter.*

*What letter, Nkosi?*

*The one I'm going to dictate to you. A letter to the king of Portugal.*

He inspects the sheet of paper which he himself has picked out, feels the pen nib, sniffs the inkpot. Then he tells me to stop at nothing in the pursuit of the ornate and florid. *I want you to use a turn of phrase appropriate for kings*, he says. *Are we who are sovereigns of whole nations not the commanders of words?* He slowly starts to dictate. He keeps his eyes closed like a singer, emotions plain to see.

My brother, D. Carlos,
King of Portugal,

I am Mundungazi Ngungunyane, the son of Muzila who, in
turn, is the son of Manukusse, the founding father, Soshangane.
I am writing to thank you for your great generosity. Rumor has
spread that I am a prisoner. It is said that I am traveling on this
boat like an animal, vanquished and humiliated. We both know
that is not true. I travel at Your Excellency's invitation. All that
has happened—my capture, my imprisonment, and this
journey—is a performance. It is all no more than a farce for the
consumption of governments in Europe. I did not have my
wrists bound, nor were my arms chained, nor my feet shackled.
I have been rendered immobile because I agreed to collaborate
in this imposture of ours. I am traveling to Lisbon in order to
talk personally with you about matters that concern us. The
privilege of this invitation would cause suspicion among
European kings and envy among African ones.

There were times, I confess, when my resolve weakened. I
doubted you, and feared for my life. I acknowledge that it was
the effect of drink. But there is one fear that haunts me: the
fear that I will not return. That is what the Zulus believe: He
who crosses the sea can never return. It is not a premonition.
This is the experience of all Africans, whether they are
enslaved, or the masters of slaves. None of them ever came
back. Those who enter the sea lose their names. And all they
can remember is before they were born. That is what we say in
my homeland.

I shall continue to govern my people from afar, as do kings
who have died. I have no fear of distance. What I do fear is
disloyalty. I am taking with me my seven wives, each one of
them with her own shadow. Of these wives, Dabondi is the
one who dreams. Each dream she has is a counselor warning
me of plots and treachery. They are going to sacrifice my
mother, Impebekezane, accusing her of being loyal to the
Portuguese. The worst thing is that this accusation is true.
Queen Impebekezane trusted the word of Portugal. I want to
ask you, my brother, to protect her as was promised. They say
that Maguiguane has proclaimed a movement of rebellion
aimed at forcing my return to Mozambique. Do not allow
yourself to be deceived, my dear Nkosi. Not even I myself
believe his motives. Why, with his military skills, did this
Maguiguane not attempt an ambush in order to free me? Why
did he let me pass through places where a surprise attack
would have been so easy? Instead of fighting for my return,
Maguiguane should have hindered my departure.

None of this surprises me, dear king. That general of mine
has a history. He comes from the VaTsonga, one of the
conquered tribes. I forced Maguiguane to go down on all
fours, and I sat on his back while I was given a bath. That man
will want to sit on someone's back. And now he commands an
army that only exists in his dreams. Maguiguane is a make-
believe general. And I pretend I am a prisoner. And you, my
dear king, affect to be my jailer. This is why I say: battles are
won with weapons. But wars are won with lies.

I speak of these things, dear king, because good manners
require me to begin one matter by talking about a different
one. The main reason for this letter is an urgent request. The
room I have been given has not brought me peace. It has
brought me protection. Now I am protected by the Portuguese

54

who are embittered toward me. What I ask is that Zixaxa should not continue to share my cell. It is from him that I most need protection. This Nwamatibjane Zixaxa is not an Nguni, he is not from the nobility of Gaza. He is an insignificant *induna* from the south of Mozambique, one of those people you call a *régulo*. If there is anyone Your Excellency should hate, it is this rebel who does not even obey me. By defeating me, you, sir, have defeated all those whom I defeated myself.

I want you to know the following: I was not, as people have told you, complicit in the attack on Lourenço Marques. Zixaxa acted on his own account and at his own risk. And now he accuses me of betrayal, blaming me for surrendering him to Portuguese forces. This is why I beg you: Do not oblige me to sleep together with someone who wants to kill me. If it is my fate to cease living, I would rather be killed by the Portuguese. Shoot me, Mr. King.

One final wish: Please convey a message to Captain Mouzinho de Albuquerque. Tell him that I do not remember him with anger. The captain detained me not as an enemy but as a companion in arms who had become insubordinate. I am a sergeant in the same army. I traveled with Mouzinho for several days. And I discovered that we are troubled by a similar problem: our knees. Mouzinho fell from a horse during the course of his duties. My suffering does not have the same glorious explanation. I merely suffer from my own weight. My pains have a long history, but they became more intense after my capture. For days on end, I was punched and kicked. I know these were not the result of any instructions. But I am still subject to beatings, a lot of beating. In the beginning, I thought it was a pretense at beating. But the blows were too painful to be false. In my hideout at Chaimite, they hit me, first to oblige me to sit down, and then they hit me again to get me to stand up. On the way to the river, I was attacked indiscriminately because I walked slowly. On the boat, soldiers tried to force me to tell them the secret of some hidden treasure. And it was Mouzinho who furiously put an end to these beatings. It was he who shouted: *No one is to touch Ngungunyane! This African is a guest of the king of Portugal!* Mouzinho, I imagine, must have guessed our secret. Keep him close to you, my brother. We should never turn our back on someone who knows our traumas.

It will not be long now before we speak in person. They did not allow me to bring you any gifts. I had already chosen three head of cattle to take with me on this long journey. But it was not possible. That will have to keep for our next encounter in Mozambique, an occasion when, apart from the oxen, Your Excellency will have the pastureland and the rivers that fatten cattle.

I salute Your Excellency in accordance with our custom: *Bayete,* King D. Carlos!

*Mundungaɀi Ngungunyane*

I round off the letter with a mischievous grin. *What are you laughing at?* Ngungunyane asks. *This can only have been written with ironic intent, my king,* I risk saying. *Why?* he asks. *You cannot have been sincere, sir,* I declare. *Did you write down all that I said?* the king asks as if he hadn't heard me. I nod. Now it's his turn to give me a malicious smile. He points his finger at me by way of a warning: *I shall send Dabondi to check whether you have been faithful to what I said.* I reply, fearful: *Dabondi doesn't know . . .* He doesn't let me finish: *Dabondi knows how to read. While you're still wondering what you're going to say, she is already reading your words.*

Ngungunyane takes the sheet in his hands and, with his index finger, follows the contours of the letters. It is his way of judging my obedience. *Do you want to know why I'm writing to the king of Portugal?* he asks. In Chaimite, he says, hunters hang the lions' skulls on a sacred tree. Everyone thinks this is a display of vanity. But it is only the hunters' humility that drives them to this: They worship the vanquished, and ask the gods of the animals to forgive them.

*Do you understand why I have written this letter?* Ngungunyane asks.

# 10

## A WHITE HANDKERCHIEF LIGHTS UP THE PAST

*The crossing of the ocean, whether on the outward or the return journey,*
*must seem like crossing a river to African eyes.*
—ALBERTO DA COSTA E SILVA, IN <u>UM RIO CHAMADO ATLÂNTICO</u>
(A RIVER CALLED THE ATLANTIC)

Ships are like cowrie shells: In them, you can listen to the voice of the sea. The *Neves Ferreira* is a gigantic cowrie, an upturned shell made of metal. Its funnels are three mouths that swallow up the clouds and then regurgitate them, thick and dirty. This ship which awaits us in the port of Xai-Xai provokes such alarm among the prisoners that the ocean becomes invisible.

Seated on bundles of cotton, the king of Gaza wants to know how long the voyage to Lisbon will take. I tell him what I've been told: It will take two days to reach Lourenço Marques. Then, more than two months to reach the Portuguese capital. When translating into Zulu, I convert months into moons. I thought Ngungunyane's reaction would be sad. Quite the opposite. His face lights up with a smile: *Two moons?* he asks, astonished. The Portuguese came such a long way just to fight him? And he proudly straightens his shoulders once more. For a few brief seconds, he is an emperor again.

The captives wait for hours on the quay for the order to board. They will travel in the hold. The Portuguese start by loading the freight. Only then will the other cargo be loaded, the one that talks, weeps, and prays.

The *Neves Ferreira* is moored with thick cables. It is tied up by its snout, like an ox. It shares its shackled state with the emperor, whose wrists have been bound temporarily with rope made from sisal.

The astonishment of my black brothers and sisters fills Captain Andrea with pride. Mouzinho's reaction is the opposite. He wants to pour scorn on the navy and on sailors. *Boats*, he says, *are only beautiful when they are on dry land. And turned upside down.*

The sailors laugh aloud. Mouzinho goes even further to belittle the navy. You need to turn a boat over, he says, in order to understand its true nature. The term *keel* applies to both boats and birds. A ship is more of a bird than a fish. This is what Mouzinho says.

Queen Muzamussi is afraid that the ship may be able to advance inland. She urgently pleads with them not to untie the monster. Ngungunyane orders the woman to keep quiet. From that moment onward, none of his wives will speak without authorization. Dabondi smiles disdainfully: the emperor has finally acknowledged the fragility of his empire and the instability of his harem. He took possession of the land with blood. He appropriated women with semen. All this power is now abandoning him. That is why he shouts at his wives. The only authority he has left is being a man among women.

On the quay at Xai-Xai, Captain Mouzinho de Albuquerque supervises the loading of his precious horse. It's not just an animal there, it's not just another piece of cargo being manhandled. The horse represents the image the captain has of himself. This is what he dreams he is, a new version of the centaur, a perpetual horseman. Luckily, the dashing military officer does not understand Zixaxa's comment: *One fine day we'll get to eat that horse.*

It is now Mouzinho's turn to smile without knowing why. He maintains this smile while he climbs up the gangway onto the *Neves Ferreira*. Once on the quarterdeck, he is greeted by the ship's captain, Lieutenant Jaime Leote do Rego. The commander of this ship is a very different man from Álvaro Andrea, and Mouzinho thanks God for this. For him, the change of captains is a relief. As far as I am concerned, it's a nightmare. Freed from his duties, Álvaro Andrea has more time to seek me out. It's not his company that I find unpleasing. It's my lack of courage to insist on what he owes me: Germano's letter.

We set sail and for a moment, it seems that the land itself is moving. Maybe it's not a ship we shall be traveling on. We shall lay our course like all voyagers do: through memories and dreams. But I no longer remember nor do I dream. I am fifteen years old. I am traveling far away from myself, without any luggage or documents. But I carry with me my child, the beginning of my eternity.

In the middle of the night, Dabondi and I are summoned to Captain Jaime Leote do Rego's cabin. At the entrance, Dabondi clutches the captain's arms. It is rare for one of our women to be so forward. But the queen has taken a liking to this white man with a gray beard. The attraction is mutual: the lieutenant looks at the queen as if he were examining her face. *Perfect, she is the one I want,* he confirms enthusiastically.

At the back of the cabin, there is a canvas on an easel. On a chair rest two paintbrushes and a palette, where various tones of blue have been mixed. *I want to paint the sea*, he confesses. That was why he had sent for Dabondi. *On the quay*, he says, *I heard this woman. Tell her to sing again!*

*I'm not the one who sings*, Dabondi argues. *Others use my voice. Explain to this woman that I'm not in the habit of asking.*

The queen smiles and answers: *Ask this man if he only dreams when he's told to.*

With the tips of her fingers Dabondi gently caresses the canvas. She believes she is in front of a loom and that the captain is a weaver. Gesticulating extravagantly, as if his arms were doing the talking, the Portuguese presents the work he has not yet begun: *We do not see the ocean as such: Rather, we see ourselves in it.* Then he adds: *I saw the ocean when I heard this woman singing on the quay.*

He offers the queen a glass of brandy. Dabondi knocks it back in one go. She waves the empty glass, signaling that she wants a refill. *If he heard me singing, this white man can't be an enemy*, she says. Then she adds: *The drink is good, I'm going to do what he wants.* Then the queen launches forth in song. The captain closes his eyes and the waters of the ocean gradually fill his cabin.

With his right arm half raised, his steps keeping time to the queen's song, Captain Jaime Leote do Rego comes over to me and asks:

*Have you ever danced with a white man?*

It is the morning of January 4, 1896, and the *Neves Ferreira* drops anchor in Espírito Santo Bay. In front of us lies the same city that Zixaxa had so audaciously attacked exactly a year before. The whites call it Lourenço Marques, we named it Xilinguíne. I remember how the Italian woman, Bianca Vanzini, used to complain how small the place was. But for those of us who have never seen a city, this jumble of streets, houses, and lights is a cause for wonderment. That is why we call it Xilinguíne, "the place where people live and talk like whites."

I naïvely assume that we shall soon be disembarking. But then I realize: All the crew are taken ashore in barges except for us blacks. Anchored out in the middle of the bay, the ship is a prison. The Portuguese need time. Preparations for the great celebration are underway in the city. Journalists, diplomats, and foreign dignitaries will be coming. They will be joined by the administrators, traders, and religious leaders. And then the populations of the neighboring regions will come together to see the Lion of Gaza paraded about, defeated and humiliated, his feet coated in the mud of the streets of Lourenço Marques.

Álvaro Andrea refuses to go ashore. He argues that by staying on board, he will guarantee the security of the prisoners. We all know that the Portuguese has his own reasons. This will be the last opportunity he has to make progress on his critical report on Mouzinho. Aboard that sleepy ship, and completely at his mercy, are the witnesses he is so anxious to question.

The following morning, we receive visitors on board. Dressed in civilian attire, Mouzinho de Albuquerque arrives, accompanied by a dozen diplomats and journalists. With him there is also a tall, thin black man, wearing European shoes and clothes. Mouzinho addresses me and asks:

*Do you recognize me without my uniform, girl? I've put on my Alentejo country boy's clothes—jacket, belt, and wide-brimmed hat.*

He has the prisoners assemble and then introduces the black man who accompanies him:

*This is Zeca Primoroso, the translator, the "language man," as we call him. He has come to help in the interviews with Gungunhana.* And he adds, turning to me: *You won't be required, girl.*

Photographs are taken of the king flanked by two queens. Dabondi smiles, happy that she is one of the two chosen. Once the press has been satisfied, Mouzinho turns to one side and coaxes the translator: *Ask Gungunhana if he recognizes who captured him at Chaimite.* Ngungunyane gets wearily to his feet and points at Mouzinho: *It was him!*

*You see?* the captain asks boastfully. *Even in disguise, I was immediately recognized. Write this down to keep those disbelievers quiet.*

While the interviews proceed, Mouzinho calls me aside in order to explain why he has availed himself of another translator. It was nothing personal. *It's the same problem with all spies,* the captain explains. *Later, someone has to spy on them. Paid to betray one person, they end up betraying everyone.*

In my case, suspicion ran even higher. I was black, a woman, I had abandoned my family and my beliefs. Worse still: I had chosen a white man as a lover. How could I inspire any confidence? *If you betrayed your own people, you'll betray us far more easily. You may be almost white, but one thing never changes: All the black people in the world are a black person's family.*

The party takes its leave. The same barge that had brought it now ferries it back to the city. Everyone returns except for Zeca Primoroso.

The new translator is one of those people we call a *muzwalana*, that is, a black who knows how to read and write. Once the whites have gone, Primoroso asks me:

*They have just arrested the missionary, Roberto Machava. And a number of others have also been detained. Are you from the church as well?*

*I'm from another church*, I reply abruptly.

*And what church is that?*

*You wouldn't know it. It doesn't have a name in Portuguese.*

The prisoners listen, dumbfounded, to our dialogue. It is the first time they have witnessed two black people communicating with each other in Portuguese. Zixaxa shakes his head and smiles. Sometimes, a smile is the best accusation.

Álvaro Andrea summons Zeca Primoroso to the bridge. We watch him getting his orders and nodding his head with a mixture of presumption and deference. Then the translator returns to the deck and parades arrogantly up and down in front of the startled prisoners. Apart from his European clothes, he wears perfectly polished shoes, and his hair is swept back on either side of a wide part that crosses his cranium from one end to the other. Speaking in Zulu, he starts listing the qualities which, according to him, distinguish him from others of his race:

*It is said that there are black kings and victorious warriors in Mozambique. None of this nonsense counts for anything, because I obey a distant king, King D. Carlos. And apart from that, I have worn socks and shoes for a long time now, I sleep in a bed, and my meals are served on a table. Do you understand?*

The rebel Zixaxa waves his arms in an excessive show of bowing and scraping and proclaims in falsetto:

*Si ya vuma!*

It is a sarcastic expression of approval, an "amen" uttered in irony. Zeca Primoroso's reaction is one of irritation: They should never again respond to what he says with native exclamations. They can agree with him, or rather they should agree with him, but they should never forget that they are standing before an agent of Portuguese authority. Then he warns them that Captain Álvaro Andrea will soon come and interrogate the prisoners. *We have two ears and one mouth*, Zeca declares. *Remember this, my countrymen: The ears are ours, but a mouth doesn't belong to us*, he adds.

The captain steps down onto the deck where the prisoners are lined up in silence. Álvaro Andrea orders me to join the prisoners. *You're not a translator anymore*, he declares as he passes me.

Ngungunyane is the first to be questioned. The Portuguese tries to get the king of Gaza to confess to the mistreatment to which he was subjected. It is of little value that the question is translated into Zulu. The king remains silent. The inquiries are repeated in a number of different formats. But the king keeps his mouth firmly shut. The Portuguese switches from interrogator to prosecutor. It is the fault of the man that he, Ngungunyane, is protecting with his silence that his counselors are casting suspicion on his own mother. And Andrea continues: Did Ngungunyane know the whereabouts of the silver cup given him by the English queen? Couldn't he guess? Did he know who, after he had been captured, gave the order to slaughter all his cattle?

The king of Gaza remains clammed up. Álvaro Andrea appears to surrender. He leans over Ngungunyane and whispers in his ear:

*Mouzinho must be grateful to you. Thanks to you, he has become a hero, thanks to you he's earned the praises of King D. Carlos. Thanks to you, blacks and whites will applaud him in their thousands, in the streets of Lourenço Marques. If it weren't for you, that captain would be nothing more than an illustrious unknown.*

Zeca Primoroso takes great pains to provide a perfect translation but is unexpectedly interrupted by voices coming from the sea. Dozens of small craft surround our ship in the darkness. The Portuguese asks Primoroso what is happening. His eyes closed, the interpreter recites the ditty by heart:

This is the youth, our youth they seek to kill.

He is the glorious one, our reason for glory.
He fought the whites, he fled to Cossine.
Now he's a prisoner. And they're taking him far . . .

Primoroso clears his throat, embarrassed:
*That's what they're babbling in their language.*
*Are they talking about Ngungunyane?* asks the captain.
*No, Excellency. The men are singing in praise of Zixaxa.*
The captain rushes along the taffrail, trying to make out where all the excitement is coming from. It is a dark night, and he can hardly see what is immediately in front of him. In a panic, Andrea orders the lookouts to fire a few shots in the vague direction of the noise.
*Fire! Fire on those goddamn boats!* Andrea shouts.
*But which boats?* the soldiers ask.
*Fire anywhere, keep them away from here!*
The tactic works, the dugouts move away and silence once again envelops the ship. Ngungunyane is locked away in the helmsman's cabin. Two guards are placed at the door, one black and one white.
In that improvised cell, curled up like a pangolin, the defeated VaNguni chief falls asleep. I recall my father's words: Cells are small, but prisons are for life.

The ghostly dugouts have left Captain Andrea alarmed. He suspects they want to kill the black king. But then he conjectures, with greater conviction, that he himself may be the target. And so he hastens to take the initiative. Whatever the nature of the threat, it is of utmost importance that the guard on the ship be reinforced.
As a matter of urgency, Zeca Primoroso and I are sent to Lourenço Marques. Our mission is to ask a certain Sergeant Duarte Amaral for help, for, apart from being an experienced soldier, he

is a loyal friend of the captain. We should look for him in the houses of ill repute. Before we leave, Álvaro Andrea warns us that Mouzinho should not know of this precaution. Such a request for help would certainly be an excuse for mockery. That was why Andrea chose us, unknown civilians, to carry out such a delicate errand.

*Take care as you go*, he warns us. *And bring Sergeant Amaral back with you.*

He has a deranged look in his eyes, and sweat runs down his face. I barely recognize the calm man who overcame the fury of the *xidʒedʒe* wind.

After only a few minutes, we go ashore next to the fort, which Primoroso identifies as the Fortress of Our Lady of the Conception. We hurriedly cross a wide square surrounded by narrow lanes. *It's the street here, this is the Rua dos Mercadores!* Primoroso proclaims. *Let's be careful! At night the city is so dangerous even God gets in a panic*, he warns. He keeps talking as he walks: *I've got my travel permit, but you, as a native black woman, aren't supposed to be out at this hour.* Self-important, he waves the document that allows him to travel in places that are exclusive to Europeans after dark. We'll have to avoid the police who ensure that the curfew is observed. Zeca Primoroso justifies their patrols:

*The Portuguese, poor souls, don't mean it badly. But it's not good to have blacks out and about when it's dark. A white might get a fright because he only becomes aware of a black man's presence once he has already bumped into him.*

We walk along the Rua dos Mercadores. I may speak Portuguese like few Portuguese can, I may have read many books, but I have never been in a city, I have never walked under the light of streetlamps. With pride, Zeca Primoroso translates the city that my eyes cannot read. In the doorways of bars, half-dressed women display themselves. There are hundreds of revelers on the street, almost all of them drunk, exchanging jokes and improprieties in the most incomprehensible tongues. The discovery of gold in neighboring lands has flooded Lourenço Marques with adventurers. English came, along with Boers, Syrians, Lebanese, Italians, Greeks, and people from such distant parts of the world that no map could do them justice.

While Primoroso lectures me about the city, he examines the fronts of the establishments. He peers from the other side of the street, from the shadiest parts of the sidewalk. Then he lifts me up as if I were a child. From that position, I am able to see into the smoke-filled rooms. The women are at once almost naked and overdressed. *I only just avoided becoming one of those women*, I confess out loud.

*How did that happen?* Zeca asks, putting me down on the ground again.

I tell him about Bianca Vanzini's proposal to employ me in one of her nightclubs. *In* The Bohemian Girl? Zeca asks, astonished. I shrug my shoulders. *I don't know*, I reply. *I know I would have been called Black Lilly*.

*That's a magnificent name*, remarks Zeca. *You should use it*, he suggests.

It is almost midnight when Zeca Primoroso stops in front of an establishment displaying the sign LA FOLIA. *It's here*, he murmurs excitedly. He goes up to a security guard at the entrance to the brothel. Uproar immediately ensues. Zeca Primoroso is stopped from going in, and not allowed to explain the situation. *You fucking nigger*, the bystanders shout in a chorus while they assault the defenseless translator. In despair, I search the crowd: Where can this Sergeant Amaral possibly be?

I go to Zeca's aid, as he lies sprawled on the sidewalk. I drag him across the road. I wipe away the blood dribbling down his face while he busies himself with an attempt to tidy his hair. In the scuffle, the heel of one of his shoes has come off. He asks me to look for it. A shoe is more important than any travel permit. That is his priority: to recover his composure. While I crawl around on the paving stones, the translator forgives his assailants: I shouldn't misinterpret the cause of such violence, which, according to him, was an "accident" of no importance. *They probably confused me with someone else. Everywhere I go, I'm treated with the utmost respect.*

*Don't say any more, Zeca,* I insist while I clean his bloodstained face. *If you don't stop talking, that wound will never heal.*

Then he starts tidying his hair again, his finger, covered in blood, straightening the part that divides his thick mass of hair. I clean his hand with a piece of cloth, that same hand which had forged so many letters of recommendation in order to get his brothers out of tight spots. This is what he tells me as I tend to him. Countless times, he had donned a white man's skin, signing letters of safe conduct by using a false, thoroughly Portuguese name. His handwriting was so perfect that no one could believe that those documents were composed by a black man.

*See, Imani?* Zeca concludes. *They say I betrayed my black brothers. No one has helped them as much as I have . . .*

Someone is calling my name from the other side of the street. It's Bianca Vanzini. We hug each other so extravagantly that passersby give each other suspicious looks. I don't see Zeca pushing through the onlookers, searching for Sergeant Amaral.

*I knew you were in Lourenço Marques*, Bianca reveals. *Germano wrote to me. He's already sent you two letters. Haven't you received them? Hasn't Andrea given them to you?*

I shake my head. *Andrea?* I ask, my voice faint, my mind vacant. Someone tugs my arm. It's Zeca Primoroso, who is in a hurry to return to our ship. That's how he put it: "our" ship.

*You go, Zeca. That ship isn't mine.*

*Come on*, the man insists. *Sergeant Amaral is here, don't keep us waiting.*

I clutch Bianca's dress more tightly, I lay my head on her chest and beg her:

*Let me stay with you, Bianca. Hide me among your women. I'll wait for Germano here.*

That would be a foolish idea, Bianca argues. Firstly, because they would come and fetch me. Secondly, because no one knew when Germano would pass through Lourenço Marques. And finally, and most importantly: If I missed that ship, I would never get another chance to travel to Lisbon. Portugal was where I should wait for my man.

*Go back to the ship. Zeca is right: It's your ship, your only ship.*

I let go of Bianca, and allow myself to be dragged off in the direction of the *Neves Ferreira*. The Italian woman is left standing in the distance, the streetlamp casting its light on her hair, when I suddenly see her waving her arms. I realize she's shouting, but I can't hear what she is saying because of the loud music coming from the brothels. Then it looks as if she has an envelope in her hands. Or maybe it's a white handkerchief she is using to wave goodbye.

# 11

## LETTER FROM GERMANO DE MELO TO BIANCA VANZINI

In one of the wars, the soldiers who had left on a mission turned around and headed back to the garrison. The astonished general watched the battalion return. They had not found the border they were supposed to defend. This was how they explained themselves:

*You don't know about the border?*

*So where is it, my general?*

*Well, the border . . . I mean the border . . . do you mean to tell me you didn't find it?*

*That's why we have come back, my general.*

*Well, the border is where the land ends.*

The soldiers left once more. And they never came back.

**—ANONYMOUS STORY COLLECTED BY GERMANO DE MELO**

*Inhambane, January 2, 1896*

Dearest Bianca,

I am writing to you in despair. I have sent Imani two letters and have not received a reply. I do not know whether she received them. I sent these messages via Álvaro Andrea, a captain in the navy whom I trust like a brother. I have had no word from him, or from Imani.

Wars have a deforming effect on the minds of those who are left waiting: We maintain an irresistible desire for news, even if we are certain that this may be the worst possible news. Hell is preferable to the absence of everything.

Not knowing the whereabouts of Imani has awakened feelings of anguish in me I thought I had left behind. And once again, I am left without hands, without body, and without any willpower. Sometimes, I wonder whether Imani has found another man. Or worse still: that, for no particular reason, she has ceased to love me. These are fantasies that destroy my peace and quiet, but not my hope. I shall soon find Imani, back in my own homeland. I shall take her to my village to introduce her to my mother. And then I shall announce, pointing to Imani's belly: Here is your grandson! Me in another life!

I have thought a lot about you, my dear Italian friend, and about the circumstances in which we met. I remember that day when Zixaxa attacked Lourenço Marques and how we sought refuge amongst the ruins. In the midst of the rubble we momentarily forgot that outside there was a world in a state of collapse.

One of these days, I shall pay you a visit again. I shall not arrive in time for Gungunhana's parade. That would be the best time to meet Imani once more. However, other absences will weigh far more heavily than mine. And one of these, the greatest, will be that of António Enes. The Royal Commissioner will receive the good news while on passage to Lisbon. Most of the military leaders are already back in Portugal. With the exception of Mouzinho, the heroes are all on vacation, exhausted by the only three battles they were ever obliged to fight. They will disembark in Lisbon having earned the right to a triumphal reception, acclaimed for a deed they tried desperately to avoid carrying out.

Your hero, that wandering cavalier, will have no cause to complain about a lack of recognition. Messages, medals, and other decorations have been sent from England, France, and Germany. Only Portugal has forgotten to take him back to Lisbon to receive the honors destined for him. The orders were very clear: Mouzinho will remain in Mozambique. The war is over. But not to the extent they want people to believe. Who knows; your wandering cavalier may visit you in Lourenço Marques. Who knows whether he won't take lodgings in your establishment?

I am sorry, my dear Bianca, but I cannot remain indifferent to your affection for Mouzinho. You are as free as I am to choose who to fall in love with. But for God's sake, anyone but that idiot! Just consider the childish enthusiasm the captain has for England. You, Bianca, know the consideration the English have for us Portuguese and Italians: They think of us as we think of Africans.

And that is how things are, my dear friend: The more narrow-minded a nation, the more difficult it is to choose its heroes. Not because there are none, for if there's one creature which proliferates in such nations, it is the hero. There are more heroes than inhabitants in Portugal. The difficulty in choosing them comes from the fear of displeasing anyone.

Amid this raucous victory celebration, the monarchy is concealing a future that it knows is uncertain and somber. They have captured Gungunhana, and they are sending him off into endless exile. One would require a ship the size of a whole continent to save Africa from the covetousness of the Europeans and the Africans themselves.

The ruler of Gaza always was a hindrance to Portugal, not so much because of what he did but because of what he did not allow to be done. Within days of his capture, our soldiers were already over-running villages, eliciting payment of the so-called hut tax. From now on, each family will have to pay half a gold sovereign. It may not seem like much, but it is a fortune for someone who, as a peasant farmer, lives far from any place where coins are used. The women weep, the elderly lament: To earn a wage, the menfolk will have to migrate to the mines of the Transvaal. In the absence of any public functionaries, they send soldiers and sepoys from Lourenço Marques. We know their ways only too well: They threaten, demand drink, order ducks and chickens to be slaughtered. And they take any cattle away with them that is not diseased.

I myself witnessed the arrival of one of these brigades in a village, and a Portuguese soldier sitting on top of a mortar, which, curiously, they call a *pilão* here. *Don't do that*, an old man begged. To use a mortar as a seat is an extreme sacrilege, an offense against accepted local custom. This is what the peasant humbly explained to the tax collector. Without moving, the soldier looked at the complainant nonchalantly and said: *I am going to correct the mistake I inadvertently made*. Then he set fire to the house and all that poor family's possessions. The fire spread uncontrolled through the village. And that was not an isolated incident. This arrogance became so widespread that those who lived under the suffocating tyranny of Gaza now yearn for it.

And so I shall bring this already long letter to a close. I took my time over it, perhaps, because I sensed that my stay in Africa is coming to an end. I confess I am sorry to be leaving this land. The truth is that Mozambique is leaving me. I go back to my home country without the glory of great deeds, I return without any great stories to tell. The only compensation that a war may bring a soldier are the friendships created during its course with his comrades in arms. I did not even gain any of these. I was a soldier without an army, I was the only occupant of a lifeless, empty garrison. I gained love and a child, you will say, Bianca. And I met you as well, I might add.

Let me tell you, and you alone, of an episode that occurred during my journey from Portugal to Mozambique—for I probably will never have the courage to share this memory with Imani. While I was passing through Cape Town, a brown-skinned, full-lipped Malay woman called me from the bottom of some stairs and, pulling me firmly to her, kissed me long and hard on my mouth. *It's a war kiss*, she murmured, and she disappeared into the darkness. That war kiss was supposed to bring me good fortune in future battles. In the end, there were no battles. But that kiss still comforts me even today during my long, lonely nights.

In Africa, I acquired an urgent desire to sleep and an incurable fear of falling asleep. I close my eyelids and the dead open their huge eyes inside me. And only the sweetness of that endless kiss brings me peace.

A fond farewell from this, your good friend,

*Germano de Melo*


P.S. It may happen, by happy coincidence, that you will meet Imani during the festivities in Lourenço Marques. If this occurs, I beg you to mention me and the letters I have sent her. If she has not received them, she should press the captain to give her what is rightfully hers. In any case—and in order to prevent any disappointment—I made copies of what I wrote. Along with this missive, I enclose these copies. Give them to Imani, I implore you.

# 12

## FOOTPRINTS IN THE DEW

*Your ancestors were great men who commanded the armies against the*
*Zulu invader, many decades ago. But they were forced to submit and to*
*pay taxes to the Zulus who occupied their territory. [. . .] Our Zulu*
*oppressor, Gungunhana, who wanted to expel the whites, was captured*
*by them and sent to the North. He was never seen again.*
—THE WORDS OF THE MOTHER OF EDUARDO MONDLANE, FIRST PRESIDENT OF THE FRONT
FOR THE LIBERATION OF MOZAMBIQUE, WHEN SHE SPOKE TO HIM AS A CHILD.
CITED BY KHAMBANE CHITLANGO AND ANDRÉ-DANIEL CLERC IN
<u>CHITLANGO: FILHO DE CHEFE</u> (CHITLANGO: SON OF A CHIEF), 1990

Zeca Primoroso and I are ferried back to the *Neves Ferreira* in a
dinghy. In fact it is Sergeant Amaral himself who takes the oars.
The silence seems to make the crossing shorter. The little pirogue
bumps against the hull of the *Neves Ferreira*, producing a familiar
sound, identical to that of the old water pail lowered into the well of
my childhood. I visualize myself, back in my village, receiving the
weight of the sky on my shoulders. How many clouds had women
already carried on their heads?

I climb up a rope ladder onto the deck. I am assailed by the same
dizziness as when I hunted bats high up in the trees. I'm climbing up
out of my past, I think to myself. If I lose my footing, I shan't fall
into the sea, but onto the floor of my girlhood. My father still ex-

tends his arms to catch me. His arms have grown and embrace the world.

I take my leave of Primoroso and advance through the darkness until I stumble into a shape. It is Dabondi. She is sitting in the middle of the deck contemplating her own feet. *Look!* she exclaims enthusiastically. *See this footprint on the floor!* I bend over in disbelief. The deck is paved with iron. Dabondi insists, pointing at what she alone can glimpse. *My son, Mangueᴢe, traveled on this same boat.* The queen reads the ground in the manner of a hunter: *My little boy passed this way, he sat down over there and wept. He was sad and very hungry when he went to bed.*

I help her to her feet. She interprets my gesture not as help but as a reprimand. She explains herself. At that moment she wasn't being a clairvoyant. She is just a mother who misses her son. And she reconstructs the scene: a young black boy boarding a ship all on his own, sailing across the sacred ocean and traveling exclusively in the company of white people. On that deck there are still traces of footsteps taken in fear.

❖

The queen is adamant: That ship, made entirely of iron, was built with the residue from cannons and rifles. On the outside, it smells of the sea, but on the inside it smells of gunpowder. All the other women of the court have lost count of the children they have given birth to. Only she had just one child. So fragile and small, what warmth would he find in a place made out of old guns?

I look at Dabondi and think: The young queen is lost. If there were any fairness in life, being a woman would justify her being a queen. But this queen is the saddest and most desolate of creatures. In order to feel alive, she needs her husband to desire her. That is why the women of the court, all of them, need to be beautiful. Dabondi is pretty but she knows that beauty, in her vulnerable situation, does not last long. That is why she imitates the shadows and disappears every day. A mirage never grows old. And that is how she would like her husband, the emperor, to surprise her: as a mirage traveling over the sea.

*The king wants to see you*, Dabondi says. *Me?* I ask. *Not a day goes by without him seeing you in his dreams*, the queen replies.

Dabondi leads me to the captain's cabin. This is where we find Ngungunyane. He has just been interrogated. The interrogation has gone well. Only this can explain why Álvaro Andrea has allowed the king of Gaza to use his quarters. Ngungunyane asks Dabondi to withdraw. The ruler of the VaNguni is worried: His brother, King D. Carlos, has not responded to his requests, while Zixaxa still shares his cabin, sleeping and plotting against him in the darkness. *They didn't deliver my letter to D. Carlos.* He is convinced someone has betrayed him by diverting the message to another recipient. *The letter hasn't had enough time to reach Lisbon*, I say. To no avail. Ngungunyane only listens to himself.

*Do you want me to write a new letter?* I ask.

Smiling, the king of Gaza waves a sheet of paper and declares: *You're too late, my girl. Andrea has just helped me. I told him some secrets and in exchange, he composed this letter.* It was Godido who served as a translator. He knows less Portuguese, says the king, but he is more familiar with the concept of loyalty.

*If you chose another scribe, why do you want to speak to me?* I ask with unexpected anger.

I am surprised by my own contempt for their having chosen

another scribe. Writing, I then realize, inverts hierarchies: The person dictating a letter has less power than the person writing it.

The king leans up against me, rubbing himself voluptuously. I stand motionless, waiting for him to stop. He asks me to stroke his knees. He is puzzled that I don't obey him immediately.

*My knees*, the king repeats. *I'm going to explain to you why a man needs good knees.*

Before leaving for war, the father of a family kneels in front of his wife and asks her to declare the names of her lovers. The warrior is supposed to stay on his knees until he obtains her admission of infidelity. If, by any chance, a soldier dies in combat, this is proof that his wife lied.

*There's something wrong with this story, my king. No man kneels in front of a woman.*

Ngungunyane laughs, amused by my impertinence. *You haven't understood anything at all*, he says. *The request that the heads of family make is not to their wives. That would be a waste of time, for women always lie. The men kneel so that their wives will think they are being submissive.*

I gradually move away while the monarch continues to digress. By the time he becomes aware of me, I'm already on the far side of the cabin.

*I'm not going to waste any more time*, Ngungunyane says. *All I want is for you to read a letter I dictated to Andrea—I just want to be left in no doubt as to what he wrote.*

I take my time in accepting the sheet he wants to give me. I give myself airs, as my mother would say. And I can see, from the first lines of script, that Álvaro Andrea took great pains to embellish the text. We both exaggerate the Portuguese ornateness of the words uttered by the king of the VaNguni. I translate slowly so that Ngungunyane can accompany me:

My brother,
King of Portugal,

I wish to speak to you of treason. Is this not the matter that most occupies kings throughout the world? It was ever thus: The blood of the royal family is the same as that which courses through the veins of its assassins.

From the start of this voyage, my feet have been bound to a traitor. He who tied the knot was not white. For this reason, I am grateful that you allowed my trusty aide-de-camp, the young Ngó, to travel with me. We both know our cook has another hidden function: He is the king's taster. And we both have to acknowledge that we have abused this silent weapon. We poisoned so many wells that eventually we killed our own people. Let us keep this secret. And here is another advantage of poison: Death occurs far away, at a time that belongs to no one.

Once again, I ask you, now that our great voyage is about to begin: Separate Zixaxa from me. Keep that cursed Mfumo away from me, somewhere he can't see me sleep or listen to my dreams. Those who share my cell have seen me sleep, eat, urinate, and defecate. What authority do I have over them? Please, D. Carlos, my brother, remove this traitor from me. Eliminate this man, no one will notice, no one will complain. Like the poison, which we use to excess, this will remain our secret.

*The King of Gaza*
*Lourenço Marques, January 4, 1896*

After I have finished reading, Ngungunyane peers into my face, trying to read in me what he is not capable of deciphering on the paper. *Do you think I lied to you, Nkosi?* I ask. *I swear I didn't make anything up, at all*, I then insist.

*I know,* says the king. *I know why you have become so similar to whites.*

Everything people say about me, Imani Nsambe, is a lie. People, the king promises, know about my past. And it isn't true, Ngungunyane says, that I spent my childhood in a Catholic mission, far from my parents and my village. It's because of witchcraft that I have become so like the whites.

*Dabondi realized who you really are,* Ngungunyane continues. *There's nothing like a witch to recognize another witch.*

Then once again, he approaches me, all blubbery. I am aware of his predatory eyes devouring my body. *You're a witch, Imani Nsambe, that's what you are,* Ngungunyane affirms.

*And you know what we do to a witch: We either kill her or . . .*

He pushes up against me, brushes his hand around my neck so that I don't know whether it's a caress or a threat. His fat fingers run down my shoulders and then to my waist. Then they slide down as far as my knees. There, they stop. *Drop your* capulana, he orders.

Deep within me, I listen to another woman's voice. That woman tells me I should feign obedience. This king whom I have always hated is now an ally. It will be in his company that I shall travel to Lisbon, where I shall once again meet the man I love. I pretend to undo my *capulana* and whisper in his ear:

*Your mother, Queen Impebekezane, told me that a husband shouldn't fear his male rivals. A male rival can steal your wife. But alcohol steals the man who lies within the man . . . do you understand what I'm saying, my king?*

He listens to my words and his hands suddenly grow limp. With ill-contained anger, he stamps his feet on the ground. He pushes me as he gets up.

*Who are you,* he screams, *to talk of my mother? You're nothing but a poor little VaChopi. Your people are dominated by the whites.*

Then he becomes more menacing: He would write to the king

of Portugal and ask him to send me back to Mozambique, tell them to get another translator. The Portuguese, in any case, have already shown their preference for Zeca Primoroso. It should be a man providing such services.

*Your friend Captain Andrea has gone. He should be ashore by now. He left you this letter*, Ngungunyane says, giving me an envelope.

# 13

## LETTER FROM ÁLVARO ANDREA TO IMANI

*Gungunhana agreed to surrender to the captain of my ship, only asking*
*that they should not cut his head off, and that the lives of his children*
*and uncles should be guaranteed. This sworn commitment was given*
*solemnly by me and betrayed in a cowardly way later at Chaimite,*
*where his uncles Queto and Manhune, who were accompanying the*
*ruler, were shot in cold blood.*

—EXCERPT FROM <u>A MARINHA DE GUERRA NA CAMPANHA DE LOURENÇO MARQUES E</u>
<u>CONTRA O GUNGUNHANA, 1894–1895</u> (THE NAVY IN THE LOURENÇO MARQUES
CAMPAIGN AGAINST GUNGUNHANA, 1894–1895), REPORT AUTHORED BY ÁLVARO SOARES
ANDREA, PUBLISHED IN THE <u>ANAIS DO CLUBE MILITAR NAVAL</u> (ANNALS OF THE NAVAL
MILITARY CLUB), 1897–1898

*The blacks, Manhune and Queto, died heroically and courageously*
*when they were shot. After they had fallen, the artillery lieutenant,*
*Aníbal Miranda, went over to each of them in turn and stabbed them in*
*the heart with his sword in full view of the soldiers, inflicting suffering*
*on dying defenseless men, a fact that constitutes a grave breach of the*
*laws of war, punishable by death according to military law. [. . .] These*
*men merit a statue raised to them by their followers for they fought*
*without turning their back, courageous Vátuas who chose to*
*die at their battle station.*

—CAPTAIN ÁLVARO SOARES DE ANDREA, ARTICLE PUBLISHED IN THE NEWSPAPER
<u>O LIBERAL</u> (THE LIBERAL), DECEMBER 27, 1908

*Lourenço Marques, January 6, 1896*

Dear Imani,

This is Álvaro Andrea writing to you. This letter is at once a decla-
ration of surrender and an apology. My surrender is as sincere as my
shame for having used you. I was motivated by a blind rancor
against Mouzinho. Maybe I went too far in my resentment. I did to
this adversary what Portugal did to Gungunhana: I magnified him
so as to give meaning to my life, I treated his victory with such luster so as to forget my own defeats.

There are a thousand questions I never got to ask you. For example, is it true that Mouzinho was drunk at Chaimite? Is it true
that he consulted a soothsayer to find out the likely result of his
audacity? Can it be confirmed that, during the march to the Limpopo, his prisoners were continually beaten?

Let us forget these questions. This letter is, after all, motivated
by another, possibly more selfish intention: I want to show you the
wounds that the war opened in my soul. Maybe I am telling you all
this because you are a woman, and because you are black, and because the simple fact of you reading me alleviates my torment.

Over the last two months, I was one of the commanders of the
so-called Limpopo squadron. Our mission was to bombard the population on both sides of the river. And that is what we did: Not a day
went by when our gunfire did not cause the corvette to shudder. At
the same moment, like some illusion of a watercolor, the sky was
filled with gigantic flashes of light. From the banks of the river, thick
smoke belched in anticipation of the sunset and nightfall.

When the deadly bombardments had finished, my soldiers
would leap off the boat and spread out over the savanna like crusta-
ceans emerging at low tide. The black folk contemplated those

shapes advancing through the mist. And what they saw were gigantic crabs bearing burning torches in their claws. With these flares, they set fire to homes and plantations. Dozens of villages were ravaged, and fishermen's dugouts sunk.

From the corvette, I watched the clouds of smoke, my half-spread fingers protecting my face. I feared being struck by a spark and returning to Portugal a blind man. However, without knowing it, I was already blind. The marines brought me news of the devastation. They did not speak of military bases destroyed or soldiers killed. Those who died were defenseless civilians. When they had completed their accounts, there was nothing but darkness around me. I am a naval captain. I should have been visiting villages in order to assess the damage. I should have had the courage to bury the dead and give succor to the survivors. I did none of those things. I remained there, indolent and quaking, until a soldier came and led me by the arm to my tent. I collapsed onto my camp bed like someone sinking into the final abyss.

I was so burdened by guilt that even when Gungunhana agreed to his rendition, I did not realize the extent of this change of heart. Perhaps the Nguni chiefs were not serious in their intentions. But the message was clear: The emperor would present himself on my ship provided that no harm would be inflicted on him or any of his relatives. I gave him my word of honor that these procedures would be observed. This was my promise. It was Mouzinho's fault that nothing happened as foreseen.

It is this weight that I carry inside me, my dear Imani. Some days ago, one of the marines tried to comfort me, convinced that my state of depression was caused by some unhappy love affair. Would that this were the case. My love life always was a desert. I remember the most beautiful, mysterious woman who would invariably appear on the quayside in Lisbon. I even thought she had come to say goodbye to one of the crew. But I later found out that she did this with all departing ships. All dressed in black, as sadness requires, the woman would remain on the quay until all the others had gone home. She would not leave the harbor until the ship had melted away into her tears. One of my adjutants told me she was the wife of a sailor who had long died somewhere in Africa. Gradually, the woman acquired the look of one who is sightless: The horizon was the only land she knew. The same sailor later confirmed that the "loiteress"—that is what he called her—came to say farewell to me. The woman had told him the story of how she and I had met. I asked the sailor to keep the matter to himself and said that I myself would go and look for her. However, the mysterious character never appeared on the quay again. It was said she had been found insane, and put away. I never visited her, nor did I try and find out the location of the asylum that had taken her in. I was scared she might recognize me. Bravery, my dear, does not emerge from the act of thought. Courage does not dwell in the brain. It comes from the gut.

Let me now confess: That woman never existed. I created the character, and for many years, I kept up the pretense. I invented the story and told it so many times that I ended up believing it had all happened. Though a lie, the solace of having someone waiting for me was always true.

The only stories worth telling are those about misplaced love. Like this passion I feel for you and which has caused me countless times to imagine that it is you who waits for me on some quayside at the end of some fanciful journey.

Even today, I tell my companions the story of that woman who experienced a love fashioned from waiting. The last time I did so, we were sailing up the Limpopo and a black sailor declared: *I've got a story to tell too*. He began by recounting a legend from his village, which lay somewhere along the banks of the river. In the old days, he started, the firmament was jet-black, starless. Then a young girl, maddened with longing, decided to walk through the gloom to look for her sweetheart. Halfway through the journey, she prepared a fire, the height of which had never been seen before. When there was no more wood left in the world, she threw the clothes she was dressed in on top of the pile. And now, stripped naked, she lit the fire and watched the sparks rise into the night. That was how the stars were born.

*Why are you telling me this story, boy?* I asked. Pointing to the nearby riverbank, the sailor replied: *One night, guns were fired from this very boat, and the gunfire lit up my village like stars. These stars,* he continued, *kindled the curiosity of the children who, in their excitement, ran out into the yard. None of them survived.* He paused, before concluding: *It's because of those stars that I shall never be able to leave this ship.*

The sailor's intention was clear: He wanted to plunge the blade of remorse into me. However, the opposite occurred. For me, his words suggested an escape: Unable to expunge my crimes, it was my duty to punish the guilty. I decided not only to confess my guilt, but to denounce the suffering inflicted by our navy. I sent a first version of the report to the Royal Commissioner, without any expectation of a reply. To my great surprise, a messenger brought me a response from António Enes. I attach part of his answer:

In any civilized country, acts of war such as those practiced by our Limpopo squadron, apart from being condemned by humanitarian principles and appearing repugnant to spirited cavalrymen, would provoke violent reactions, reactions of hatred and vengeance among peoples punished by the sovereign ruler; but in Africa, such reactions are not in evidence, because these can only be produced by elevated notions of morality and desire for justice and dignity, all of which are lacking in Negroes.

I should spare you these insults against your race. But I want you to know how these people who command us think. After receiving António Enes's reply, I abandoned my epistolary lamentations. I concentrated on writing a report on the immoral acts committed by Mouzinho de Albuquerque. I am naïve but I am not stupid: No one is interested in these incriminations. The adventure at Chaimite, the *Chaimitada* as I call it, is a lifesaver for the monarchy. All the celebrations will have to fade away before another version of this invented epic may be accepted.

Perhaps Mouzinho told you how he found me at the post at Languene. It was Christmas, and the heroic captain made a point of ridiculing the party which I had so zealously prepared for our soldiers. He asked me to lend him a sword and in one absurd flourish, he plunged it into the marsh. It was Lieutenant Miranda who picked it up, and in a moment of forgetfulness, took it with him to Chaimite. And it was there that the unthinkable occurred, my dear Imani: It was precisely that sword of mine which they used to pierce the hearts of the two men they had shot. I close my eyes and see blood. That sword pierces my sleep, every night.

You will not see me tomorrow at the parade. I may well be far away, on my journey back to the Limpopo. I could not bear to witness such a circus. In truth, it will be no different from many of the performances put on by the other European peacocks. What a grand illusion! We claim we are the lords of a continent of which we are ignorant. It is a lie that Europe has conquered Africa. We mistake a desire for reality. All we do is to command small, dispersed trading posts near the coast. I am familiar with these places, and they can be counted on the fingers of one's hand. All the rest of the continent continues to be governed by African kings and emperors. Two Africas alternate with each other like mysterious women, one by night, the other by day. We know neither of them.

In order to maintain the appearance of our power, we need to exhibit the king of Gaza on the streets of Lisbon. This is not a question of banishment. It is a funfair.

*Fond regards,*
*Álvaro Andrea*

# 14

## PARADES AND PANDEMONIUM

*When walking through a forest, a man was attacked by robbers. They beat him, stripped him of his clothes, tore his eyes out, and tied him to a tree. In the middle of the night, the poor man's eyes started to climb up his legs. They were trying to get back to his face. The man felt his eyes clambering up his body and asked them to leave him in peace.* Please don't come back, *he pleaded.* I don't want to see myself anymore, I never want to see the world again.
*Toward the end of his torment, he heard animals growling as they approached. In a matter of seconds, he was devoured. Not even his bones were left. A few lengths of rope hugging a tree trunk were all that remained. As they no longer had a body in which to dwell, his eyes wandered through the woods. And it is through these eyes that travelers in the forest glimpse their own dreams.*
**—DABONDI'S TALES**

I forgot about my race long ago, it is a long time since I distanced myself from the customs of my people. But I still sit like a black woman: my legs folded next to each other under me, knees together. The emperor's eyes are glued on me as he assesses how faithful I am to ancient fears, and watches my hands, which I keep respectfully crossed.

It is morning. Only a few hours ago we were still on the boat. When the prisoners entered the city, they breathed a sigh of relief.

And the queens even smiled. But their joy was short-lived. They were merely changing penitentiaries. And now, at the rear of the Lourenço Marques jailhouse, the prisoners are divided into two groups. An Angolan soldier pushes them, shouting:

*Landins over here, Vátuas over there!*

*There's no such thing,* Zixaxa mutters through gritted teeth.

In the shade of a mango tree are Ngungunyane and his family. Under another tree sit Nwamatibjane Zixaxa and his three wives.

Zixaxa murmurs sarcastically: Instead of worrying about getting his royal crown back, Ngungunyane should ask his wives to dress him in the white man's uniform. *Or can it be,* he asks, *that the ruler of Gaza is no longer a sergeant in the Portuguese army?*

He wants to humiliate the king, and he wants to belittle his queens. What Zixaxa does not know is that he himself, the proud, emblematic rebel, has been incorporated, this very day, into the Portuguese army. All those prisoners are, from today, members of an army against which they always fought. Strictly speaking, they ought to march in boots and uniform in the upcoming military parade. But instead, they will march barefoot and almost stripped of any clothing. Their race will be their uniform, the only one the colonials recognize.

I go over to Ngungunyane. It takes time for a king to notice the presence of someone approaching. It takes even longer if the visitor is a woman. I have been warned about these whims and that is why I am not offended by the wait. Finally, with a slight nod, Ngungunyane authorizes me to speak.

*They have told me to explain to you how the ceremony will proceed.*

*Will I be led along with my wrists bound?* the king asks.

I was the one supposed to be asking the questions and dragging secrets from him. That's why they sent me: to guarantee that no conspiracy would spoil the party. I definitely have no talent for keeping a watch on others. With a frown, the emperor scans the distance. He is looking for kraals, herds of cattle. But he cannot make out any horned animal. What kind of a miserable place was this, where all you could see were people?

Busy weaving the crown into the monarch's hair, his seven wives do not share their husband's concerns. Ngungunyane may parade with his hands bound, but he will never be without his *chilodjo*. No hair stylist in the world can compete with the gifts these women have. The crown is festooned with threads of the rarest material: slender tendons taken from the loins of oxen. It takes the sacrifice of several heads of cattle in order to obtain a dozen of these nerve threads, each of which is plaited with the emperor's hair. Each member of the Nguni nobility wears a wax crown. But none of them is woven with these delicate braids.

Dabondi leaves the group and offers me a gourd containing *ukanyu*. I refuse it initially. I know what my reaction will be to what they say is the most aphrodisiac of drinks. But in the end, I give way.

*Did they invite the English?* the king asks.

It was a predictable question: The main intended audience for the ceremony are the English, who covet the colony of Mozambique and who, according to Lisbon, always backed the king of Gaza.

*Do you know what day it is today?* Ngungunyane seems to ask himself. Without waiting for an answer, he continues to hold forth. *Today is the day of Umnkosi Nkwayo, the Festival of First Fruits.*

This festival doesn't belong to the Portuguese. It is his, celebrated in his honor. The whites merely authorize it. They were unable to forbid it. The Portuguese paid all the expenses, but the festival is against them. This is what the deposed king of Gaza thinks. And raising his arm, he orders:

*Go and tell this to your paymasters: The Portuguese defeated my soldiers but they will never disarm our gods.*

I think to myself: The king is drunk. His hands are trembling when he pours himself another round. *Make the most of it, my girl,* he urges me. *This is the last time we shall be able to enjoy our drink.*

Ngungunyane is like one possessed. His half-tended hair gives him a ridiculous air, with a spiky tuft standing erect on top of his cranium.

The disheveled emperor wanders around and imagines out loud how the festivities would be if we were at his court in Mandhlakazi. He would be the one to choose the cattle to be sacrificed. He would choose cows, as tradition demands. They would have to be blinded before their throats were cut. They cannot watch themselves dying, otherwise their meat grows tough. This is his secret request, which he confides to me: That they should tear his eyes out when they are about to kill him. Blindness is a gift in a time of horror, Ngungunyane says.

I am not surprised by the rapture with which his wives listen to him. What does astonish me is the fact that the king is aware of the preparations for the parade. For example, he knows that his prime adversary, the warrior Xiperenyane, is sweeping the streets at that very moment.

*That great hero of your people, that fellow Xiperenyane, agreed to ally himself to the Portuguese,* the king comments. *Now he's a slave of the whites. They made him work, preparing for my party. He's one of my slaves. That is the fate of those who dare stand against me.*

They can keep the emperor in chains, far from his army, removed from his court. But the truth is that he still has a weapon that is more powerful than gunpowder at his disposal: networks that relay news and rumor. Whoever told him about the VaChopi chief was not lying. I too had bumped into Xiperenyane. In front of the governor's residence, there he was, carrying a broom and bucket. The man who had been my people's guiding light, he who had done most to assist the Portuguese in defeating Ngungunyane, was now an anonymous servant. When, surprised and disturbed, I greeted him, he showed no sign of vexation:

*I'm helping to celebrate the imprisonment of my greatest enemy. Isn't that any warrior's reason for joy?*

Bibliana's prophecy had come about after all: Xiperenyane had become blinded to the false respect once shown him by the Portuguese. There he was, as she had so aptly foreseen, the image of us all, poor blacks, sweeping the world for other peoples' parties.

I never thought there were so many whites in the world. Or blacks, for that matter. But now I see them all, feverishly cheering the Portuguese troops marching down the only avenue in the city. Soldiers of all races stand to attention before a tribune full of colonial worthies. In the center of the podium is the acting governor, Correia Lança, surrounded by diplomats from various nations. The best seats have been reserved for the captains of German and British battleships visiting the port. All around the rostrum, Portuguese and English journalists jostle together. And finally, on the tribune, all the dignitaries are present except for the one who most deserves to be there: Captain Mouzinho de Albuquerque. His absence riles the governor, who keeps repeating the order under his breath:

*Call Mouzinho! Call him quickly. Everyone wants to hail him.*

A hardworking emissary rushes off to find the hero. I know where they'll find him: sitting next to Major Caldas Xavier's deathbed. Mouzinho confided in me yesterday: This was the worst possible moment for celebrations. Struck down by a tropical disease, the great architect of the Portuguese military offensive in Mozambique now lay dying. And it struck Mouzinho that life is made up of missed opportunities. For months, Caldas Xavier had been an administrator for the Zambezia Opium Company. A field of poppies as far as the eye could see had, for months, nursed the Portuguese major's dream. That sea of red flowers is now vanishing under his eyelids.

For the whites, Caldas Xavier was overcome by a disease. For us blacks, the man was the victim of a contract killing. In our homeland, people don't die of something. They die of someone. Death has no cause. Only a perpetrator.

Mouzinho de Albuquerque eventually appears in public and, without greeting the dignitaries, he crosses the tribune to address the crowd. In a split second, his eyes meet mine. I acknowledge him, bowing my head. Like this, I thank him for reserving me a place right next to the tribune. Standing stiffly at the very front of the podium, his voice shaking and trapped in his chest, Captain Mouzinho speaks:

*I don't merit this fanfare*, he starts by saying. His voice gathers volume. *One does not render homage to one soldier when another is dying.* Then he announces, full of emotion: *Gentlemen, Caldas Xavier, the bravest of Portuguese, is dying.*

He pauses, discreetly wipes the sweat from his face. He breathes a deep sigh and babbles:

*I envy him his good fortune, because he is dying for the fatherland.*

We then hear the crowd clamoring: *We are forever Portuguese!* I notice the contorted faces of those yelling, possessed, so fired up that they seem to have changed their race. It's too hot for such an exalted demonstration of patriotism. But then I understand: What is being celebrated there isn't just a military victory. What the captain has brought those people is a miracle cure for their downtrodden lives.

Suddenly, whether because of the heat or the effects of the drink, I am also thrown to the ground by a feeling of dizziness. I have nothing to hold on to. I am surrounded by untouchable people. I shut my eyes. The giddiness doesn't stop. I shouldn't have drunk so much *ukanyu*. It's too late to go back.

When the speeches have finished, the Africans are allowed to celebrate as long as they remain on the opposite sidewalk. I am holding on to one of the supporting struts of the podium, while the dizziness has worsened and the world has become misty and remote. I can hear the beating of drums, women are dancing wildly, songs are being sung in countless different languages. The racket the blacks are making becomes so deafening that the prisoners recoil in far greater fear than the whites. They remain forlorn even after Ngungunyane raises himself onto the tips of his toes and starts bellowing. The king is gripped by high spirits. Among the whites, no one understands a word he is saying. The delirious king announces: It is not a military parade taking place on that avenue, but the Festival of the First Fruits. *This is the Nkosi Nkwayo*, he proclaims euphorically.

Pointing toward me, the king of Gaza asks me to explain to the whites the reason for his ecstasy. The blacks are paying him homage as tradition requires: They insult him on the day in which nothing is sacrosanct. These ugly names, which are impossible to translate, merely confirm his divine authority.

The beating drums make me dance and the ground sways, intemperate like the sea. In a split second, I am leaping around in the middle of the avenue. My heart is a drum and my body is no longer mine. I look around me, and everything is blurred. I cannot distinguish the prisoners from the thousands of black people taking part in the parade. They are all mingling, those who weep and those who celebrate. And all dance together, the tyrants and the slaves. Those who fought each other before are now arm in arm in the white man's city. In their right hand, they carry a Zulu spear. In their left, the curved hatchet of the VaNdau. From their shoulders hang the bows with which we VaChopi resisted the occupation of the VaNguni. And they all wave the same weapons used to kill them, as if they were the banners of victory. United by failure, the vanquished take possession of the city. Africa has conquered the fortress of the Europeans. Xilinguíne has swallowed up Lourenço Marques.

Terrified, the colonial authorities retreat in disorder, protecting their hats as if in a storm. The white women take off their shoes in order to keep up with their husbands in flight, and all of them seek refuge in the governor's palace.

I am pinned against the edge of the podium when Xiperenyane dances past. Behind the warrior come Bibliana, praying as she walks, and Chikazi, my dead mother, dragging the rope with which she hanged herself. The two women cross the avenue and come over to me. They hug me. The seer, Bibliana, whispers in my ear: *Those dancing are the warriors who fell at Marracuene, Magul, and Coolela. They're all together now. This is the army of the dead, those who will never have to give up their weapons.*

I take my mother's hand and keep it on my belly while tearfully begging her:

*Mother, help me. Take me home.*

*There's no return for you, my daughter. When the party's over, you'll be pursued by the blacks as a traitor. And you'll be rejected by the whites because of the incurable flaw you carry in your skin. This is the fate you chose, Imani.*

The two women dance off and disappear into the throng. I climb up onto the rostrum and cry hysterically:

*Save me, for the love of God. Save me!*

That heartrending appeal is more than a scream. It is a soul I expel from me with the violent pain of giving birth. All of a sudden, everyone stops speaking and that huge clamor recoils like a snail into its shell. I shake my head as if cleansing myself on the inside. I come to my senses at last.

In front of me, the white dignitaries are seated, staring at me, astounded, their eyes popping. Round about us, the crowd waits, in suspense, for what will follow. As they say where I come from, a knot has been tied in the silence. I must seem so unrecognizable that even Mouzinho remains cold and distant.

*Who is this black girl?* the governor asks. Then he orders the police to arrest me. At this point Bianca Vanzini bursts through the ranks on the tribune. The Italian woman gives a hurried curtsy and declares: *Your Excellencies, this girl is ill, I'll take her away with me.*

Without saying a word, Mouzinho raises his arms and then lets them drop in a gesture of indulgence. I am led away by the Italian woman among the massed ranks of the inquisitive, who peel away from us as if to avoid a contagious illness. Bianca guides me through the deserted streets of the city, in a hurry to distance herself from the celebrations. After a while, she pauses and places her hands on my shoulders. She seems exhausted. Her voice is almost tearful when she asks me:

*What's happening to you, my dear girl?*

There isn't a soul in Bianca's brothel. I walk along the corridors, I explore the bedrooms with their pink wallpaper. The Italian woman allows me to try on a dress of red silk. She beautifies my hands with long black gloves. She praises my figure, lamenting my not having accepted her invitation to be one of her ladies of the night. I wave my gloved hand.

*I'm pregnant, it won't be long before my body just turns into one big belly.*

She takes some dog-eared sheets of paper from a drawer. They are Germano's letters. The Italian woman hastens to explain: *These are the copies that Germano wrote in his own hand.*

I hardly have the strength to hold the papers she hands me, as my heart is thumping so hard, it is causing my body to shake. *I tried to give you them last night,* she says, *but they dragged you off down the road back to a boat.* Something is dripping onto my shoes. The papers are sopping wet. They hang from my hands as heavily as something that has died.

*Why have you kept them all wet?* I ask. *How do you expect me to read them if they are dripping with water?*

Bianca's anguished look is that of someone who does not recognize me. *There isn't a single drop of water on those papers,* she assures me. She wants to touch my face, but hesitates. She wants to caress my hair, but her hand holds back. Then eventually, she gently coaxes me: *Give me back the letters, Imani. Let me read them to you.*

I pass her the papers, which are soaking. She examines me slowly, incredulous. She cocks her head and starts to read. Her lips move but all I can hear is the murmur of a river, that same river where Germano and I made love.

When she finishes reading, I feel empty. What is left inside me is no more than a blind rage directed against Álvaro Andrea. How dare he keep what didn't belong to him? I walk round and round the room, cursing the narrow-eyed captain: *I'll kill that white!*

*Calm down, girl,* Bianca orders. Then she tells me to sit down and write to Germano. *I'll give him your letter*, she says, *when he passes this way.*

I languidly take off the gloves, with the sluggish sadness of a snake shedding its skin. I want to write. But I don't know how to start. My hatred of Andrea is greater than my yearning for Germano. I'll write later, I promise Bianca. Her hand brushes my curly hair and, just as happened on our first encounter, I dissolve under her caress.

*I'll visit you in Lisbon even this year*, Bianca declares. *Because I'm also leaving. I'm going back to Italy.*

Bianca opens the windows and her breath mingles with the dust released from the curtains: *Mouzinho wants to leave life; I just yearn to leave Africa.*

She pretends to peer out the window. Her hand strokes the fabric of the curtain as if she were seeking support.

*It isn't death that captain desires*, she says.

Mouzinho is waiting for a love that can never happen. Everyone talks of his impossible passion for Dona Amélia, the distant queen of Portugal. *At least he still waits in hope.* The Italian woman sighs.

Bianca blames life, blames the city that had once been her salvation. She looks out at the movement in the street that is now buzzing with people. At that hour, blacks and whites still share the same space.

*Do you know what tires me most about your country, Imani? It's the wailing of the children.*

In other places, Bianca declares, children cry in the same way that we learn to pray: They hope things will get better. That doesn't happen with African children. They wail voicelessly, for themselves, as if they were living their last day. Their tears imitate their bellies: swollen but empty.

*I'm going back to Italy, we always return home eventually.* Then she smiles sadly. *The first time I went back, no one recognized me in my village.*

*You'd been away a long time*, I suggest by way of an explanation. *It wasn't because of the time. They didn't recognize me because I returned happy.*

The Italian woman folds Germano's letters and puts them in her purse. There's an ink stain on her dress.

# 15

## A SUBMISSIVE ACT OF DISOBEDIENCE

*Priests tell us that after we die, we go to heaven. My heaven is on the
ground, Imani. Every day, I go around treading on my future abode.
I've been living in the heavens for a long time. When I die, I would
like to go and live somewhere else.*

**—ZIXAXA**

*You are an idiot, my dear Álvaro. I could simply ignore you. But life
has taught me that it is idiots we should fear the most.*

**—EXCERPT FROM A MESSAGE TO ÁLVARO ANDREA FROM MOUZINHO DE ALBUQUERQUE**

I spent the night in a bed in the brothel, between sheets that had
never welcomed anyone's sleep. I had long forgotten what it was like
to sleep in a bed. Maybe that's why I slept so long and so soundly.

Early the next morning, I am roused by the gentle voice of
Álvaro Andrea. The Portuguese waited for the parade to finish in
order to come ashore.

*What are you doing in my room?*

*I brought you something that'll please you.*

*Have you brought me the letters?*

*The letters?*

*The letters from Germano.*

*I must confess something*, Andrea says. *I no longer have those letters. Mouzinho took them.*

Captain Andrea looks downtrodden. He hadn't given me the letters, he admits, because he meant to use them as a bargaining chip in exchange for any statements I might provide. But gradually, he began to realize that there was another reason for his delay. He hoped, he confesses, that I would forget Germano.

*I beg your forgiveness, Imani. I betrayed a good companion, and I disappointed a lady friend.*

Then without looking up, he continues. His despair at not being loved poisoned his soul. Love moves mountains. But unlove can open up an abyss. This was Andrea's lament.

*Go away, Captain*, I mumble.

He raises his arm. The gesture is authoritarian. He is no longer asking me. He insists I listen to him. Then he recalls what happened: Some days ago, Mouzinho surprised him concealing some papers in his pocket. Believing it was the accusatory report, he gave the order to search the pockets of his uniform, and the drawers in his cabin. This was how Mouzinho got hold of Germano's letters. And he never returned them.

*So why didn't you ask for them back?*

*I shall go to my grave before I ask that impostor a favor!* Andrea says. *I know Germano won't forgive me. And you will hate me. But I could not have acted differently.*

*Go away, Captain*, I request, now impatient. *Please leave me alone.*

The Portuguese stands there, impassive. After a while, he holds out his arm with the amiability of a suitor:

*Come, let me show you the city.*

I refuse, gently but firmly: *I don't want to be with you*, I say. *I don't want to talk to you.*

From the window I watch Álvaro Andrea walking away. And I have to admit that he is a very handsome man. There is a vulnerability and a delicacy about him that do not match his military status. These attributes leave me confused.

I wait for a while and then I leave the house without noticing how inappropriately dressed I am. The same place I thought resplendent yesterday now appears dull and sad. The streets are still damp from the overnight drizzle. I drag the dress Bianca lent me along the muddy sidewalks.

Signs in Portuguese show the names of the streets. All the other signboards are in English. Even the city is designated Delagoa Bay. I walk along the Rua dos Mercadores which, in the light of day, looks drab and empty. A little farther on, I turn into the Rua da Gávea and pass Indian traders standing on the sidewalk, who call out to me in their strange accent:

*Come into my shoppie, girlie! You can just lookee, no problema!*

I pause in the last street, the so-called Rua da Linha. Along it, there are rows of old streetlamps that used to be lit by burning whale oil. All this is now no more than a memory. The lampposts evoke a terrible recollection: my mother's body swaying from the tree where she hanged herself. I turn my back on time, and walk away from the marshes that start here. The lights are the sentinels on a border separating two worlds at war.

Suddenly, three sailors burst from a doorway. They surround me menacingly. One of them comments: *This is the first time I've seen such a ladylike black whore!* They push me toward a stairwell. They share their tasks in silence, as if raping a woman were some inherited skill. One of them holds my legs, the other pins down my arms. A third one lies down on top of me, tears my clothes off, and dribbles over my breasts. I shout out for help. My screams seem to excite them even more. I know I have given up the struggle when, more than any other pain, I feel a tear rolling down my cheek. Then something happens that I shall never be able to describe properly. For all of a sudden, I'm wrapped in shadows that gesticulate furiously, collapse, and then get up again and run away. I feel the relief of someone coming up for air. I open my eyes wide again and come face-to-face with Álvaro Andrea. He helps me to my feet. He waits quietly while I recover my composure.

We return in silence to Bianca's bar. The Portuguese holds out his hand to help me step across puddles. I do not immediately accept his kindness. Finally, our fingers touch. But then I free myself abruptly. *That's fine, we're here*, I hurriedly defend myself. Bianca, who has already got wind of the incident, is waiting for us at the door. She takes me in her arms and comforts me: *Good, you're home now.* Never has a strange house felt more like my own home.

For some reason, Bianca recalls how her late husband arrived home late one night. The man was drunk, and sought refuge in a corner of the house to defend himself from embarrassing questions. *I don't know what time I got home, woman*, he said. *When I arrive home, time stops.*

*Men.* Bianca laughs, helping herself to a lemon liqueur. *Men are just like this liqueur: sweet when we want them to be bitter, acerbic when we want them to be cordial.*

*Dona Bianca, I beg you: Give me back Germano's letters. I know they're copies. But they're worth more than the originals.*

The Italian woman hesitates, as if she were searching the confines of her memory. I remind her that she had read me two of the letters the previous day.

*I put them away among a pile of clothes. I'll have to look for them.*

*Do you remember what they said?*

*My dear, love letters never say anything.*

I have lunch with Bianca. The woman serves up more words than food. She tells me stories. She knows everything about all her clients, from the soldiers to the missionaries. One day, she'll write a book divulging secrets that will compromise the most notable figures.

*They call me the lady with the hands of gold. But nothing sells for a higher price than silence.*

Prostitutes who have just woken up pass us. They have the brazen look of night birds.

*I remember perfectly the first time we met. You were the first white woman I had ever seen.*

I remember that moment, months ago in my village. I recall the Italian woman's sweet-smelling perfume and her even sweeter accent. And I once again feel her hands combing my hair. It seemed such a simple gesture but few moments have lasted so long in my memory. There was a white woman telling me I had beautiful hair, assuring me I didn't need to hide it under a headscarf. It was impossible to forget her sad confession: that she had come to Africa in order to stop living. And that Lourenço Marques had then seemed to her like a good place to die.

*And your Prince Charming?* I ask.

*What prince?* Bianca retorts.

*Your mad passion for Mouzinho?*

*That's all water under the bridge*, she affirms with a smile.

Love, she adds, is the briefest of all fatal diseases.

Late afternoon I pay Ngungunyane a visit in prison. I received the order from the director. He is worried about the prisoner's depressed state. He spent the night under extra surveillance. Straight after the parade, they shut him away in isolation. They fear him being in the company of other prisoners. But they are also scared that isolation may aggravate his already fragile morale. For this reason, they urgently require my assistance.

The guards turn the key loudly, rousing the sleepy prisoner. Ngungunyane looks at me, surprised: He is aware that visits are forbidden. Sitting with a bottle on his lap, the king is the image of despondency. I ask permission to keep him company.

*You who are white almost from birth: Do you know when they are going to kill me?*

I say nothing, leaving him to suffer a while. Each second of my silence is a blade that slashes through his soul. I know he is watching me, perplexed. He is admiring, as he has already confessed, my beauty. But he cannot conceive of me being disobedient. That is why he speaks again.

*I have a proposal to make you: Let us forge an alliance.*

He starts by acknowledging that I have powers. And that my powers are greater than any he once had. I am, he says, the only black woman the Portuguese listen to. His proposal is that I should invent another version of events. A version that heaps all blame on Nwamatibjane Zixaxa.

*I took risks to protect Zixaxa that no one can gauge. The Portuguese waged war on me because of Zixaxa. And now this fellow blames me for handing him over to the Portuguese?*

He resisted them for longer than many expected. He only surrendered the Mfumo fugitive when he no longer had a choice. There's no gratitude in life, Ngungunyane laments.

*Zixaxa goes around proclaiming I'm as bad as the whites and that I persecute my black brothers. He says I harass the least fortunate, and that I mistreat my slaves. But I ask you: What does he do with his people?*

The emperor of Gaza is right, I feel like saying. This is what always happens: The humiliated end up the same as the oppressors.

*I'm very sad, I need a little consolation*, the king complains. *Lift up your dress, I want to look at your legs.*

I close my eyes, and take a deep breath. The mere request is offensive to me. The king perceives my unease. And he mumbles: *All right, then bring me another bottle of sweet wine.*

I withdraw. Ngungunyane is still grumbling before they close the cell door. When he meets the king of Portugal, he won't have anything to offer him by way of a gift.

*I shall offer him you*, I hear him shout. *But first, I've got to satisfy myself with the quality of the gift.*

The next day, Álvaro Andrea once again drops by Bianca's establishment. Yet again, he invites me out for a walk in the city. Faced with my refusal, the Portuguese points out:

*This shall be the last time we meet. Your ship sails tomorrow.*

So I end up giving in. The Portuguese takes me to a hillside covered in kitchen gardens. Here and there, Indian women in brightly colored saris toil in their plots. We sit here and gaze at the early morning bustle of the city. Ox wagons bring Boers from the Transvaal and English from Natal. These wretched people, the Portuguese remarks, are attracted like moths by the bohemian nightlife which is forbidden by the puritanical customs of their own homelands.

The first stone and mortar buildings were built by blacks. A stone mason, a carpenter, and a blacksmith came from Inhambane to carry out the work. They were joined by a local caulker. From working so much with tar, the caulker's hands were completely black. He would proudly wave them around and proclaim: *I'm the true black man here.*

We laugh. And once again our fingers intertwine until, gently but resolutely, I move away from Andrea. Then I ask myself what I am doing here, hand in hand with such an unusual, distinctive man. Somewhere, Germano is waiting for me. And I wait for him with the same devotion. That place, though, is slowly fading away like the footprints Andrea and I leave behind us on the damp, sandy road.

❖

Farther on, we meet an elderly medicine man. Andrea greets him, addressing him as "doctor." And there he intends no irony. Until recently, there was no doctor anywhere in the settlement. The whites were treated by this *nyamosoro*, who was of Mfumo origin. The old medicine man laughs when Andrea recalls those times. For every soldier he cured, he recalls in his improvised Portuguese, he would get one *capulana*. And as the whites never stopped falling sick, the man accumulated so much cloth that he ran out of space to store it. He lost count of all the marriages he contracted in order to find homes for so much fabric.

*Be careful of women,* the old medicine man warns, pointing at me. *There's no nicer illness.*

It is at that moment that the translator, Zeca Primoroso, appears, in a state of great excitement. He is unrecognizable, his eyes wide, his hair in a muddle. He asks the medicine man to stand aside. What he has to tell us is confidential.

*I've been called up, Captain. They're going to send me to the war front.*

Primoroso has just come from an emergency meeting of the

High Command where he acted as translator. Worrying information has reached the city concerning the situation that has developed in Gaza ever since the king's imprisonment. There are signs that the VaNguni army is reorganizing.

*Have you heard Ngungunyane comment on this matter?* he asks me in Portuguese.

I shrug my shoulders. I try to forget what the deposed king has never ceased repeating over the last few days: *This war isn't returning. It never got going in the first place.*

Until a few moments ago, I was the center of the world. Then in a flash, I became invisible. The news from Gaza absorbs Andrea and Primoroso completely. It was an elite composed of white soldiers or Angolan Africans, along with local sepoys, who took possession of the emperor's domains. They were given ranks but no means of subsistence. They live by raping women and pillaging the possessions of the local population.

*And what about Maguiguane?* Andrea asks.

*Maguiguane is going from village to village, mobilizing people to rebel,* Zeca replies. Wherever the Nguni warrior goes, he yells his proclamation: *Vambuyisa inkosi. Give us back our king!* This is his demand.

*Here I go, back to the inferno of the Limpopo,* Andrea complains.

If the war starts again, then fresh contingents will be sent to Gaza. It is more than likely that they will transfer him to reassume command of the corvette *Capello*.

Zeca and Álvaro bid each other goodbye. The translator's slender figure disappears among the buildings. Our return to Bianca's house takes place in silence. At the door of the brothel, I ask the captain:

*And Germano? Do you think he will be mobilized too?*

Álvaro Andrea shrugs and starts: *I couldn't care less* . . . But then ashamed, he changes his tone of voice: *Germano will get out of it. It'll be enough for him to raise the issue of his war wounds. I'm the one without any wounds to save me* . . .

I think of Germano's hands. But it is another man's hands that squeeze mine in a clumsy farewell.

# 16

## NEITHER A MANE NOR A CROWN

At the beginning of time
there was only one village and one well.

The world was contained in this:
a village and a well.

One day, as he was filling his pitcher,
a man dropped his eyes into the well.

He plunged his arms sightlessly into the dark
and realized that the well had no walls.

And the man felt himself
summoned by the bottomless waters.

By the time he found his eyes
the sea had been born.

**—LEGEND TOLD BY DABONDI**

I am not allowed to leave the prison where I have just spoken to
Ngungunyane. For a moment, I am merely one more prisoner. The
soldiers say that we shall all go together straight to the quayside. It
is the dead of night when they make us leave in silence for the port
of Lourenço Marques. We are led away like this under cover of
darkness, for fear of an ambush. Until we glimpse the distant lights

of a ship waiting for us in the bay. Afraid of falling, I lean on Dabondi, who is walking next to me. She pushes me away. *Let me stumble, what I most want is to fall down*, she declares. And then she adds in an undertone: *It's the last time our feet will touch our homeland. It's a pity you're wearing shoes, Imani.* All of us women will leave accompanied: The dust of the dead will cling to our feet forever.

If the boat we came this far on was big, this other one seems bigger than the city of Lourenço Marques. The *África* is so vast that it cannot tie up at the quay. For if it did so, the entire continent would break once it touched dry land. That is why we are transported out to it in barges. During the brief journey, the women remain with their heads bowed. Only I contemplate the starry sky. Dabondi tells me to lower my eyes. I am going to be a mother, and I should not look up at the stars.

The captain is waiting as if to welcome us at his front door. He is a bald man with a wide face and a friendly smile. He is in full uniform, his navy blue coat offset by the four golden flashes on his shoulders and sleeves. The medals on his chest are so many that he seems to be wearing a coat of armor.

*I am a lieutenant commander and my name is António Sérgio de Sousa*, the captain announces. He points to a stocky creature standing to attention beside him: *This is my adjutant, Sergeant Júlio Araújo.*

The sergeant is the exact opposite of the captain: he is squat, sunken-cheeked, with black hair fading into a thick beard, his deep-set eyes almost hidden under thick eyebrows.

Ngungunyane is the first prisoner to step aboard. He stands stock-still before the captain, blocking the way for those behind him. All of a sudden he bends over, kowtowing deeply. Leaning on my arm, he instructs me:

*Tell him I am his son.*

The captain smiles, unable to understand. He asks the king of Gaza to get up, but he insists on falling to his knees. Tugging at my *capulana*, Ngungunyane asks in Zulu:

*Isn't this King D. Carlos?*

It pains me, I must confess, to see someone who forced others to kneel before him humiliated in this way. *Translate, Imani!* Ngungunyane urges. *Tell him I am his son, I am the son of the king of Portugal!* Seizing the captain's hands, the prisoner moves from flattery to supplication: *Don't take me away, please, I am already dead, I am as dead as can be.* At the orders of the sergeant, Ngungunyane is dragged off, continuing all the while to proclaim his own death.

After the first prisoners have filed past, another thirty or so detainees pass by, headed by the Protestant missionary, Roberto Machava. These other blacks, captured in Lourenço Marques, are bound for somewhere else: they will be exiled in Cape Verde, accused of conspiring against the Portuguese fatherland. None of them are aware of this charge, none of them know what fatherland it is that they have offended so seriously.

Sergeant Júlio Araújo takes charge of operations, yelling: *Split the prisoners into two groups, otherwise we'll lose control! These jokers all look alike.* Then he orders them to be searched. We don't want any of them killing themselves along the way. He himself proceeds to inspect each of the prisoners. He pays meticulous attention to the women.

*God protect us, Captain, we've got a cargo of demons down below,* Júlio Araújo declares.

All the whites cross themselves when they hear the sergeant's words.

We are escorted down an iron companionway. Then we are led down a passage lit by flickering ceiling lamps. I hear Ngungunyane babble: *This boat is my iron coffin.* The queens burst into tears when they see the dark cubicle where they are to be accommodated.

*Explain to them how they'll be distributed,* the sergeant orders me.

It is a miracle that sixteen people can fit into such a tiny compartment. Two wooden boards hanging one above the other will serve as a bed for all the prisoners, men and women. I translate his instructions: the upper bunk will be for the king and all his wives to sleep. The lower bunk, near the entrance, will be for Godido, the cook Ngó, and Mulungo to rest on. Toward the back, the same bunk will accommodate Zixaxa and his three wives.

The sixteen prisoners from Gaza are pushed into the cubicle and the door locked behind them. I am given a separate cubicle, a kind of storage space located right opposite the cabin housing Ngungunyane's people.

Roberto Machava and the thirty prisoners from Lourenço Marques are led down to the cargo hold. When the hatch is opened, the pastor and his followers step back in horror. It is a common belief among them that a ship's hold is a dark chasm that opens onto the bottom of the sea. It is down there, in such depths, where slaves are burned and then the ash from their bones is used to make gunpowder.

*I don't believe that,* I say.

*You don't believe it?* one of the prisoners asks. *What happened to our brothers who were taken away? Did any of them return?* Then convinced, he concludes: *They'll eat us.*

Another prisoner warns: *On this journey, no one should agree to eat meat! We'll be eating our own people.*

*Do as you wish,* I say resignedly.

*They want to fatten us up. That's what they want.*

Before we weigh anchor, I ask the guard to allow me up on deck. *I need a bit of air*, I argue. Only then do I notice that the soldier is a mulatto. I am absorbed by his bronze skin color and loose curly hair. And I think to myself: My child will be like that.

*Where are you from?* I ask.

*I'm from the engine room*, he answers. *I'm dirty, covered in coal dust.*

He didn't understand my question, nor does he understand my smile. We climb the companionway in silence. At the door onto the deck, he gestures as if he were opening some invisible curtain for me. Then he returns to his guard post.

The deck is full of passengers witnessing the ship's departure. There is some irony in this sad trick of fate: A ship named *África* is taking me away from the African continent, with a mulatto baby in my belly and leaving my white man in the land of black people.

*You cannot stay here*, someone tells me.

But I immediately hear António de Sousa countermanding the order.

*Leave her with me, sailor.*

*I'm pregnant, Captain*, I blurt out, ashamed of my rueful figure. He points at my feet and shakes his head in disapproval.

*I'm sorry, sir*, I mumble. *My shoes no longer fit my feet.*

We are surrounded by other passengers, both civilian and military, who want to watch our departure.

*The sailor was right, you'll have to go back inside.*

*Let me stay, please. I'll put my shoes back on . . .*

It wasn't my feet that were worrying him. The captain's concern is the number of people, but he doesn't want to offend me. There are two hundred and sixty civilians and more than two hundred military personnel on board. Around five hundred people, all wanting to see us leave, and none of them would want to be near a woman of my race.

Carrying my shoes in my hand, I am about to head belowdecks when António de Sousa changes his mind.

*You can stand over there in that dark corner, no one will be aware of your presence.*

I squeeze back into my shoes. And I remember my brother Mwanatu, so happy in his muddled mind, praying to God to make him stop growing so that his feet would always fit into his only pair of shoes.

❖

Dabondi was allowed to join me by the deck rail. The queen sat down with her back to dry land. I urge her to watch the lights of the city.

*The one who wants to run away never looks back*, she affirms.

A couple pass us, and are astounded at our presence. The husband, never imagining that I understand Portuguese, comments: *I bet they are part of a folk dance troupe to entertain the first-class passengers.* To which the wife retorts: *Dancing is all they're good for.*

And they walk off laughing. The queen watches the couple and, when their voices and laughter have faded away, she confesses that she didn't wait for me to start her Portuguese lessons. Her teacher is Godido. In response to my smile, she says that all she needs are a few basics.

I promise to give her some classes. I suggest we share the same cabin space. Dabondi declines: She will sleep alongside her husband for the rest of her days.

*But the king sleeps between Muẕamussi and Tuka.*

*I'm not interested in whom he goes to bed with*, Dabondi argues. *It's only me he dreams of.*

The queen goes over his other wives by name. She counts them on her fingers, as if checking the beads on a rosary. Then she recites their names once more: Muzamussi, Namatuco, Patihina, Machacha, Xesipe, and Fusi. *There are seven wives*, she says. *But only I keep watch over his dreams.*

That night, Dabondi did not protect her husband against nightmares. In the early hours, Ngungunyane wakes up screaming: *It wasn't me, it wasn't me!* There is uproar in the cabin, the noise of kicking on the iron door echoes down the passageway and alarms the guard on duty. They open the door, bind Ngungunyane's wrists, and send the prisoners out into the passageway. Only I, the king, and the furious Sergeant Araújo remain in the cubicle.

The king takes time to catch his breath. He is completely naked, his wax crown spoiled, spittle running down his chin. Terrified, he reveals the demons who were depriving him of his sleep. He hasn't yet rid himself of the nightmare: A dugout is approaching the beach with a body in it. While it is still some way off, he recognizes that it is his brother, Mafemane. The king keeps himself away from the water: The sea is forbidden territory. When the boat runs onto the strand, he realizes that it is, in fact, a coffin. In this open casket, his brother starts talking as dead people do: without moving his lips.

*Brother Mundungaꝫi*, the dead man tells him, *you've got to close this coffin.*

Ngungunyane stays rooted to the ground: In order to place the lid on the dugout, he needs to wade into the sea, an unthinkable heresy. But if he doesn't close the coffin, he will be haunted for the rest of his life by the dead man. Horrified, he walks into the waves and tries in vain to pull the boat up onto the shore. The craft is temporarily stuck on a sandbank. Mafemane speaks once more: *Get into the coffin and together we'll row it to shore.* By now, the waves are bigger, the king is almost out of his depth. He has no choice but to jump into the improvised craft. The moment he does, the coffin lid slams shut over him. The darkness is the same as that of the cubicle in which the Portuguese have locked him away. The ship is the coffin carrying him and Mafemane, his ephemeral brother, forever in his death throes.

The sergeant orders me to help the emperor regain his composure. In order to do this, he is taken up on deck and allowed to walk. Wrapped in a blanket, Ngungunyane moves forward with tiny, halting steps.

*That's the king of the blacks,* one of the passengers declares.

I translate for Ngungunyane to see that someone recognizes him. He appears to smile, but his face is marked by no more than a saddened wince. The emperor is well aware of the power he has lost.

*Tell me something, Imani: Isn't there some bit of earth anywhere on this ship one can dig?*

More than ignorance, it is illusion that rules Ngungunyane. When it comes down to it, we all know: It is not in the soil that we bury our dead. Those who have departed only find peace in our hearts. The brother whose death he had ordered left life more alive than when he entered it.

With his bare feet, Ngungunyane feels for an impossible crack in the metal floor. He yearns for the sand that absorbs the rain, the dew, and the blood. He closes his eyes and sees a river of red flowing through the arid landscape of his kingdom.

Ngungunyane's nightmare has upset the false harmony among the prisoners. When the king returns to his cell, the detainees are gathered in the passageway. Zixaxa is shackled to a beam and the moment he sees the king arrive, he bursts out:

*Don't delude yourself, Ngungunyane. The Portuguese aren't taking you away because you're great. They're taking you away because of the English. Don't convince yourself that they're killing you. Quite the opposite, they're saving you from being killed by your people in your own kingdom. The VaTsonga don't respect you, the VaChopi hate you, the VaNdau don't acknowledge your authority. The Mabuiendjela, the people who once worshipped you, spat at you when you were captured. You're nothing now, you've got no friends, no brothers, you're alone with your wives. You're just one of them, you're a dowager queen. As for the Portuguese, you're no longer any use as an enemy. By the time this journey is over, you won't have any more use even as a trophy.*

Godido and the cook Ngó await a signal from him to silence Zixaxa. The queens look anxiously at their husband. Ngungunyane merely curses him under his breath:

*You haven't uttered a word. All you've done is bark. You're nothing but a dog.*

The soldiers reestablish order, and the prisoners are pushed back into their darkened cell. On my way back to my cubicle, I push my way past the soldiers gathered in the passageway. The men's eyes tell me I'm a woman. I hear their lewd comments. But they don't touch me. The curve in my belly announces my imminent motherhood. I open the door with only one certainty: I'm no more than a young girl. Maybe even less than that, because I fall asleep all curled up, my knees touching my face. Just as my child sleeps inside me.

# 17

## BARTHOLOMEW AND THE SEA ROUTE TO THE SKY

*Dabondi is right when she says that the ship is a prison. The ocean is so*
*endless that it induces a feeling of enclosure. The noise of the hull*
*tearing through the waves, the subterranean vibration of the propellers,*
*the solemn lament of the siren, the metallic clank of the anchor chain:*
*All this leaves me in the grip of an existential fatigue.*
*Gungunhana is right when he laments that there is no stone on this ship*
*where he can sit down. There are almost no wooden fittings on ships*
*nowadays. Modern vessels require little from the wind. Just like those*
*women who have abandoned their dreams and allow themselves to grow*
*fat, these ships have indulged in the luxury of weight.*
*I cannot say how tired I am of these mobile prisons. In spite of it all,*
*whenever I remain on dry land, I am once again tempted by the call of*
*a distant sea. And once again I set off for the quay, once again*
*I leave on a voyage.*
*This is the sea's inexplicable seduction: No voice is so human, no*
*silence so full of stories.*
**—EXCERPT FROM THE DIARY OF ANTÓNIO SÉRGIO DE SOUSA**

As we left Lourenço Marques, Queen Dabondi predicted it was going to rain. *One water can be read in another water,* she said, staring
lingeringly into my eyes. The queen was right: It has been raining
so hard ever since yesterday that one can no longer see the ocean.

I slowly make my way across the deck as if walking through a cloud. I have been summoned by Captain António Sérgio de Sousa.

I shake my clothes and apprehensively enter the captain's cabin. It is a large, well-lit space. The first thing I see is a bird perched on the Portuguese man's shoulder. The creature examines me, curious, its hybrid posture somewhere between princely and clownish. Then, suddenly startled, it flutters up to a cage hanging from the ceiling. The captain calls it: *Bartholomew!* And the bird, a Congo parrot, replies: *Aye aye, skipper!* It hops down to the table and walks across it with the swaying gait of a dwarf.

*He sometimes soils my charts*, the captain complains.

The parrot tries clumsily to fly, causing its red tail feathers to poke out from its gray plumage. I ask whether I should close the door. *You can leave it open*, Sousa recommends. Bartholomew has his little routines: He flutters around the deck on the high seas, but when the ship is in port, he doesn't leave the cabin for fear of the gulls.

*It's not the bird that worries me. What I'm not so sure about is whether we should separate that fellow Zixaxa from the king of Gaza.*

*Zixaxa isn't going to harm Ngungunyane.*

*How can you be so sure?*

*Zixaxa believes that if Ngungunyane dies, the Portuguese will throw him overboard. Without the king, none of the other prisoners are of any value.*

António de Sousa intends to give the parrot to his son, who will soon be eight. The little boy was born in India but spent his first years in Africa. Now he's in Lisbon and suffers from asthma. The captain believes his son misses the African skies. It's not on the ground but in the skies that he comes closest to finding Africa again.

*It wasn't because of a parrot that I called you here*, the captain says, shaking his hands as if he had burnt his fingers. He seems to be swatting me away. My visit cannot be prolonged. *I am the captain*, he says, *and I cannot be seen shut away with you in my quarters*.

He has called me because he is worried. One of the prisoners down in the hold, from the Machava group, committed suicide the other night. The captain fears others may follow his example. He gave orders for their food to be improved. It hasn't worked. Those people are in need of spiritual comfort. What they are lacking in general comfort may be mitigated by faith.

*These people*, he says, *are strong in their beliefs*.

It would be extremely beneficial if the prisoners were to believe that the gods were protecting the ship and had given their blessing to the journey.

The previous day, he had summoned Roberto Machava. He knew of the pastor's influence over the other blacks. The meeting had occurred in this same cabin. Sousa explained his intentions. He would gather together the prisoners in a great assembly so that the pastor could lead an African blessing and so assure them that the ship would arrive safely at its destination. *An African blessing?* Pastor Machava asked. *Forgive me, but there's some mistake here. I'm a Christian missionary. I don't hold any African beliefs. You and I, sir, share the same God, the only one who can bless this ship.*

Without a word, António Sérgio de Sousa allowed the pastor to leave. But he was not going to give up. That is why he called me this morning and gave me this hurried message:

*It didn't work with the pastor. But it will work with the witch queen. You must bring her to my cabin. I want the prisoners to know I am going to receive her. And they should also know that she is going to bless our voyage right here in my cabin.*

I accompany the queen to the captain's cabin. Dabondi resists at first. She doesn't want the other prisoners to know that she is casting her cowries in the captain's quarters. They'll say of her what they do of me: that she's sold out to the whites. At the entrance, the queen reacts in a brusque manner:

*I'm only stepping into this room if that white gives me news of my son.*

The captain reacts in a solicitous manner. He notes down the name that the queen dictates while also spelling it out loud: "Man-gue-ze." Why, I wonder, are our names such a mouthful for Portuguese people?

*I'll send a message to Lisbon right away!* António de Sousa promises. *By tomorrow we should know the boy's whereabouts.*

Even so, the queen hesitates to go in. *That bird*, she says, pointing at Bartholomew. So the captain hurries to shut the parrot away in its cage.

Eventually, the soothsayer sits down on the carpet and takes her magic bones out of a satchel. The captain's instructions are clear: *Tell her to take as much time as she needs. It's good that everyone knows she has been here.* The queen starts to invoke the names of the dead, which the Portuguese slowly gives her. She pronounces these names in her own way and most of them are unrecognizable to António de Sousa. The *tintxolo* are scattered over the floor: there are more little bones, seeds, shells, than there are cowries. *Careful with the seeds*, the Portuguese warns. *Bartholomew considers those a delicacy!*

Dabondi sways, snorts, sneezes, coughs, and eventually falls into a convulsed trance. With her eyes turned upward and her voice distorted, she announces: *There's a barefoot man crossing a river that flows down from the sky. In those lands, it rains so much that no one needs to dig a well . . .*

*It's the Congo! It can only be the Congo!* Captain Sousa exclaims.

*The captain thinks he's transporting us as prisoners*, the queen declares. *But you, sir, are the only prisoner. This boat is your prison.*

With her eyes shut tight, the queen emphasizes each word with a roll of her body. I have surrendered so completely to her words and gestures that the captain asks me:

*Why do you gesticulate so much when you translate?*

*Because when I translate, I am her.*

I dream I am traveling on a ship under the command of a black captain. The ship is called the *Europa*, and its hull is painted in bright colors like African textiles. Its masts are trees and provide the deck with shade. The wind scatters leaves over the sea.

A light tap on the door interrupts my dream. It must be Dabondi, I think, still half asleep. I tidy my hair and, with uncharacteristic difficulty, tie a *capulana* around my waist. I'm five months gone, and before long I shall be devoured by my own belly.

There's another tap. I open the door slightly. It's the missionary, Roberto Machava. My visitor's hands hurriedly anticipate his face:

*Look at this sketch*, he tells me.

I tremble. It is a drawing in color which I did for my father when I was a child. It showed a burnt-out village and bodies lying across the ground. Underneath the figures, a caption is written, a promise of vengeance against Ngungunyane's troops.

*How did you get hold of this piece of paper?* I ask, alarmed.

*Let me in. I can't talk out here in the passageway.*

*Come back another time.*

*Now's the best time. They're all busy preparing for our arrival at the next port.*

The pastor comes in and remains leaning against the door as if he wanted to reinforce it. He stops talking in Portuguese and explains himself in his mother tongue. Machava had crossed the River Save and visited my father, Katini Nsambe, and his current wife, the sorceress Bibliana. My father was sure the missionary would find me in Lourenço Marques. When he gave him the drawing, my old father was categorical: *Give this to Imani so that she won't forget what she promised.*

*I made the same promise,* Machava declares. *I am also seeking the same revenge and I need your help.*

*Ask Zixaxa to help you.*

*Anyone but him. I and my companions are prisoners thanks to that traitor.*

He opens the door, peers down the passageway to make sure no one is listening. Then he closes the door again. His face is close to mine as he confesses: *I'm preparing a revolt.* I shake my head and he repeats: *That's what I'm preparing, a bloody rebellion.* The plan is simple, but of a chilling logic: He is going to kill the king of Gaza. Without Ngungunyane, the Portuguese will arrive in Lisbon empty-handed, without any proof of the crushing victory they so fervently proclaimed. *If we kill him now,* Machava argues, *it will be impossible for them to preserve the corpse until we arrive in Lisbon.* The European nations would think Portugal had tried to put on some clumsy show for effect. The missionary's plan has a perfect end result: In the Mozambican interior, Protestant followers would insist that Ngungunyane was still alive, wandering through the mountains of the Transvaal. And who, in such a world, could prove the contrary?

*I'm going to tell you what you've got to do,* the missionary declares.

*No, say no more! I'm not ready.*

I am assailed by a terrible doubt: If Ngungunyane dies during the journey, why would they take the rest of us on to Lisbon? We would almost certainly be abandoned in Luanda or Cape Verde. I would never see Germano again, and my baby would never know its father. It's true, I made a promise to carry out our revenge. But I don't have to carry it out now.

*Listen, girl.*

*Go away, Pastor Machava. Go away before I scream!*

*Think about what I asked*, the pastor mumbles as he leaves.

He steps past the sleeping guard. I see him disappear into the hold. I bolt the door and breathe a sigh of relief. I am afflicted by various levels of anxiety: It isn't enough for me to refuse to take part in an assassination. It is vital that the plan should be aborted. I must expose the missionary's intentions without delay. But it isn't hard to guess the consequences of such an exposure: They'll throw Machava and his followers into the sea. I'm left with an impossible choice between two crimes.

❖

The *África* is now approaching a land unlike any other. On the horizon, we can make out Cape Town. The city is framed by a range of mountains. I contemplate those mountains like a condemned prisoner glimpsing a little patch of sky.

Under military surveillance, the prisoners are allowed to enjoy the view. Dabondi joins me and the captain. She takes my hands in hers, fascinated by the sight of a continent that looks as if it has just been born. Then she issues a prophecy:

*There will come a day when a black man will pilot a ship like this one.* Then she addresses a request to me: *Translate that, Imani. This Portuguese needs to be aware of the future.*

*Only if the sea turns into a river*, António de Sousa replies, as soon as I have translated the queen's prediction.

127

*The sea always was a river,* Dabondi affirms.

The captain and I laugh. A vague smile appears on the queen's lips. The Portuguese looks around, fearing someone may have seen us in such an animated exchange. Leaning toward the queen, he asks: *It's good to see dry land, isn't it?*

He doesn't wait for an answer. He just wants to be heard. Last night, he didn't sleep a wink, thinking about Dabondi's words. The queen was right: That boat was a prison. During his bout of insomnia, he thought about the colleagues who had left the navy in order to wander through Africa. They hadn't chosen to be pioneers. They were just tired of the confinement of the sea. The wild animals, the jungle, and the primitive tribes, all were preferable to the eternal solitude of the ocean.

It's good to see dry land, he repeats to himself. Before retiring, the captain transmits his commands to Sergeant Araújo:

*Take these two women back down below and get the* régulo *ready to receive visitors. Give him wine and some presentable clothes. I want the fellow as neat as a pin.*

Dressed in European clothes, the king of Gaza is left alone in his quarters. All the other prisoners are transferred to the hold. With the exception of Dabondi, who remains by my side.

*You two go to your cabin and wait for me there,* Araújo orders.

The ship has stopped, and the boilers are cooling. This is what will happen every time the *África* reaches a port. They need to save on coal. Without the heating, the ship is enveloped in cold. In the half-light of my cubicle, I lean against Dabondi as if we were one body. The queen cups her hands around my belly to keep me warm.

The door opens abruptly and Sergeant Araújo steps in. A strange glint lights up his eyes when he sees Dabondi's tender gesture. The compartment is tiny, but the soldier considers there's enough room for three. Then he urges us on: *Go on, go on, I want to see those caresses!* It's not me he desires. I'm too familiar, too European. He is attracted to the king's wives, whose names he will never be able to pronounce. But his fear of contracting a disease is greater than any desire he feels for them. He limits himself to raping them in his dreams, without having to look into their eyes and without the inconvenience of having to smell their sweat or the risk of catching a disease.

He probably imagines that Dabondi and I are caressing each other out of shamelessness. And that we're doing so in order to excite him.

*Get closer together. I want to see you like a husband and wife*, the sergeant orders.

Araújo slips his hand into his trousers, his eyes drooling in expectation of what they are about to see. As we remain motionless, the soldier raises his voice and insists:

*Show your tits!*

It's not the ones who shout whom you should fear. This was my mother's advice. The real villains, she used to say, never raise their voice. If her warning is true, this man's bellowing shouldn't scare me. And yet there's something about him that makes my flesh creep.

*We are pregnant*, I warn him.

*No you're not*, the sergeant says, *but you're going to get pregnant before long.*

The queen gets to her feet and lets her *capulana* fall to the floor. The sergeant steps backward, surprised to see a bare woman, her dress lying helpless at her feet. I'm even more dumbstruck when the queen asks me to undress too. I shake my head, fearing that she is unaware of what is happening here. In one tug, Dabondi tears my dress off. We are both naked, defenseless against the bewildered Portuguese.

Dabondi's hands advance provocatively toward the sergeant, who closes his eyes. But her gesture is intended otherwise. With a sudden pull, the queen opens the door and hurriedly pushes me out into the passageway. *Let him follow us, like a bull in heat*, the queen declares as we advance, hand in hand, through the bowels of the ship. We climb the companionway onto the deck. *How far will this white man go?* Dabondi asks. Only then do I understand Dabondi's tactic: The nudity which in other circumstances makes us so fragile was, in this instance, our best form of defense. In an open space like the deck, we would be protected from Araújo's advances. Below us, far below, we hear the sergeant kicking the ship's bulkheads.

# 18

## AN INVOLUNTARY SUICIDE

A ship traversed your heart
Yet continues on its way without you
—SOPHIA DE MELLO BREYNER, NAVIGATIONS

Oh Daude! Daude! Go and tell Administrator Madekhise that
some whites have arrived and arrested the executioner.
Let's hope they find him!
—EXTRACT FROM A SONG DEDICATED TO THE ARREST OF NGUNGUNYANE. THE SONG WAS
COMPOSED BY THE MAESTRO KATINE NYAMOMBE AND PLAYED BY HIS XYLOPHONE
ORCHESTRA DURING THE VISIT OF PRESIDENT ÓSCAR CARMONA TO MAGUL, IN THE SOUTH OF
MOZAMBIQUE, IN 1939. DAUDE WAS AN OFFICIAL IN THE ADMINISTRATION AT ZAVALA.

We blacks were told we were forbidden to go ashore. This is the rule
in Cape Town. The captain allows us to occupy the deck so that we
can enjoy watching the permanent bustle on the quay as cargo is
loaded and unloaded. The prisoners point to the harborside machin-
ery, looking for names that do not exist in their languages. Then
they laugh, amused by the sight of so many mulattoes carrying
heavy bundles. They are not like the mixed-race people in our country, who avoid heavy work. And my brothers laugh at these mesti-
zos, who perspire like miners digging out the earthen floor of Hell.
I'm the only one who does not laugh. And I think of my future child.
He will be an eternal stevedore, carrying the burden of his own skin.

Hour after hour, journalists, diplomats, and missionaries come aboard to interview Ngungunyane. Cape Town is the first place outside Mozambique where the African king can be put on display. In a corner of the deck, the Portuguese prepare an appropriate venue: They have seated the king in a leather armchair, with borrowed clothes and a pair of military boots that weigh as heavy as lead on his feet. The foreigners never imagine the inhuman conditions in which their interviewee is traveling. The king smiles and waves to each of his visitors. None of them return the compliment.

At midday, when all the visitors have gone, the cook Ngó brings us food. Ngungunyane is happy and uses his short fat fingers to serve himself. The emperor is blissfully unaware that on that ship there are people of his own race planning to eliminate him.

Sitting on my bunk, Dabondi stares wide-eyed as she listens to the noises from the Cape Town quayside. *How many days are left before we arrive in Lisbon?* she asks.

*We are not even halfway*, I reply.

The queen pulls out a parasol from the jumble that has accumulated in my little cabin. She wants to take a walk up on deck but she doesn't want to get a tan. *Women grow dark and are no longer desirable*, she declares. Black men, she says, have learned to think that a dark-skinned woman is ugly.

Dabondi refuses my offer of company. She is not alone. Godido is waiting for her at the end of the passageway, with a pair of sandals in his hand. The prince had dismantled his own royal crown in order to make a kind of pair of sandals out of it. He turned the diadem into a dark paste, which he separated into two pieces, and then covered them with strips of canvas. With the two remaining strips, he made a pair of laces. The queen knows that the improvised sandals will be of little use. The metal plating of the deck is like a burning pan. After just a few steps, nothing will be left of her generous stepson's efforts. And yet those sandals are the best present she has ever been given.

I watch her walk away down the passageway, brandishing her parasol as if it were the most resplendent ensign. Leaning on Godido, she slowly climbs the steps, taking greater care to keep her sandals on than to avoid stumbling. At the top of the companionway, she is embraced by the light. The queen and her stepson enter the infinite circle of the sun.

Moments later, Dabondi bursts into the cabin. She is distraught as a result of her stroll with Godido. She leans toward me to reveal the deep gash in her wrist.

*We fought.* The queen sighs.

In her people's tradition, two long rods are tied to the body of unfaithful wives. Then in a public ceremony, their eyes are gouged with a metal spike. But it's not the idea of being punished like this that worries her. Nor is it even the fight she had with her stepson. It's the wound in her wrist. She got cut and didn't bleed, and that's what has given her a fright.

*My blood has stopped. My veins have run dry.*

She holds out her arms to reveal the most deadly of illnesses. Her entire frame is shaking, suddenly fragile. For the first time, I am the one who has to console her. I don't know what to do. Timidly, almost nonsensically, I sit down next to her and open the parasol. We lean against each other, shoulder to shoulder as if we were made of one shadow. And we remain in silence until we are aroused by yelling coming from Ngungunyane's cell. They have come to take his measurements and, once again, he thinks they are preparing him for when he becomes a corpse. I am summoned to intervene and to communicate the reassuring message to him: At our next port of call, Luanda, the Portuguese are going to buy clothes for him and all the other captives. They do not want to protect us from the cold. All they intend is that we should disembark in Lisbon with a minimum of decorum.

The explanation does not placate Ngungunyane. What was the purpose of their giving him clothes and then taking them away? He had already been undressed and dressed by me. He had agreed to it the first time because it was done by the hands of a woman. This time, it is men who are measuring his arms, legs, neck, and belly. His belly, for God's sake! There can only be one reason for such humiliation: The jailers have become executioners. That is why the emperor has been furiously trying to avoid these cursed measurements. They are not measuring him. What they are doing is assessing the size of his future coffin. Ngungunyane calls me and asks me to intercede. I pretend not to hear him. I let him suffer. Sometimes, the only courageous act is to do nothing at all.

The boilers have been lit again. Like an invisible serpent, the electricity is once again circulating around the ship. We are leaving the port of Cape Town when Sergeant Araújo comes into my cabin without asking permission. He turns the compartment over like a suspicious husband. His fingers run slowly over the dresses that I have hung on a rail. He takes his time over this gesture as if he were caressing a body. Then he asks: *Haven't you got anything for me?* I shake my head. He insists: *Are you sure?* Faced with my stubborn silence, he throws my clothes on the floor.

*Well, let's go then*, he declares. *The captain wants to see you.*

He tells me to hurry out of the cubicle but he does not stand aside in the narrow passageway, forcing me to squeeze between him and the damp wall. I smell his sour breath as he feels my breast with his fleshy hand:

*Don't act smart with me*, he warns. *I've got my eye on you, my little black girl.*

He orders me to walk in front of him. I know what he wants to do: to stroke my buttocks and thighs as I go along. The passageway is a short one, and his fingers work frantically until, once on deck, self-consciousness overcomes desire.

In his cabin on the bridge, Captain Sousa is seated at his desk, waving a telegram:

*Sad news! João Mangueze, Gungunhana's son who lived in Lisbon, has died.*

I listen to him as if he were talking of a stranger: Gungunhana's son? It takes a bit of time for me to understand. For me, João Mangueze was only the son of Dabondi.

*I've already spoken to Gungunhana*, the captain continues. *He asked me to inform his mother of the sad news.*

Ngungunyane had received the news with more fear than sadness. He confessed that he was scared of Dabondi's reaction. He fears being accused of complicity in what may have been an assassination. Or worse still, that he will be suspected of some kind of sorcery.

As a child—and long before he crossed the ocean—João Mangueze had been sent to the School of Arts and Crafts on Mozambique Island. He returned home months later with new knowledge but serious lapses of memory. He had forgotten, for example, that a young Nguni's destiny was war. Only half the person Ngun-gunyane had sent now returned. The warrior blood of the Man-guezes had become diluted in him, and the boy refused to leave for the battlefront. The very idea of killing someone reduced him to tears. The emperor ordered his guards to take his son to the kraal at night, oblige him to cut the throat of an ox, and then leave him lashed to the dead animal's horns. This experience would stiffen his son's resolve. The following morning, João's mother found him covered in blood and led him back to the house covered in a blanket so that no one should see him return in such a deplorable state.

Captain Sousa now needs my help to give the news to the boy's mother. He does not require me for my linguistic competence. I have been summoned because I am a woman.

They went to fetch Dabondi, and found her sitting on my bunk with her open parasol. Upon reaching the door to the captain's cabin, the queen hesitates. Then, her head bowed, she asks me in the faintest of voices:

*Is it about João?*

I step outside and try to take her hands, but the queen flinches. Unable to do anything, I watch her bare feet recede. Dabondi is right: There are footprints that leave their impression on iron.

Only a few moments have passed since Dabondi received the grav-est of news, but it is as if a century has gone by since she disap-peared. Alone in my cubicle, I fear that she may have thrown herself into the sea in her despair. But then all of a sudden, the door to my compartment swings open and Dabondi appears, escorted by two soldiers. She is disheveled and covered in ash. They push her onto the bunk while hurling an order at her:

*Stay here and be quiet!*

Then they tell me to translate: From then on, the queen will remain shut away in my cabin, with a guard on the door.

*What happened?*

*Your friend tried to kill herself. She went down to the engine room and tried to throw herself into the furnace. If it weren't for us, she'd be a lump of coal by now.*

*A lump of coal is all she ever was*, the other soldier comments ironically. They stop their guffaws to warn me that from now on, it's my job to look after Dabondi. The queen is of no importance to the Portuguese, but the number of black prisoners needs to remain intact. The more women on display in Lisbon, the more genuine the king's presentation as African. These were the soldiers' words. *Take care of her*, they repeat as they leave. I hear the key being turned outside. And I realize that from now on, I will be one of the prisoners.

I sit contemplating the queen for a while. She seems devoid of body, devoid of life. More than ever before, I am helpless. In the face of such deep pain, any attempt at comfort is absurd. Suddenly, Dabondi gets to her feet as if her soul has ceased to be a burden to her:

*Open the door. I want to speak to Ngungunyane.*

I negotiate with the guards. They are adamant, the queen cannot leave. On the other hand, they authorize the king to come to our cabin. Moments later, Ngungunyane appears. Dabondi does not wait for him to cross the threshold before declaring:

*Everyone thinks Mangueze was your favorite son. Everyone believes you sent him to Lisbon out of love. It was the opposite: You wanted to keep him away. You hoped he would be gobbled up by the sea.*

*Dabondi, my wife*, the king protests. *You want to blame me because you are suffering.*

*I'm not your wife*, Dabondi replies. *I was never anyone's wife. You will know what the burden of guilt is like. And no amount of drink will give you any relief.*

The threats continue. Was the emperor having bad dreams? From now on, he will have nightmares even when he isn't dreaming. And suicide won't help. Even when he dies, these ghosts will still consume him. Then Dabondi, the ruling queen, concludes by ordering the Portuguese: *Take him away, I don't want to see him again.*

Ngungunyane withdraws in silence. The door is shut. Only then does Dabondi burst into tears.

News of a death always spreads more swiftly than the wind. In the cloistered environment of the ship, news of Mangueze's death circulates in the blink of an eye. Alerted to the grief which has struck the royal family, Roberto Machava asks permission to speak to the captain. In the presence of António de Sousa, the missionary bows and then expresses himself in Portuguese with an eloquence that surprises everyone:

*The prisoners want to pray for the soul of João Mangueze. I wish to ask your permission to use the chapel.*

*I don't know whether I can,* the captain answers. *It is Father Martinho who is responsible for the chapel, and he fell ill and had to stay behind in Cape Town.*

Sergeant Araújo butts in at this point. He is familiar with António de Sousa's weaknesses, and fears he will bend the rules with regard to what blacks are permitted.

*Don't trust this black and his false act of humility,* Araújo declares. *This black who says he's a missionary is nothing more than a subversive who follows the interests of the Protestants. Ask him, sir, if he's aware that the chapel is a place of worship for Roman Catholics.*

*I was taught that we have only one God*, the pastor affirms.

*There's only one God, but there are different flocks*, the sergeant retorts.

The missionary leaves. As he passes me, he asks whether I have thought about "that little matter."

# 19

## THE AMNESIC DEAD

One day, they saw a fisherman digging a huge pit in the beach.
They asked him what he was doing. He pointed to an old dugout
up on the dune, already in pieces. It was the craft in which, for
many years, he had gone out to sea beyond the breakers. After so
much riding the waves together, man and boat had developed an
attachment to the point where the fisherman would only go to
sleep if he was curled up in the bottom of the craft.

*When boats die, we need to give them a burial.*

When he had finished, he stuck an oar next to the grave. When he
made the sign of the cross, the sound of wood being hammered
echoed in his heart.

**—EXCERPT FROM THE DIARY OF CAPTAIN ANTÓNIO SÉRGIO DE SOUSA**

*In the art of killing, we have not evolved much since primitive times.*
*What is a bullet if not a tiny stone that has learned to fly?*

**—ROBERTO MACHAVA**

All night long, the emperor Ngungunyane wailed loudly that he
was the son of the king of Portugal. This piercing expostulation
echoed clearly through to our cabin.

From shouting so vociferously for his Portuguese father, the
emperor forgot that he had just received news of the death of a son.
The boy's name was swept from his mind. He wants to invoke his

ancestors but none appear. In panic, he tells his relatives to draw near and he murmurs: *The whites want to kill me. But I'm one step ahead of them. The moment I came aboard, I was already dead.*

His wives eye each other apprehensively. They all know that there is no more serious predicament in this world than a sudden fit of amnesia. More serious than the king forgetting his dead is the failure of the dead to remember him. All efforts to rehabilitate their husband prove fruitless.

*Do something, Dabondi,* implores one of the queens.

Muzamussi, the favorite spouse, raises her arm in silent proclamation. Only she should bring peace to this chaos. She jingles the twenty-four tin bracelets that sheathe her arm. She pushes past the other wives, and lifts off her day gown, which falls at her feet. The oversized dress is one of the items of clothing that were bought in Luanda.

*Keep away from here, I am the nkosikasi.*

The "big wife," as she is called, does her name justice. She is lofty and voluminous, and wears a conical hairstyle which makes her look even taller. She kneels in front of her dazed husband. The light coming through the door hatch shines on her shoulders.

*Buia, Nkosi wa mina!* the queen calls to her husband. In a low voice, as if she were praying, she invites him to rest on her lap.

The other wives press themselves up against the walls and the king curls up in Muzamussi's lap. Ngungunyane collapses weakly, rendered ill by the lack of alcohol. He gets muddled and calls Muzamussi by the name of Vuiaze, his former and only true love. *Thank you, dearest Vuiaᴣe,* the king babbles. Muzamussi pretends she hasn't heard the slip. The king lies prostrate on her lap, and at that moment, she is queen once again. Then she makes a sign for the others to leave. The prisoners obey and crowd into the passageway. The women look up at the lights in the ceiling and stretch their fingers upward to feel the fire hidden in the lamps.

Having recovered, the king of Gaza advances down the passage-way escorted by two guards. He passes the wider hallway next to the entrance to the hold. The Machava prisoners are standing there, waiting for their improvised jailhouse to be disinfected. The king of Gaza presents himself and they all fall to their knees. They are plotting to kill the tyrant. And yet they unhesitatingly pay him homage.

*Get up, my brothers!* Machava orders, furious.

But there is nothing he can do. The prisoners display the same respect for the ruler of Gaza as they do when they prostrate themselves before Christ's cross. Ngungunyane opens his arms in front of such a submissive assembly and proclaims almost inaudibly: *I am the son of the king of Portugal!* Machava shakes his head sorrowfully: the emperor is off his head. Not because he's consumed alcohol. Quite the opposite. He is drunk from abstinence. That is why his hands are shaking uncontrollably. The missionary is struck by a thought: Who knows whether the king may die without a crime having to be committed? This is the prayer he will be directing to God over the coming days.

Machava does not bother to appeal further to the good sense of his flock. He vigorously pushes the king of Gaza away. Ngungunyane does not have the strength to resist. And he tumbles dramatically to the floor. Suddenly, to my surprise, Zixaxa comes to Ngungunyane's rescue. *Leave him alone!* he yells, while he helps the king to steady himself. Then, pointing to me, he shouts:

*Ask the soldiers to take this black priest away! We don't want to see any more of him. And tell them to bring the king of Gaza some wine.*

At the door to his cell, the guards are seated on crates of port wine. This stock of alcohol is all part of the treatment reserved for the royal prisoner. They want him jovial, but without his soul. This is the exile he is destined for, an emigrant from himself, devoid of memory or future. One of the soldiers gives the emperor a bottle, and he drinks from it eagerly. Wine is running over his chin as he stares at me at length, and repeats: *I'm going to offer you to the king of Portugal.*

*Go away, Pastor Machava*, Zixaxa requests. *Ngungunyane has succumbed to the white man's drink, while you have succumbed to his God.*

According to Zixaxa, wine and priests will finish what the Portuguese started with guns. Before long, we won't have anywhere to call home, we won't have anyone to call our brother.

*Does my presence make you feel awkward?* Machava replies. *Do I make you feel guilty?*

*I didn't denounce you*, Zixaxa defends himself. *That is the truth. Or do you by any chance believe the Portuguese more than you do me?*

The missionary signals to me to follow him away from the gathering.

*Let us pray*, he urges me.

*Here in the passageway?* I ask.

*Come with me, the captain has now authorized the use of the chapel*, Machava promises.

I follow the missionary in silence. When we reach the deck, a pair of soldiers searches us meticulously and then escorts us to the entrance to the chapel, which happens to be empty. Without taking his eyes off the cross, Machava pretends to pray. Kneeling, his eyes shut and his hands together, he intones a plainchant in his native language. But there is no prayer. What he is announcing are the plans for executing a crime. The whites are organizing some festivities over the next two days. It is a tradition of theirs whenever they cross the equator. They told Machava that it's like an African celebration, with drinks, dancing, and masks. The prisoners will be allowed to attend the party. *Your task*, Machava announces, *will be to distract the sergeant while we deal with Ngungunyane.*

*I'm scared, Pastor.*

*Trust me*, the missionary declares. *I have visions. I'm going to tell you how I found God.*

Roberto Machava's religious vocation was revealed when he was still young and traveling on foot between Lourenço Marques and the Rand. He was seeking a better life. He knew what he wanted but not how to achieve it. On the third day, driven crazy by the heat and thirst, he fell to the ground in the middle of the savanna. When he came round, he was in a farmer's hut. The man who saved him was one of those VaTsonga people who had been catechized in the plantations of the English. They both knelt and Machava, without ever having done so before, prayed as if the oration were in his native language. His host sighed and said: *No one ever arrives by chance.*

Later, he sat in the backyard contemplating the lands that were parched because of lack of rain. And it was there that he fell asleep with his hand resting on an acacia branch. During the night, his fingers became shoots of the tree, pointing up to the sky with the despair of someone coming up for air. With the longest of his fingers, the man pricked the belly of a cloud. Then it rained.

That morning, Roberto Machava crossed the Mozambique border in high spirits, surprised by his recently revealed faculties. In Lydenburg, he joined the Methodist Church and became a pastor. Returning to Mozambique some years later, he opened a school in the bay of Lourenço Marques. The Roman Catholic Church insisted he join what they called "the only true church." Machava refused. They banned his school. And that was the first of many more bans. In the end, he realized he was the one who was being banned.

The pastor asks for help to get to his feet. He had been mistreated in prison. Now he can kneel by himself, but cannot get up without support. In prison, they had told him that Zixaxa had denounced him. They had sat the Mfumo warrior down in front of a list of names that were read to him in some unfathomable accent. When the priest's name was mentioned, Zixaxa nodded. *Was that the man who told you to fight against the government?* they asked him. And Zixaxa confirmed this once again. Hours later, the pastor was arrested. During his interrogation, he was beaten so badly that he accepted all the charges made against him. The next day, he was put on board the *África*, ready for deportation to the Cape Verde Islands.

*There are things you should know*, the pastor declares. *The hold where they locked me up is a weapons store.*

*A weapons store?*

*All my followers are armed.*

*What are they armed with?* I ask.

The pastor answers by half opening his hand. *These!* At first, I cannot see anything. Then I notice a piece of glass shining between his fingers. It is a shard from a bottle. Of the sort that lie smashed outside Ngungunyane's door every day.

*We shall kill Ngungunyane with these weapons*, Machava proclaims, squeezing the glass, not noticing the blood oozing between his fingers.

A surprise awaits me on the slippery deck: Ngungunyane is sitting on a solitary wooden bench in the rain. Water flows over his bare chest, while the cloth draped around his waist drips steadily. The soldiers guarding him from some distance explain: *He asked us to leave him like that, he said he wanted to feel the rain.* I reply in a maternal tone: *It would be better if he covered himself. Otherwise, he'll get sick.* And the soldiers agree: *Go and speak to him. And take him this cape.*

I drape the cape around the king's shoulders. His body trembles more than his voice when, in an undertone, he confesses he missed the feeling of rain falling on him. He gets up and walks beside me as if he were sleepwalking, his bare feet splashing on the metal deck. While climbing down the companionway that leads to our cabins, he leans one arm on me and the other on Dabondi, who has just arrived. But it is toward my face that he directs his sour breath:

*How do you say* gold *in Txitxope?*

He does not wait for an answer, and rambles on disconnectedly. The whites, he says, measure their fortune in gold, a word we do not have in our languages. When he thinks of wealth, the king of Gaza sees herds of cattle as far as the eye can see, hooves and horns furrowing the sun and the earth. And he sees rain, drops of rain, like these ones running down over his body.

The king seizes my hands and begs me to intervene on his behalf. He needs Dabondi to sleep with him again. They must allow her to go back to the prisoners' cabin. He is talking as if Dabondi weren't there. *I've had so many women that I've become the most solitary of men,* he mourns. Now that they have taken Dabondi away from him, he has ceased being a man. He is silent for a while, lost in his thoughts, until he turns to his wife and begs her: *I want you to put me to sleep, Dabondi.*

*Why are you in such a hurry, my king,* Dabondi asks. *Aren't you afraid of being visited again by nightmares?*

*Sometimes,* the king replies, *nightmares are the only way of preserving the past.*

# 20

## HOW MUCH DOES A TEARDROP WEIGH?

*I look at the ocean and I see life.*
**—EXCERPT FROM THE DIARY OF CAPTAIN ANTÓNIO SÉRGIO DE SOUSA**

First thing in the morning, I am at the captain's door. I greet him at the entrance to his cabin and he does not respond as he leans over a table covered in charts. The empty birdcage lies neglected on the floor in the middle of the cabin. There's no sign of the parrot.

*I let it go as we left Luanda*, the captain comments without looking up. *I couldn't offer my son a caged bird.* Then suddenly, in a change of tone: *I'm busy, what do you want?*

The purpose of my visit is clear: I have come to denounce Machava's underhanded plans. I don't mention any names, nor do I expand on the details, but I am categorical when I reveal the existence of conspiracies to assassinate Ngungunyane. I must have sounded so vague that the Portuguese, who is completely absorbed, goes on moving his little ruler around on the nautical charts. I repeat my warning, now in a calmer manner.

*It's urgent*, I stress, *that the guard outside the hold should be reinforced. They want to kill Ngungunyane, and the perpetrators will come from there.*

*Have you dreamed all this, Imani?* asks António de Sousa sarcastically.

Captain Sousa stares at me with tired incredulity. He hasn't understood the gravity and urgency of the situation. Brandishing his ruler, he draws an arc in the air, suggesting he wants to be left in peace.

Before I leave, I ask about Germano. Who knows, maybe news from Mozambique has been received by telegraph? António de Sousa shakes his head. I then ask for news of Álvaro Andrea. The captain puts down his ruler and sighs: *Please, Imani, don't ask me about anyone. I'm so tired of people* . . .

He had always been a man who kept himself to himself, he admits. Many of his colleagues complained of isolation in the overseas colonies. For him, solitude was the most precious of gifts. Making peoples' acquaintance, he confesses, was the most exhausting activity. In Africa, he was free of such a duty. The whites were passing through. The blacks, no offense intended, were all one person. Like that, he was always alone. This is António de Sousa's explanation.

When I signal my intent to return to my cabin, he suggests, with a spin of his ruler, that I should stay for a moment.

*I know about him*, the captain confirms.

*About Germano?*

*About Álvaro Andrea*, he answers. *They say this man Andrea has returned to the battlefront, in the Limpopo estuary.*

António de Sousa feels sorry for Captain Andrea, for whom the Limpopo is the worst place to be in this troubled world. He knows of the remorse that tortures his compatriot over the massacre of innocent civilians. This guilt, Sousa confirms, was invented by the adversaries he had created within the army. That man Andrea is mistaken: The vast majority of the targets he bombarded were not centers of population. It was uninhabited bush.

*Andrea is convinced he killed many people* . . . *did anyone ever see the bodies?* Sousa asks.

He didn't, I feel like answering. No Portuguese soldier ever sees us blacks, even when we're alive.

*Álvaro is a good man*, he concludes. *They want him to abandon his causes.*

He goes back to studying his charts and then murmurs in an offhand way: *You did well to warn me. I'll transmit your disclosure to Sergeant Araújo. We'll reinforce the king's security.*

*Please don't involve the sergeant in this matter*, I beg him anxiously.

*You haven't told me anything I don't know, my dear*, he reassures me. *I've known about Roberto Machava's plans for a long time now. I have my sources.*

He gets to his feet with a scrape of his chair and peers into my face as if he no longer recognizes me. I step back fearfully.

*Why are you so scared of Araújo?* he asks quizzically.

He examines me closely, looking for signs of a complaint. *What has my sergeant done to you?* the captain insists. Faced with my silence, he rubs his hands and concludes in a whisper: *I think I know why.*

<br>

Darkness has fallen and the ship's deck has become unrecognizable. Hundreds of passengers sing and dance in fancy dress. We shall soon cross the equator, the spine of the world as the sailors call it.

In the middle of the crowd, on an improvised dais, a masked man is sitting. He is covered in a golden cape, and is wearing a false beard and crown. Ngungunyane exclaims enthusiastically: *Look, it's the king D. Carlos!* And he calls to the Portuguese monarch at the top of his voice. The soldiers laugh playfully.

The crew are sprinkled with oil and then bathed and purified. They call this rite a new baptism. It is incredible how similar we blacks and whites are in our ceremonies. And how alike are our rituals for cleansing the soul. The angels of the whites are not, after all, as austere and watchful as we were led to believe. Like ours, they are drunken and fun-loving.

The chaotic luster of the celebration makes me recall the festivities of my childhood by the River Inharrime. All of a sudden, I see Bibliana once more emerging from the crowd. With her red tunic and the white cloths tied around her waist, the sorceress proclaims: *The seas are like blood: They appear to be many but they are all one.*

Then I do what I have always done: When people are making merry, I stand on the fringes, well away from all the lights and the noise. António Sérgio de Sousa joins me, his hands plunged into his coat pockets. Two soldiers pass us, dragging old Mulungo, Ngungunyane's uncle, along with them. They take him over to Sergeant Araújo. *This bastard got away from the hold*, they say, saluting. Mulungo is thin, dignified, and impassive. He does not want to learn a word of Portuguese and is ashamed of the king of Gaza's panic fits. Captain Sousa recognizes him, and tells them to free him. *This is Gungunhana's elderly uncle. He is authorized to attend the festivities. But not the others.*

The "others" are Roberto Machava's congregation. They have remained in the hold, under extra surveillance. My warning worked, I think to myself, not without a little guilt.

*This whole voyage is a farce.* Sousa sighs. *We are busy inventing a king who never existed.*

The ritual associated with the crossing of the equator has a history, according to António de Sousa. Those who celebrate it are unaware of this. But the captain is determined to tell me. In the time of the caravels, he begins, it wasn't the storms but the doldrums that the sailors most feared. The region of the equator is rich in sunlight but poor in winds. Every time a ship was becalmed, it wasn't just the food stocks that deteriorated: Discipline and the sense of hierarchy also disintegrated. They needed to create an escape valve, a kind of carnival in which everyone could be anyone. That was how the ritual of crossing the "spine of the world" was born. The ocean was a woman and the sailor's fingernail, like a sharp blade, drew a line across this woman's back. The Atlantic smiled and this laughter was the license they needed. The frontier between North and South, like a torn dress, fell at the sailors' feet.

The Catholic and Protestant churches banned this ritual. They saw some lingering remnant of paganism in it. But it wasn't the churches' prohibition that was to weaken this age-old practice. It was technological advance. By freeing itself from the caprice of the winds, the steamship came to the rescue of Christian efforts. Though weakened, the ritual resisted. As long as fear survives, the gods will not be destroyed by machines.

✤

I take my leave of the captain and on my way back to my cabin, I am accosted by Sergeant Araújo. He is accompanied by half a dozen soldiers.

*I need you*, the sergeant warns me. *I'm going to talk to that scoundrel Machava.*

*Permit me an opinion, Sergeant*, I say apprehensively. *It's just that in this case, I can be dispensed with. The pastor speaks perfect Portuguese.*

*I couldn't care less what Machava may have to say*, the soldier declares. *What matters to me is that the other reprobates understand what I have to say.*

I have never been inside a ship's hold before. Now I feel the dizziness of a cold, musty, lackluster inferno. It is so dark that I lose the ability to breathe. And thank goodness: This saves me from the pestilential stink. One of the soldiers decides to lift the entrance hatch and we are bathed in a beam of light and a timid flow of air. One can make out prisoners' bodies huddled together in the same confined space. The sergeant addresses them with a shout. He announces that he is aware of the serious plots being hatched in this enclosure. He demands that the detainees talk. The prisoners obey in a strange way: Instead of talking, they pray together.

*What are you doing? Are you praying to keep the demons away? I'll show you what Hell is.*

The sergeant's yells reverberate through the hold and he keeps leaning toward me as if he is about to check my translation.

*There's a problem here, sir,* I declare timidly. *It's just that we don't have a word for Hell.*

Araújo doesn't pay any attention to me. He is determined to display his anger, pacing up and down, his steps echoing throughout the hold. Eventually, he stops in front of Roberto Machava and orders him:

*Choose which one of them is going to die.*

The pastor remains impassive. He behaves like we used to in our village when we were visited by whites or the VaNguni: We became inscrutable. All that is left before him is a mask, made of dark stone.

*If you don't choose one, we'll kill three,* Araújo threatens.

Not a muscle moves in Machava's body. And he remains like that even when they grab three of his companions.

*I'll take these three with me as they look the youngest,* Araújo declares. *I've got to kill some of you, so I might as well start with those who've got the most reason to live.*

The missionary steps forward, arms open, and announces:

*I've chosen one.*

*And who's that?* Araújo asks.

*It's me,* Machava declares. *I've chosen myself.*

*In that case,* the Portuguese says, addressing his soldiers, *kill these three.*

*But I've chosen . . .* the missionary stutters.

*You chose yourself. And you're nobody.*

They drag the terrified young men out into the passageway. The sergeant and I bring up the rear of this improvised cortege. One of the soldiers shuts the hatch behind us. Then he asks timidly:

*Forgive me, sir, but are we going to kill them for real?*

*Is there any other way of killing?*

*It's just that they told us to protect the prisoners . . .*

*Those are the others,* Araújo insists impatiently. *No one knows about these ones in the hold. The fewer get to their destination, the better. Kill them down near the engine room because, like that, no one will hear the shots.*

Outside, the party goes on. I don't hear the shots. It would have been better if I had. A truncated memory is one that never heals. On the nights that follow, I am visited by the terrified faces of the boys who have been killed. And I shed all the tears I did not shed for my own dead. Then I fall asleep. And my weightless tears remain imprisoned in my eyes.

*Why did you kill them, Sergeant?* Sousa asks.

Araújo is standing to attention at the door to António de Sousa's cabin. The sergeant's look is tense, but his answer is serenely confident.

*Do you want me to answer, sir, in the present situation?* Araújo asks, pointing at me.

I am the "situation" to which he refers. It was I who brought him the news of the execution. António de Sousa's silence is an accusation that obliges his subordinate to defend himself.

*My commanding officer gave me an order to solve a problem,* Araújo explains. *Well, I solved two for you: the one you were facing here, and another one that would be caused in Cape Verde, if a bunch of insubordinate blacks were offloaded in a territory over which we have little control, even though it is ours.*

*What crime were they accused of for such a summary execution?* António de Sousa asks.

*What crime? For the love of God, Captain, those rascals wanted to kill Gungunhana, a Portuguese, a sergeant in our army.*

*And the bodies?* the captain checks. It is not a question. It is an admission that he is resigned to the facts. The executed men, the sergeant informs him, were thrown into the sea.

The truth is that not a day goes by when a body isn't thrown overboard. Many of the Portuguese soldiers are fatally ill, weakened by sores and fevers, when they board. Most of them are aware of their eventual fate: They will die without a grave, left to rot at the whim of the currents and the monsters of the deep. They prefer this to being buried in African lands.

António de Sousa stares at the horizon, which is a way of abdicating from sight. The sergeant understands that his silence is an order to withdraw.

# 21

## ON THE EVE OF ARRIVAL

*Whoever is scared of water ends up drowning in the soil.*
### —A PROVERB FROM NKOKOLANI

In the early morning, a pale, skinny sailor knocks on my door. He comes on behalf of António Sérgio de Sousa and is bearing two envelopes. The captain wants me to read these two letters and then return them with the messenger. *You must start by reading this one,* the sailor says, waving the envelope in his right hand. He holds out his arm and then hesitates, as if he were assessing the weight of the two messages. *I've made a mistake,* he admits, correcting himself. He hands me the other envelope and withdraws. He will wait in the passageway until I have finished reading.

The first letter has been written by Captain Sousa and is addressed to Sergeant Júlio Araújo. Dabondi asks me to translate it while I read. She closes her eyes as if she could listen more attentively like this.

Dear Sergeant Araújo,

Tomorrow, we shall arrive in Lisbon and I shall have completed my last voyage. I know what happened to my colleagues who retired. In a few years, I shall fade away, as they did, yearning for what I always complained about. In contrast, you, Sergeant, will pursue your career in the navy. It is highly unlikely that our paths will ever cross again. We have shared the same limited space for so many months and yet, in spite of this—or perhaps precisely because of this?—we have never had what one might call a conversation.

I know what you think of me, I do not intend to try to change your perception. You think I am a weak man, and that I am too condescending toward the Africans. I have no defense, nor do I wish to have any, against this impression. Those words of yours, brandished like some accusation, are the greatest compliment you can pay me, as far as I am concerned. Thank God for these petty dislikes.

I wish to speak of myself. The act of writing permits confessions that we would not have the courage to make in other circumstances. I was born in Africa, in a land where the trees reach higher than the sky. My mother—God rest her soul—taught me to love those creatures of nature as if she could guess that I would miss them more than the land itself. *Trees are like people*, she used to say. What we do not realize is that we only see the surface. What we fail to see, in trees and in people, is time itself, that infinite weaver. The roots, my mother assured me, are like the stories of our lives. Who sees them? Well we, my dear sergeant, we passed each other like people passing a tree and only seeing the shade. We have not got to know each other, my dear Araújo. And perhaps it is better like this. We do not need to pretend to bid each other farewell.

My father died out in India. He thus accomplished what he had set out to do. So many times did he tell us: No one knows how to die in the place where they were born. He could not have died farther away. After we buried him, I went to sort out the piles of papers he had allowed to accumulate over the years in his study. They were not just papers; it was his life that slowly sifted through my fingers.

In a folder labeled "Documents from the Congo," I discovered a photograph of three slaves flanked by two whites. It was a picture taken in the Belgian Congo. The blacks were holding the severed hands of other slaves. One could barely distinguish between the fingers of the living and those of the dead. As if the severed hands were still clinging on to a living body. As if they did not know how to die.

It was not just that macabre sight that robbed me of my sleep forever. It was the looks on the faces of those slaves, their numbed expressions. The faces of those men were empty masks, as if that most human of qualities—which I call the voice of the face—had to be concealed from the photographer's indiscretion. They were thus defending the last vestiges of their dignity.

It was not we Portuguese who committed such a barbarous act. That is what you will say. It was not us, that much is true. But all of us, all Europeans, have woven a blanket of silence around this huge crime which was slavery. The young men you shot—on a ship of which I was the captain—will be your Hell. Until your dying breath, my dear sergeant, you will be marked by that memory.

Countless times I have listened to you proclaiming that the end of the world has already happened. Not one of us—not even God—has been aware of this fateful event. The truth is different, my friend. It is not we who have our reasons to believe in the apocalypse. It is the blacks who see their lands attacked, their hands severed, and their dreams bleeding to death. While we philosophize about the apocalypse, those people are experiencing the real end of the world. And this theory of yours about a hecatomb is very convenient: If there is no future, then we become the same as the beasts of the wild. And there is nothing better for wars than a wild beast in a soldier's uniform.

I enclose the photograph that robbed so much of my soul. Do not limit yourself to just looking at it. Let yourself be looked at by the image. As the eyes of those black men pierce through you, perhaps you will understand that the weakness of which you accuse me is not as bad as the courage which serves as your pennant.

I hope, my dear sergeant, we shall not meet again. I bear you no ill will. I just want to forget. That is what I want. To forget me, to forget you and all the others. Perhaps I want a little more than this: I pray that you, Sergeant, might never have existed in my life. And that this letter might never have been written to anyone.

*March 12, 1896*
*António Sérgio de Sousa*

My translation may, perhaps, have been lacking, because when I finish reading, Dabondi appears to be completely indifferent. At first, I thought she might have fallen asleep. But I am surprised by the sight of her shaking her arms and jingling her bracelets. She is chasing away the spirits that emerged from the letter.

*You told the white man*, the queen reminds me, *that I was praying to my gods. You were wrong. There's no such thing as other peoples' gods, my dear girl. They are always ours.*

The soldier knocks on the door. He wants to know whether he can collect the letters. I ask for a little more time. Dabondi closes her eyes again, waiting for me to read the second letter.

Most Esteemed Captain,
António Sérgio de Sousa,

We are taking leave of each other in this curious manner, exchanging letters as if we had lost the gift of speech. But it is good that it should be this way. This, Captain, is your last voyage. But my journey does not end here. I shall die at sea and be buried in unknown waters. Without ground, your Africans tell us, the dead man never finds death. I'm talking like a black, God forgive me.

To begin our conversation, I have to acknowledge that you, Captain, are a good man. However, I ask myself the value of goodness in this world. Of one thing I am certain: I do not have the least desire to be good. My only intention is to be just. And justice requires men who are not afraid of being cruel.

You are right, Captain: I am obsessed with the end of the world. It is not just the nineteenth century that is ending, it is not just the monarchy that is on its deathbed. It is the entire universe that is emptying away like sand between our fingers. It has been written in the books, Captain. There were times when I asked blacks what notion they had of the creation of the world. They all gave me the same answer, astonished by the absurdity of my question: *But the world has no beginning or end.* The substance of the world is time itself, they said, there are no words to distinguish one from the other. You, sir, with your

THE DRINKER OF HORIZONS

incurable paternalism, will say that this answer conveys some
deep wisdom. I would claim that it shows a total lack of
insight.

Why do I speak of this now? The truth is this: There can
be no justice if there is no notion of a final judgment. Without
the idea of a divine reckoning, the Africans won't give a fig for
anyone else. A people like that, devoid of civic responsibility,
should be guided by civilized folk. Our failure to assume such
a mission would indeed denote a lack of courage and goodness.

If the world is in the middle of an apocalypse, then I would
rather sink to the bottom on the back of a demon. That is the
only advantage of traveling through southern seas: they are
peopled with devils. These malign creatures are nowadays my
only counselors and protect me far more effectively than all the
angels together. They say we bring back ships full of "zinc
coats," which is the polite term we use for coffins. In my case,
the opposite is happening: There is a part of me that is not
returning to Portugal. Part of me has remained among blacks
and above all, among black women.

God the Father Almighty was cautious: Europeans and
Africans were not made from the same mold. And so much the
better. Because I don't have the time or the patience to
disentangle the good from the bad. Did you want me to treat
the prisoners like people? If it was the other way round, if we
were the prisoners, tell me, Captain, would the blacks have
given us the same chance? Do you know any white who has
been held captive in the jungles of Africa? And do you know
why you don't? Because they were all killed.

Once, in the middle of a battle, I heard the commander
shouting: "Don't kill the women and children!" I thought to
myself: this fellow is a naïve greenhorn. In Africa, there are no
women or children. Here, they are all enemies, they all want to

kill us. That is why I say: The happier they appear to be, the more I hate them. I can't bear it when they laugh, I can't stomach it when they talk loud, sing, or dance. Tell me frankly, Captain: What is so important in life that it needs to be celebrated?

There is no point in us wasting any more time. I am a man of action and, for me, the issue is perfectly straightforward: You, sir, have been poisoned by that woman, Imani. That is what women do: They inoculate us with a sweet venom, which we only realize we've taken when we are already dead. I can imagine the untruths that girl has told you about me. I never touched her. Not that I didn't get the urge. That harlot—I'm sorry, but that's the only term to describe her—is no more than a fraud. And let me tell you something else: There are rumors doing the rounds among the crew. Just gossip, you will say, sir. And in your defense, you will argue in this case that there's no smoke without fire. But on a number of occasions, Imani was seen entering your cabin. I hope you took advantage. Because, to be quite honest, that girl isn't my type. The last thing I want are black women speaking Portuguese as well as I do, and looking at me with pride in their eyes. The ones that attract me are the others, the real black women who are more authentic, more savage. I've even played the Peeping Tom when they were washing themselves. And did they wash?! Twice a day! But I never saw them up to any hanky-panky with their husbands. The cook told me they are forbidden from having sex when traveling or at war. The ones who forgot this prohibition were Dabondi and Godido. I even caught them in the fuel bunker. That was where they lay down and fornicated among the coal dust.

Let me return to the photograph you sent me, and suggest the following: The image doesn't prove anything. Photos are like us sergeants: They say what they are told to say. It's the captions that give them their meaning. And I don't see any inscription here. I don't deny it. Some act of barbarity was no doubt committed. But it was the Belgians who did it, and they are more foreign than any other Europeans. Or who knows, maybe it was the blacks themselves? Haven't you ever heard of scenes of cannibalism, witchcraft, tribal revenge?

In any case, we Portuguese aren't capable of such gratuitous cruelty. We are not like Northern Europeans who hunt butterflies in the morning and kill blacks at night. We Portuguese are different. Even when we punish, we do so like zealous fathers. Those receiving their punishment—no matter how severe this may be—never cease being our children. We hate with love, and you, sir, are well aware of that. No other people have mingled and created so many mulatto children as we have. Look at Imani. Isn't the child she carries in her womb one of ours? I am sure he will be a beautiful youth. You can be sure, other Europeans rarely make mestizo children, and when they do, it is never with the same degree of pride.

With all due respect, Captain, be very careful with that photograph, which is a double-edged blade. For I have witnessed, with these very eyes, white folks being massacred by enraged blacks. There was no photographer there to record the horror. What I can say is that the truth is not something that can be captured in a photograph. The truth is in the eyes of the person looking at it. That is why I beg you: Throw that photograph away. For that image, God forgive me, merely perpetuates desires for vengeance against whites.

It is easy to be good when we have once been happy. Life for me was an adulterous wife. Better to be a widower, my dear captain. A widower closes his eyes and dreams. A man whom life has betrayed loses the gift of dreaming forever more.

I am returning your letter and the wretched photograph. I won't go to the trouble of tearing them up. Maybe you will wish to keep them, sir. They will provide easy fodder for your uneasy conscience.

*Sergeant Júlio Araújo*

# 22

## THE LIGHT OF LISBON

I put to sea
in a perpetual dream of a ship
and islands left me
with the orbed illusion of infinity.

And I never encountered a strand
where I failed to hear my mother's voice:
wherever there is sea, it said,
you will have a berth for your yearning, distance, waiting.

Later,
the oars were shattered
and the bottom of every ship ripped open.
They say it was the work of the devil.
But it was time
that smashed those oars
and extinguished my desire for travel.

I ran aground
without any grandeur,
a mere ebbing of the tide.
And on the sands of the beach
the memory that there was ever an ocean
was erased forever more.

  —VERSES IN THE SHIPBOARD DIARY OF ANTÓNIO SÉRGIO DE SOUSA

We have arrived in Lisbon, the final port, the end of our voyage. On the ship, the soldiers, in tears, wave their camping bags at those waiting on the quay. Something unexpected joins both Africans and Europeans in war: On the other side of the sea, in the distant land where we were born, everyone thinks we are dead.

With vigorous steps and a tense face, the queen Dabondi crosses the deck pushing her way past members of the crew. She has brought a shovel from the engine room, which she drags noisily behind her. She feels the dry sand of anxiety in her mouth and has to spit in order to breathe. She is looking for the ship's captain, and wants to know where her son, João Mangueze, is buried. The first thing she will do when she disembarks is visit his grave. If she doesn't do this, the earth left from his burial will grow within her. All mothers who have lost children experience an inner burial, according to Dabondi. And she spits sand again.

The captain explains that it will be hard to find out where his grave is. It is a great city, he argues. Dabondi is puzzled: How great is a land which doesn't know where its dead have been sown?

*Worse than seeing a child die*, she says, *is learning to forget one who is still alive.*

Captain Sousa shakes his head, confused. Then he asks me in an undertone: *But didn't her son die?* To which I reply: *When they die, our children become even more alive.* The queen coughs, and the floor is covered in sand. The Portuguese, startled, takes a step backward. When she regains her breath, Dabondi affirms: *Women and the earth have the same mouth.* Then she hands the shovel to the Portuguese. *Dig me up, Captain*, she beseeches him. *Dig me up before I suffocate.*

A soldier whispers in António de Sousa's ear: *Bind her wrists, in Africa there are women who commit suicide by eating soil.* The captain sits down, the shovel across his feet. He doesn't know what to do. All that occurs to him is to listen to this mother's lament.

*Every day, we give birth to the same child*, says Dabondi. Every day, the umbilical cord is reborn in order to be cut once more. A mother goes into labor again and again throughout her life, she listens to the first cry, feels the same smile. Every birth repeats itself endlessly.

Dabondi does what all mothers have done since the beginning of time: They gather up the footprints of the children who have left. In this way, the ground becomes more alive. And the earth gains the curvature of a belly.

A soldier brings a request for an audience from Ngungunyane. The king wants a little bit of attention on the eve of our disembarkation. *Well, I'll give him a few minutes*, António de Sousa agrees. And down I go too, the eternal translator, to the cabin of the VaNguni prisoners. *I waited until the end of the journey for you to come and pay me a visit*, Ngungunyane begins by declaring. Then he continues slowly: *I may be a prisoner, but I am still a king.* For more than a decade, he had treated the Portuguese ambassadors with respect. He still hoped that they would finally take him to see his counterpart, the king of Portugal. António listens in silence to all he has to say.

*Today is Friday the thirteenth*, the captain declares. *Aren't you afraid?*

The king is puzzled. *Is this white man scared of some sorcery?* he asks. Because for him, the ruler of Gaza, that day brings him some relief. He is interrupted by a violent coughing fit. Ngungunyane's breath smells musty. The king shivers. It is not from the cold, but from fever.

*I miss Dr. Liengme*, he complains, almost voiceless.

*We've got better doctors here*, Sousa placates him. *Don't die now, Gungunhana!*

And they both laugh. There is another coughing fit and the Portuguese hurriedly says goodbye for fear of contamination. Ngungunyane stretches out his hand. For the first time in his entire life, the captain shakes a black man's hand. The salutation lasts longer than he expected. He delicately frees himself from the other man's grip. Ngungunyane seizes him by the arm, and murmurs: *I am very frightened, my friend.* Once again, the Portuguese sits down next to the prisoner, unsure of what to say. Eventually, he takes a bottle out of his coat pocket and hands it to him with this advice: *Drink this wine. It would be better not to be sober today.*

In the end, he retires to the bridge. Ngungunyane offers me a drink. I thank him, but decline. The emperor lifts the bottle to his mouth and I listen to the slow gurgling of the liquid. The ship's siren sounds like the lowing of a giant ox. Ngungunyane raises his eyes, childlike, to the heavens.

*It's precisely what you are thinking, my king*, I declare. *They are sacrificing a head of cattle to celebrate your arrival.*

The king smiles weakly. But his whole soul lights up. For an instant, the gods return and Ngungunyane's fears are abated.

*This ox we are listening to now is the same one that bellowed at my father's funeral.*

His wife, Muzamussi, suggests he shouldn't remember sad events. Now I must talk, Ngungunyane says. And he recalls the burial of his father, King Muzila. The dead man's body was wrapped in the skin of a cow and hung from the ceiling of the big house. There he remained in order to receive the due honors. And it wasn't the royal counselors who headed the cortege. Nor was it the military chiefs. It was the *inkomo ya mdloẓi*, the bull from the great shadows.

It is this great bovine that is now booming through the skies over Lisbon.

There must be a sun in this river. Only this can explain the light in Lisbon. That is what I say to the captain as we contemplate the city's hills. António de Sousa admits, smiling, that the city ought to be called "Litbon."

It is the morning of March 13, 1896. The ship is progressing, slowly and proudly, up the Tagus estuary. Around us, there are more boats than there are gulls. And they are of all sizes and shapes: launches, skiffs, frigates, boats propelled by motors, sails, and oars, all packed with people waving in an endless clamor. For the Portuguese, it's a cause for rejoicing. For the prisoners, it's a prelude to the end of the world.

As we approach the quay, we see how the crowd extends and undulates as if it were another sea. We can hear shouts:

*He's arrived! Gungunhana's arrived!*

The engines are shut down. In the distance, the land sways, shapeless and dazed. I go down to the cabin to get rid of my nausea. I peer at the steps beyond my belly. I'm in the sixth month of my pregnancy.

We haven't yet tied up and there is an invasion of journalists, who arrive on barges. They climb aboard with such enthusiasm that no one stops them from visiting the cubicle which has served as a prison over the last two months for my fellow countrymen. The sergeant hurries me to follow the journalists. At this point, Araújo warns me, it would be better if I gave the impression of being one of the king's wives. And when I translated, I would have to adopt more of an African accent. Press people, the sergeant says, are experts in telling stories and fabricating scandal. Then, addressing

the visitors, he allows himself to be overcome by vanity. Like a circus magician, he announces at the cabin door: *Here are the blacks,
gentlemen!*

Covering their faces with handkerchiefs, the journalists peer
into the tiny space. Zixaxa's voice can be heard commenting in
his own language: *All the better that we smell bad. So they won't come
near us.*

*Is that Gungunhana?* the journalists ask, pointing at Zixaxa.
They don't understand a single word of what has been said, but the
mere fact that the man had dared to speak suggested he was different from the others.

Sergeant Araújo lifts the blanket Ngungunyane has used to
cover himself. He didn't need to hide. The emperor's face has been
lost. All that can be seen are two round eyes, like those of a new-
born child. He doesn't understand why the reporters are so vora-
cious. They could only be after his soul. And the king's soul was
left behind on the other side of the ocean.

Ngungunyane weeps, and the reporters are puzzled. They expected a more dignified posture. And the photographers hesitate to
take the anxiously awaited portrait of the king. The space becomes
too small, there is a black woman coughing clouds of dust, and
there's a king sobbing profusely. They need to get out of there.
Araújo euphorically leads away the platoon of scribes: *Come with
me, let's take this bunch of vagrants up to the deck canopy.*

Ngungunyane staggers forward at the head of the prisoners.
He has taken the captain's advice: He has drunk so much and
so quickly that the alcohol has caused his brain to float away from
him like a cloud. Drunkards aren't satisfied with sadness. They
want tragedy. And he is convinced of his fate: He is going to be
shot like his counselors were at Chaimite. He sobs, begs, hides
his face in his hands, and offers all he no longer has to obtain his
rendition: pounds sterling, cattle, gold, ivory, slaves, lands. And

he begs to be received by D. Carlos. He wants to prove they are lying to him, he wants to swear his loyalty to his Portuguese counterpart.

He waits for me to translate his supplications. I ask Godido to take my place in this task. The emperor's son doesn't need to be asked twice: his haughty demeanor and mastery of the Portuguese language make him the center of attention. The sons of chieftains are almost always unbearable. What they lack in maturity, they make up for in arrogance. Later, when it becomes apparent that this Godido can write his name, a number of distinguished ladies will pester him for his autograph.

Red-and-white-striped shawls are distributed by the queens. These are the colors they use to summon rain. I was not included among the recipients of this warm garment. Up until then, *winter* was just a word I read in books. Now it is a white arrow piercing my body. I am scared it will affect my baby. Captain Sousa drapes a black cape around my shoulders. And he says: *It suits you, it's yours, take it with you.*

Unexpectedly, the journalists are joined by a dignitary: António Enes, the Royal Commissioner. He came out on a special launch, and on the deck, everyone steps back to make way for him and to bow respectfully. He asks to see the prisoners. He shakes his head when he sees the tearful emperor.

*It isn't a good idea to exhibit him to the public*, António Enes says regretfully. *He'll inspire fellow feeling and compassion. Certain sectors of the press will jump at the chance to defend a poor black man.*

*Can't we display Zixaxa instead?* António Sérgio de Sousa suggests.

A resigned smile is the immediate reply. It's tempting, Enes admits, but it's a risk that should be avoided. The worst thing that could happen to Portugal would be some failed propaganda coup.

*Gungunhana looks jaded*, the Royal Commissioner says. *He must be revived. Tell him he's going to be received by the king of Portugal.*

*But is that true, Commissioner?* Sergeant Araújo inquires.

*Let's allow him to think so. We'll lie. That's what he did to us for years.*

Sergeant Araújo walks around the commissioner's chair. He is tense, and uses his feet to abuse the ground. When he summons up the courage, his voice is shrill:

*With all due respect, Your Excellency, isn't there someone missing here?*

*I don't understand.*

*Isn't our Captain Mouzinho de Albuquerque missing?*

António Enes straightens his glasses. He didn't hear that. It's Friday the thirteenth. On a day like that, there are things one shouldn't hear. Then he withdraws. He excuses himself, saying that urgent matters await his attention in Lisbon.

An uneasy silence lingers on the deck. Sergeant Araújo is insistent and addresses António de Sousa: *Answer me, Captain: shouldn't Mouzinho be here?*

Sousa keeps his eyes on the sea as he answers. He tells the sergeant that he should already know the difference between a politician and a soldier. The politician knows, or thinks he knows, when he should speak. The soldier has learned to hold his tongue. And thus, by holding his tongue, he is always right.

At long last, we are led onto the quay. The women disembark first, carrying their bundles on their heads. Then it is the men who file off, flanked by a cordon of soldiers to keep the crowd away. They lodge us first in a huge warehouse they call the Arsenal. In this huge building, government figures, journalists, gentlemen, and their ladies are waiting for us. Outside, the noise is deafening. *Where are we, Captain?* I ask António de Sousa. *We're in an armaments factory,* he answers. *It's a good way to enter this country,* he says. *Our factories,* he adds, *aren't factories, nor do they belong to us. What they make comes already made abroad.*

Ngungunyane sits down on a wooden bench. It is a lofty seat, and the king's feet swing in the air. He calls for me, and asks me to stay near him. He needs to know what the whites are saying. Dabondi sits on the other side of him. The wooden boards creak. The queen's thin hand caresses the wood. *We are in Portugal now, Nkosi,* I say. *I'm nowhere,* Ngungunyane declares. *I'm keeping my son João company, I'm under the ground.*

Look at the trees, Dabondi urges us. They're dead, so lifeless that the crows are even scared to perch on them. The trees have been sucked dry by a creature that has a master. On the streets and sidewalks, dry leaves shrivel like widows suffering from the cold. That is what the sorcerer queen says. And then she asks: *Tell me honestly: Have you ever seen such desolation? I have,* Ngungunyane replies. When he felt he was dying, his father, King Muzila, shot an arrow into the sky. In an instant, the clouds lost their feathers and plummeted in pieces to the ground.

Five horse-drawn carriages pull up in front of us. The parade is going to start. The soldiers push us toward the carts. *See?* Ngungunyane says. *I'm not a prisoner, but a visitor. They're taking me in a carriage, as they told me they do for kings.*

Dabondi breaks away from the other prisoners. The cold is such that shadows stick close to their bodies. She kneels in front of the horses and uses her fingers to dig between the cobblestones. *What is that woman doing?* Araújo asks. *We are walking over a cemetery,* the queen declares. *The whites place stones over the dead so that they won't return.* Where other people presumed a street, she saw a graveyard.

The horses scrape the cobblestones like the *tingoma*, the drummers of my homeland, play their drums. The horses, Dabondi claims, are scared of their own shadows. That is why their hooves are restless. A military band takes up its position in the yard. The drums now beat to the same rhythm as the horses. The animals now shake their hooves like the *ikanyamba*, those creatures that live in the waters and in the dreams of the Zulus. And there is fire bursting from their nostrils. Their eyes are full of rivers and dark plains. *Horses' eyes are good for crying,* Dabondi says. The dead leaves swirl upward and the emperor watches them, believing them to be swallows. Long ago, he had ordered the extermination of swallows. But they have revived and are emerging from the ground where his son was buried. The Portuguese soil is also his. That land has belonged to him ever since it received his blood.

They start distributing the prisoners among the carriages. They make the wives sit in the first ones. The fourth is occupied by the cook Ngó, who installs himself on top of the bundles and sleeping mats, which are our only baggage. Ngungunyane, Godido, Zixaxa, and Mulungo follow in the last carriage.

For a moment, they are undecided about where to put me. The press had already disclosed that there were ten wives. My presence would give rise to questions. Eventually they decide that I shall travel hidden in the cook Ngó's carriage.

And so the procession begins. Escorted by thirty soldiers, the carriages push their way through the tight throng. Thousands of people are packed onto the sidewalks and the streets, are perched in trees and up lampposts, and lean from windows and balconies. They all form one creature, which undulates like a roaring sea. Insults and threats rain down. They spit on the ground, hurl objects, and demand that those who dared to rebel should have their throats cut.

As we jolt along, I peer out from behind our luggage. With the exception of Dabondi, all the queens appear to be curious and relaxed. They believed Ngungunyane's version: that all the uproar is a demonstration of their welcome. And the hoots of the white women are understood to be like the *mukulungana*, the ululations with which they themselves greet visitors in their homeland. From time to time, they catch a glimpse of black people in the crowd. And they wave at them as if they are encountering old friends again. But gradually, reality imposes itself and the women follow the example of the pangolin: they huddle together as if they are of one body, under the same curved protective carapace.

From the outset, the men are subdued, gripped by cold and fear. Slowly, though, Ngungunyane assumes a peaceful, confident posture. It isn't dignity that emanates from him. It's indifference. If the monarch's intention was to escape humiliation, then he had more than enough wine to do so. And the swaying of the carriage causes him to nod off. This sleepiness is badly received by the Portuguese, who hoped to detect in Ngungunyane's face the submission of an entire race. The African is absent, absorbed in himself as is to be expected of an emperor. They insult him and he does not react.

They throw things at him and he does not try to dodge them. Dabondi smiles, and raises her right fist, causing her bracelets to jingle. The dried leaves pick themselves up from the ground and flutter back up to the trees.

# 23

## A ROOM UNDER THE GROUND

*Here is what they do: With a sword they kill people with no god;*
*with the cross they kill the gods of the survivors.*
**—NWAMATIBJANE ZIXAXA**

In the Monsanto Fortress, they lead us down an underground stair-
way, as if we were visiting our final dwelling place. Not even the
dead live so far down, Ngungunyane sighs. The dungeon is dark,
damp, and cold. There is water running down the walls, and there
is a smell of old things. *They are burying us alive*, groans Godido.

Sitting on the stone floor, the king asks for help with taking off
his boots. *I don't need them*, he says. *I no longer have any feet. The cold
has eaten them, the cold is ravenous.* The king rattles on: If the winter
continues for much longer, maybe he'll get used to walking without
feet. And if they don't kill him, who knows, maybe his feet will
grow back again?

My eyes get used to the darkness and I see that the cell is larger
than our previous accommodation. But in the depths of the earth,
everything seems narrower. We sleep huddling together. Dabondi
nestles up to me. For the next few nights, the queen will be my blanket, my pillow, my stove.

We do not know whether we wake early or late, for there is only
one small window at the top of the wall. Through this narrow
opening, we can see a tiny sliver of Lisbon sky. Godido climbs up

to peer at the crowd which has gathered on the nearby waste ground. And that is how things will remain over the next few days: On the open ground in front of the fort, hundreds of inquisitive people have established a fair, with stalls selling snacks. There are postcards of Gungunhana on sale, along with leaflets containing epic accounts of the African king. The stalls exhibit cookies, going by the name of "Gungunhanas," with a cutout of a tubby, large-headed man. The emperor himself will claim to be a fan of these cookies. Not a day will go by when he does not consume himself.

*The Portuguese rejoice like all unhappy people do*, Dabondi murmurs. *Because they don't realize that the city is cursed*. And the queen spits on the floor. On those same streets where we processed today, the blood of the king D. Carlos will be spilled. And Mouzinho de Albuquerque will drop dead. His body will fall like a dead leaf onto the city's paving stones.

We live like moles, in a hole burrowed in an alien land. Queen Dabondi recognizes our unhappy condition, but she does not seem sorry. One of these days, she says, water will spring from the paving and rise up the walls. We have a clear challenge, she predicts: Those who turn into fish will be the ones to survive. That is what happened to the Portuguese.

A week has gone by since we were imprisoned in the gloom. I hear footsteps. A guard arrives carrying newspapers. He stuffs them through the bars on the door. *It's for you to read out loud to the others*, he tells me. I show the photographs to the emperor of Gaza. He smiles, content. *It was the king of Portugal who ordered them to be published*, he insists. I refrain from translating the captions. They call Ngungunyane the "cruel beast," "the bloodthirsty chieftain," "the brutal tyrant, ally of the English."

The papers are then distributed among the prisoners. They patch them together as if they were making clothes. They will use these sheets of paper to keep warm. They who never learned to read are now covered in letters.

On the eighth day, they came and cleaned the cell and white-washed the wall. It is rumored that D. Carlos is to visit Monsanto. Ngungunyane is not startled by the news: *I always welcomed royal emissaries from Portugal. They are going to receive me, for that is what they do with kings.*

The next day, they stop their cleaning and painting. King D. Carlos has canceled the visit. It's a political decision, they explain. They brought Ngungunyane to Lisbon so that he would become a focus of attention. But the presence of the Lion of Gaza has ended up becoming an embarrassment. This unease has a name: women. Ngungunyane may be an African, he may be an enemy of Portugal. But he cannot display the sin of polygamy with such impunity. The Church protests, the press complains, and society echoes this discomfort. D. Carlos's counselors advise him that to visit Ngungunyane would be to legitimize such immorality.

Disappointed, Ngungunyane orders his son to block out the only window providing any light in the dungeon. *If they won't receive me, then I too reject the light they are charitable enough to send me*, he declares. In a loud voice, as if someone were listening beyond the walls, he asks rhetorically: *They invited me here along with my seven wives. Did I ever count their wives when they visited Moçambique?*

It is not so much the sun that I miss. What I yearn for most is the moon. I no longer see it gleaming. Maybe that is why I find myself thinking so much about Germano. His memory reaches me like the moonlight I can no longer contemplate. Dabondi asks me to distance myself from recollections. She tells me to sing. And that I should do so in my language. *What language?* I ask her. In silence, she moves away.

On the following days, we are visited by ladies from the court. They speak through gestures and we soon realize that they have one purpose: to civilize, so they say, their African counterparts.

And the first lesson focuses on the appropriate use of cutlery. Black women can direct insults at them in some incomprehensible language. But it is unacceptable that they should eat with their hands. To use one's fingers to eat with is, like polygamy, unacceptable and obscene.

After their visits, the Portuguese ladies pass by the church to confess. They have just come from a den of iniquity. *God doesn't accept that a man should have various wives*, one of them explains to us. *Do the men here only have one spouse?* Dabondi asks. The Portuguese woman smiles, and does not answer.

In the end, the court women are forbidden to visit us. From then on, the queens spend most of their time playing cards. While they play, they also comb each other's hair. They remain unfazed by their endless inactivity. Their lives have never been very busy. At the court of Gaza, there was always someone to do the work for them. Ngó, Godido, and sometimes Mulungo make baskets and bead necklaces. Zixaxa studies Portuguese, using a little exercise book he was given on the ship. Ngungunyane drinks, coughs, and sleeps. Old Mulungo paces up and down from one side of the cell to the other. He does what all prisoners do: He counts his steps so that the cell will lose its dimension. He is happy that he doesn't understand a word of Portuguese. Just like the Zulu warriors, who daub themselves with the juice of *impundu* leaves to protect themselves, he has become invisible. This self-abnegation renders the walls meaningless. The old counselor is the only one who has never been captured.

In my corner of the cell, I only have one thing to keep me busy: pregnancy. My belly is my sand clock. It fills up as time empties, and I am now in my seventh month. So I follow Dabondi's advice, and I sing. But I sing wordlessly. We do not choose the language we are born with. What one sings to a child is a womb that lasts for longer than the act of childbirth.

Every night, I fall asleep in Dabondi's arms. The cold requires a supplementary body. In this double womb, my child now nestles. By the time he is born, he will already have several mothers. At night, when everyone is sleeping, I draw back the cloth that covers the window. Unable to sleep, I peer out at the night like a drowning person breaking the surface of the water. There is no such thing as insomnia, Dabondi says. There is only another way of sleeping. In this different kind of sleep, I listen to the king groaning and coughing convulsively. It isn't an illness, Dabondi assures me. Someone is trying to get out of his body. The emperor is more pregnant than I am. A malign spirit has taken shelter in him and is consuming his chest and crushing his knees.

We have not heard the infernal racket coming from outside since yesterday. The fair has been banned. The traders have dismantled their stalls and gone off somewhere else to sell their caricatures of the Lion of Gaza. *They are afraid of me*, Ngungunyane remarks with irony. *I was starting to compete with their king.*

Each prisoner may have their pastime. There is, however, one activity we have in common: sleep. Old age and a prison teach the same lesson: that sleeping cancels out time. Next to me, the man the Portuguese call the Lion of Gaza snores away endlessly. The title confers upon him the nobility of a king. But the Europeans reserve one of three fates for lions. To be hunted, to be caged in a zoo, or to be domesticated in a circus. The king of Gaza unites these fates in one person.

Days pass by uneventfully until, one gloomy afternoon, we receive a visit from the doctor at the fort. They have alerted him to Ngungunyane's chest pains and febrile state. While the patient is being examined, Queen Dabondi announces her diagnosis: There is a bird inside the emperor's chest. One can hear the bird hooting at night. It's a *xikhova*, an owl, says Dabondi. It must be scared off, the queen claims. The doctor shakes his head firmly. It's an illness, pleurisy, he declares haughtily.

The following day, they come and fetch Ngungunyane, carrying him away on a stretcher. Godido goes with his father to translate. The piercing cry of the women mingles with the siren of the vehicle transporting the king to the hospital. The queens go into mourning. They do not know how to bid farewell to their husband in an alien land. They ask for a razor and shave off their hair. They will only let their hair grow again when their husband returns. Dabondi no longer hugs me during the night. She cannot touch me while the king is absent. I'm impure, she explains. I carry a mulatto inside me.

Ngungunyane returns from hospital brimming with health and with a plan in his head. During his stay in hospital, his son Godido overheard conversations. And he realized that there was a matter which was keeping the Portuguese court awake at night: Álvaro Andrea's report. This other version of the epic of Chaimite is a ticking time bomb. The republicans are anxious for the document to be divulged. The monarchy's heroic deed risks dissolving into dust.

Ngungunyane asks to see the commander of the fort. He wants to negotiate with the prison authorities: He will corroborate Mouzinho's version of events as long as he is given better prison conditions in return. His demand brings results. On the following day, we are given two large, airy cells, with clothes at our disposal. In addition, we are allowed to spend the mornings in the outer courtyard. On that same day, I lie down on the grass, pull up my blouse, and let the sun warm my stomach. My son must know that he is from other lands, full of warmth and light.

The sun isn't just a gift. It is a remedy, for I had stopped praying. Every morning, I stretch out in the courtyard with my feet pointing south. The tips of my toes touch my home village. And there I remain until my skin burns. Slowly, I begin to like the city of Lisbon, with its clear, azure mornings. Can someone love a land only because of its sky?

During these sunlit hours I think about the women of my homeland. And I come to the following conclusion: If there is a queen in this fort, then it's me. All these women who accompany me are not very different from the humble folk who inhabit my country. If I had never left my village, I would have remained one of those creatures who, for centuries, have trekked into the forest and come home again loaded with dry branches. This is a task reserved for them from the time they learn to walk. Their arms grow faster than the rest of their body, the better to serve their menfolk. In appearance, they are working for their households. But they are doing far more than that: They are gathering firewood to set fire to the world. There will come a day when the girls of my homeland will enter a school, their arms laden with books. This is what I dreamed on those sun-filled mornings in Lisbon.

Some days later, they give me a room to myself. I thought this was a privilege. But it is a punishment. It is in these quarters that I receive a visit from the commander of the fort. His instructions are clear: I am to extract information from the prisoners and disclose anything that is said and who says it. Ngungunyane and Zixaxa harbor secrets. The Portuguese are sure that the prisoners are still directing resistance operations in Mozambique from afar. It may be too much of a conspiracy theory. But the truth is that the war did not come to an end with the king of Gaza's detention. New hotbeds of rebellion have sprung up around Maputo and in the district of Magude.

This news puts a damper on Portuguese propaganda. If the news is bad for the Portuguese, it is a real calamity for me. Every night, I transition from being a translator to being an informer. I have no choice: Either I denounce my racial brother or, after I have given birth, they will send me back to Mozambique. I shall travel without my baby, without Germano, and shorn of my dreams.

I decide to make things up in order to please my tormentors. The only difference between illusion and reality lies in the degree of conviction. And so, every night, a secretary transcribes imaginary conspiracies. The worst thing is that I start to derive pleasure from these false disclosures.

Until we receive news from Gaza: they have killed Maguiguane, the warrior who could turn into a bird. They murdered the man who kept the flame of Ngungunyane's empire alive. They decapitated him. They needed proof of his death: They stuck his head on an iron spike and took it from village to village. After a few days, it was so putrid and covered in flies that it could have been any creature's head. The people looked, bowed their heads, and ran away.

They didn't need proof. They knew the truth, conveyed through channels unknown to the Portuguese.

The man who brought us the news was an Nguni who traveled from Mozambique. He brought with him a twig from the *umphafa*, the holy tree. The twig was cut at the very spot where Maguiguane died and they asked the dead man to migrate into that little piece of wood.

They gave the twig to this messenger and asked him to travel to Portugal. Throughout the journey the man talked to the sprig. When he went to sit down, the messenger asked for two chairs, one of which was to accommodate the twig. He always had a second place set at table. Standing at the handrail, the messenger described out loud the ports where they stopped. The sailors laughed at the messenger's raving. They never believed they were giving passage to the late Maguiguane Khossa, the feared leader of the enemy troops.

This same twig is now delivered to the emperor, whose fingers grasp its leaves and thorns. Drops of blood fall on the stone floor. *Who killed him?* asks Ngungunyane. *It was Mouzinho*, the messenger answers in Zulu. The king of Gaza orders the courier to leave. He lays the sprig of *umphafa* on his bed, and covers it with a cloth. Then he addresses it in a low voice: *You've come to join me, my warrior. In our homeland, there is no longer any soil left for you to be buried.* He is interrupted by a fit of coughing. Then he continues: *I told the Portuguese you were a traitor. I lied in order to protect you. And you carried out my orders to the end.*

In a furious outburst, Zixaxa tears the twig from Ngungunyane's hands, snaps it into pieces, and throws the fragments out the window. Ngungunyane is dumbstruck, while the queens weep. They never thought they would witness such a heretical act, the dwelling place of a dead man being treated with such impudence. *All this is a lie*, Zixaxa shrieks. We have scarcely arrived ourselves from Mozambique, and already someone brings news from Mozambique? What ship did this messenger travel on? Only a drunkard, Zixaxa assures him, could believe in such a fantasy. Or who knows, maybe Ngungunyane is only trying to prove Maguiguane Khossa's death?

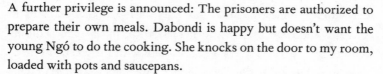

A further privilege is announced: The prisoners are authorized to prepare their own meals. Dabondi is happy but doesn't want the young Ngó to do the cooking. She knocks on the door to my room, loaded with pots and saucepans.

*Hide them in your room and only give them to the queens,* she says. *We can't allow a man to prepare Nkosi's food.*

*But why not?* I ask.

*That's the way things always were: Men light the fire, but women put the fire to use.*

There are strict traditions in the kitchen: The ashes are thrown to the four cardinal points. Only then is the village cleansed. Prison is now our village.

*Let Ngó do the cooking,* I beg her. *If the man is left without anything to do, the whites will throw him into the sea.*

With a piece of charcoal, the queen makes a cross in each of the saucepans. *Right, they have been blessed,* she says with a sigh. *The whites have powerful magic. Cooking, dear girl, isn't about making food. It is seating the gods at our table.*

We forget, Dabondi continues, how our houses were prepared so as to receive these invisible guests. In our front yards, the men sit facing south. Their wives take up the opposite side. They give the north wind the name *nwalungo,* the "man." The south wind is called *dzonga,* the same word used to designate women. These precepts are no longer respected. In this new house—which Dabondi says is a buried boat—no one knows where the cardinal points are. If the spirits come to rescue us one day, they won't know where to find us. They will know how to cross the wide ocean, but they will get stuck outside the door to our cells.

My only visitors are dreams. That night, I dreamed of someone I should not dream of: my child who is soon to be born. In my dream, my little boy is going to be baptized in the church at Nkokolani. All the family is present, both the living and the dead: my father with his orchestra of marimba players, my mother carrying in her arms the rope she hanged herself with; my brother Dubula wearing his warrior's dress and Mwanatu with his patched Portuguese army uniform. The last one to arrive is my grandfather Sangatela, who is all covered in dust. When he coughs, he twists his body as if to expel the dust from all the mines he worked in. And he declares in a grave voice:

*I have journeyed across the land to be present at this baptism. This great-grandson is me.*

The names of those taken away on slave ships or killed in wars are solemnly invoked. Each name is blessed with a drop of seawater. The sorceress Bibliana summons those who have disappeared and the walls of the church begin to creak. She raises her voice and cracks open up in the masonry, until the roof is released and floats higher and higher. In the end, it is lost in the heavens like some wayward bird.

Bibliana brings the bowl with seawater. She asks Father Rudolfo to pour the water over my son's body. The boy wails and coughs, choked. The sorceress raises the child on high: *The rivers are like blood; they seem vast and varied, but they all fit in one body.*

Bibliana stands behind me and hugs me with conviction. I squeeze her arms to strengthen her act of affection.

It is morning. And I awaken, startled to find myself touching Dabondi's bracelets.

# 24

## A TORN BODY

*Not all savages are my enemies. But it is enough for them to be enemies to become savages.*
**—SERGEANT ARAÚJO, CITED BY ZIXAXA**

One night, Patihina and Xesipe burst into my room, interrupting my sleep. The queens tell me to be quick, the king is having a fit. They lead me to a cell shrouded in darkness. I become suspicious: Why have they doused all the lights? There is the shape of a body lying on the bed. Suddenly, I am surrounded by arms pushing me. It is the queens who are assaulting me and pushing me toward the bed. I am so taken by surprise that I forget to scream. The women hold my arms and legs. Queen Muzamussi places her knee on my chest and exclaims: *See who's here with us!* At one signal from her, Zixaxa's three wives step forward.

The same mysterious smile deforms the faces of all the women. The eldest queen vehemently accuses me: *Do you think you're a white woman? You go around shamelessly wearing shoes and a dress, and even though you're not yet a mother, you speak to men without lowering your eyes. We know why: You're a witch, you want to drive men crazy. And you already have. We see our husbands' eyelashes burning during the night. They're dreaming of you, it was Dabondi who told us.*

Muzamussi goes on, with emphasis: They are the most respected mothers in the whole of the kingdom of Gaza. But they are still only women. Everywhere they go, they will be treated as intruders.

The matriarch addresses her husband, uttering her verdict: *The guilty woman is here, here is the woman who doesn't respect you as a man, the woman who offends your dignity as a person. Punish her, show her your power!*

*Dabondi!* I call out in despair.

The queen isn't in the fort. So the other wives tell me. She's been taken to the city. *You're all on your own, without your protectors, without your godmother.* Ngungunyane drags himself up like a vast slug, dark and slimy. Half of me is submerged under his weight. There's a hand clasped over my mouth. I peer through the darkness. I see the king's face bending over me.

*Don't hurt my baby, Nkosi,* I implore, struggling against the hand that is gagging me.

The king respects my request: He sits on the side of the bed, his feet on the cold stone floor. He commands his wives to leave. He wants to be alone with me. Muzamussi insists: *We want to hear the bitch groaning.* Then the women abandon the room.

Now we are both alone in the cell. Seated on the edge of the bed, Ngungunyane remains for a while contemplating his knees. Then he speaks, without raising his head: *You're nothing more than a wretched little VaChopi woman, hired to spy on me.*

There is no point in denying it. Godido heard the guards talking. They didn't realize the prisoner understood Portuguese. They were talking about me, Imani Nsambe, and the secrets I was telling the commander of the fort. No one had any doubts about my role anymore.

*It was my spying that saved you, Nkosi.*

*When?*

*During the voyage. It was I who aborted Machava's plot.*

With unexpected vigor, Ngungunyane seizes me by the arms as

if he is dragging me down into the abyss. In the darkness, I sense the whole weight of the universe falling on top of me. The emperor of Gaza, stark naked, has now irrevocably collapsed over my thighs. I am tormented by his fetid breath, sickened by his sweat that reeks like that of a wild animal.

*Groan, struggle, scream!* he whispers in my ear.

I don't understand. *Pretend I'm raping you,* the king insists. And he starts shaking his body shudderingly, causing the bed to creak. Suddenly, it all becomes clear. I agree to participate in this playacting. I scream for my mother, I scream with such conviction that my whole body hurts and tears flow down my face. And no true suffering would have given me such pain.

The king gets up and, in the corner where baths are taken, he pretends to wash himself. The water flows from one bucket into another while he talks. *They know,* he says, *I'm impotent.* He swishes his hands around in the bucket, he needs the consolation of hearing the sound of water. *You were right: I haven't been a man for months now.* Dr. Liengme attributed the cause to alcohol. But the king doesn't believe it. *The Swiss are not familiar with our sorcery,* he says. *It wasn't the wine, it was my wives who caused me to wilt.*

What they had just done, delivering me into the hands of their husband, was nothing more than a trick. This is what Ngungunyane assures me. The queens were certain of his failure just as they were sure of my humiliation. But the king had engendered an appropriate response for the occasion.

*Now it's my turn to punish those women,* the king declares. *Keep up the pretense, Imani.*

*I don't need to pretend, Nkosi. I was raped.*

Ngungunyane shakes his head with a vague smile. For only now does he understand: The Portuguese haven't brought him here to kill him. When he set sail, he was already dead. At the precise moment when Mouzinho had spared his life, in front of his subjects, that was when he was executed. An emperor dies when he shows his mortality, when he declares himself fragile and human, when he kneels meekly before another emperor. *You can't have been raped, my girl*, he declares fiercely. *For you didn't lie down with a living person.*

I withdraw from the darkened room. My soul torn, my eyes moist, I pass the queens waiting in the hallway, who stand aside, astonished. I feel their eyes like knives plunging into my back. I close the door to my room, cross my arms over my belly and think that it really is sad, what the queens have just put me through. Sadder still, however, is what life has done to these women. Their envy of me makes absolute sense. But none of them ever dreamed of taking control over their own lives.

Early in the morning, they come for me. There is someone in the waiting room, they tell me, someone who has come a long way to see me. It can only be a mistake, I think, as I cross large rooms and austere corridors. Maybe it's Germano, I ponder, my heart thumping hard in my chest. He has arrived in time to witness the birth of our child.

The soldier leading me points to the high ceilings and proudly declares: *It's all made with reinforced concrete, there isn't a bomb in the world capable of demolishing this.* I eventually walk into a strange room, with large red carpets on the floor. In an equally red armchair, a thin woman is seated, her white hair emerging from a black headscarf. She is knitting a garment the same color as the seat and carpets. For a moment, it's as if she is knitting that whole dark place. She moves her elbows to avoid the thread getting entangled around the needles.

*It's for my grandson*, she says. *He will be born on the day I finish this little coat.*

Now I'm sure: I am standing before Laura de Melo, Germano's mother. The lady sweeps to her feet, causing the ball of wool to roll onto the carpet. It follows her like an obedient cat. She holds the knitted piece next to my face and shakes her head disapprovingly: *You are blacker than I thought. I should have chosen a lighter color.*

I crawl after the ball of yarn, trying to make myself useful, and wanting to show my submissiveness. Still on my knees, I lift the ball of wool cupped in my hands. Laura de Melo does not appear to see me. *Don't come near,* she tells me. All of a sudden, she raises her arms and, with a violent thrust, she sticks the needles into the woolen threads. The ball of yarn recoils like a live body in its death throes.

As if returning to her senses, Dona Laura crosses herself and turns to face me: *I don't want any intimacies. We might even start to like each other, and there could be nothing worse than that.*

She looks me up and down. Her eyes are the same blue as Germano's.

*I am here for only one reason,* she says. *I have come to give you a letter that came from my son.*

From the pocket of her dress, she takes an envelope: *Take it. It's for you.* She holds her arm out in my direction. Reacting to my passivity, she starts waving the message nervously. Then she moans: *Germano always was given to writing. I hope he abandons that obsession. Writing letters is a woman's thing.*

At last I accept the envelope. I don't open it. I lift it to my face and breathe deeply. *That's what I did too,* Laura says, smiling. *In previous letters I never got a hint of my son's smell. Now I have: Germano has become my son again.*

Her old mother, Laura says, used to smell her hair to establish her state of health. As she lay dying, and was unable to eat, the old lady fed on smells. In the morning, they left orange peel on her bedside. At night, they crushed mint leaves and put them on her pillow.

And her old mother would fall asleep with a smile on her face. And Laura concluded:

*There's no point in smelling that letter, my girl: You won't find your sweetheart.*

Clutching the envelope, I walk back toward the corridor, when I hear her fire off these terrible words:

*He's not coming, my dear: My Germano is going to stay in Africa.*

I walk back along the cold hallways, following the same soldier who escorted me before. I look up at the concrete ceiling, wishing that the edifice would collapse on top of me.

I have just settled back in my room, which has never seemed so narrow. The door swings open, and I don't open my eyes. I hear Dabondi lamenting. She has no inkling of how downcast I am myself.

*They killed him*, the queen wails. She has come back from the city, where she went to visit her son's grave. It was Godido who had accompanied her to the cemetery.

*He died and then they killed him*, the queen mumbles. This is what she discovered that morning. They buried him in accordance with white customs. They didn't go to the trouble, though, of getting the news to Mozambique. So the proper prayers were never said over there. Her only son, João Mangueze, came to Portugal as a prince and was buried like one who has been disinherited, with no name or family. Now he roams, turned into a *xipoco*, one of those souls without relatives.

*Do you know why I went to the cemetery?*

The question is so obvious that I remain silent. Dabondi is calmer now, there's even the shadow of a smile on her face.

*I went to see the dead man, but I also went to introduce him to his new brother.*

I rush to give her a hug. Ever since the beginning of the journey, I suspected that Dabondi was pregnant. And this is such a happy moment that I decide not to tell her about the rape I have suffered. But there is something I am unable to conceal. The queen takes a step back in order to take a better look at me. *Why are you so sad, Imani?* she asks. *Germano isn't coming*, I answer. She says she already knew. That's what the queen always says, that she already knows. And I believe her.

Dabondi contemplates the infinite while she scratches the wall. Then with her finger covered in lime, she draws a white circle on my breast.

*When you give birth*, she says, *you will be empty.*

*Empty?* I ask, puzzled. *Shouldn't it be the opposite?*

*Let's not talk about that now*, she suggests.

But as I insist, the queen elaborates: The gods will grant me the happiness of being a mother. However, these same *psikwembo* will want to express their displeasure: They are disappointed because I disregard their existence.

*They will erase you from the inside.*

*Erase me? What does that mean, Dabondi?* I ask anxiously.

I shall have the same fate as the wild fig tree, the *umbombe*: I shall be devoured by my own roots. The queen pronounces these words and then returns to her cell. Her prophecy leaves me unable to sleep. The night is now a bottomless well. And it is made even deeper when I decide to read Germano's letter. I tear open the envelope and something tears within me.

My dear Imani,

This is not an easy letter. I shall start by getting straight to the point: I am not going to Lisbon. There will be no boat, there will be no voyage. I am staying in Lourenço Marques. We shall meet again, here in Mozambique, or maybe even back there in Portugal.

I do not want to hurt you, nor do I want to lose you. All the love I felt for you—and still feel for you—is absolutely true. It is not my loyalty that you need doubt. The reasons for our separation are different. I can be your husband. But I cannot be the father of that child. I was imprisoned in a cell in Portugal. I was imprisoned in Mozambique without any walls, door, or bars. I do not want to be imprisoned by domestic routine. This is what I learned from my married colleagues. A life within a marriage is the most permanent of imprisonments. Perhaps I am ill, maybe I lacked a family. My old father professed a peculiar form of atheism: He did not believe in happiness. And he would say of the people in the village: "The stupider they are, the happier they become. The thicker they are, the more easily they fall asleep."

There is another reason for my decision: I cannot return to Portugal until the monarchy is overthrown. I would be locked up in a prison cell straightaway. You would still be without a husband. And our child would not know his father.

Do not pity me. I am perfectly at ease here, Imani. Better than I ever was in the land where I was born. My mother wept when I left for the war. She wept as if I were leaving a place of peace. It was a mistake. I found greater tranquility in the battles in Africa than I ever found in my homeland.

Forgive the brevity of these lines. But this is the most blatant of truths: War strips men. The proximity of death reveals the human soul, shorn of its vestments, without restoration or disguise. And believe me, Imani, a man's soul is not something you want to see. That is why the best thing for me to do at the moment is to keep my distance. The love we

194

had, and we had it in its entirety, will survive. There is no word to describe what love was. And there is no silence that can make us forget what love bequeathed us.

You do not know how hard it is to write these last words.

*As ever yours,*
*Germano de Melo*
*Lourenço Marques, March 21, 1896*

P.S. We may not speak again. I must have the courage to tell you everything. We are dealing with governments and powerful armies that kill, imprison, and divide people. However, there is something more powerful than any government or army, and that is the malevolent mindset that surrounds us. Against the violence of this insidious encirclement, there is little we can do. There is no island nor exile that can save us from this kingdom of stupidity.

I was sincere in all that I wrote before. It is true that I do not view with any pleasure the prospect of our being a couple leading a life of mediocre routine. It is true that I have no enthusiasm for children. But our relationship was not destroyed for any of the reasons that I invoked before. It was destroyed long before we met, long before we were born. The same narrative that paved the way for our encounter made our love impossible. We shall be nearer each other by being separated than we would have been by remaining together. You would be blamed for being black. I would be hated for being the husband of a black woman. At first, we would resist. But in the end, we would surrender in the face of the invisible army of prejudice. The only way we can win is to refuse to go into battle. Our love will live like these letters: Only your eyes will awaken the words we put to bed.

# 25

## THAT WHICH WAS GIVEN BIRTH

*He who only lives by half, gains a twofold fear of life.*
—PROVERB FROM NKOKOLANI

In my homeland, when a woman conceives, the whole family gets pregnant. During gestation, a woman's body once again ceases to be hers: It is quite simply lent out. It is handed over to her husband, her parents-in-law, the family of the father of her child. Later, not even her birth pains belong to her. For this is how tradition goes: It isn't the woman who gives birth. It is the ancestors who breathe a new life into those who are born. A woman exists like moonlight, the mere reflection of other suns.

On the night of May 25, I wake up in pain, my legs are wet, the sheets soaked. I cry out for Dabondi. Dabondi cries out for Muzamussi. And Muzamussi doesn't cry out for anyone, for she is the big woman, the *nkosikaʐi*. And she is also the most experienced midwife. All the other women abandon the room in silence. I kneel before the eldest of the queens, my arms around her neck. Muzamassi is also kneeling, holding me by my waist. Her hands slip down: I have just been daubed with oils which will help the baby emerge from me.

The birth pains are daggers stabbing me in the back. They come and go like the tides. Suddenly, I forget I am fifteen years old, that I have still not relinquished my own filial status. My body is that of an older woman and obeys the directives of another life force. Even my voice sounds strange to me as I ask:

*Am I doing all right, Muẓamussi?*

*You're not the one who has to do all right. It's the one trying to get out,* declares the queen.

She too is canceling me out. I myself begin to flag the longer the birth goes on. Tiredness and pain join each other and I no longer possess the strength in my back and my arms to remain on my knees. I am sustained by Muzamussi, who is sweating more profusely than I am. *My son,* I say in order to muster up courage, *reminds me of my grandfather Sangatela: stubborn even before his birth.* Muzamussi doesn't find this funny. For her, the delay is proof of my infidelity. I must declare the name of the man with whom I was unfaithful. *Say who it was,* the queen insists. *Germano,* I mutter almost inaudibly. *Not that one, say the other man's name!* The midwife repeats stubbornly. By now, the pains and my exhaustion are such that I decide to invent a betrayal. But at that very moment, my baby decides to come out. And it is as if I have been born again. My eyes are so full of tears that I see Germano holding my hands.

I do not feel them cutting the umbilical cord. I am not aware of them separating us, there is no blow preventing us from being one sole creature. And they carry the baby boy and place him by my face, he flies above me with his tan skin, and his little hands clutching the air. His generous light curls are those of the angels I saw painted on the walls of the church. I hear his vigorous protest. I cry along with him. Muzamussi asks me not to do that. I am calling the bad spirits.

I close my eyes and summon Germano. I do not know how to live alone now. The bulky shape of the midwife bustles around me. The placenta and the blood are carefully disposed of. *So that no one can do you any harm,* Muzamussi explains.

*Why are you helping me? Why are you protecting me?* I ask.

The queen does not respond. She asks me to take my clothes off. She is going to take my clothes away with her, and tear them up into tiny shreds. As she closes the door, her instructions are clear: Over the coming days, no man can enter my room. I smile: What man would want to? If even Germano waits for me far away, in another country, in another time.

Hours later, Dabondi visits me. *I'm pregnant*, she says. *I can pick up your child, don't be afraid.* A menstruating woman—those whom we say are jumping the moon—is forbidden to touch a newly born baby. But that isn't the case with her.

The queen dances around with the baby in her arms. *What name are you going to give him?* she asks. *His name is Sanga*, I reply. It was my grandfather Sangatela who chose the name. The queen shrugs her shoulders. The decision should be the father's. Let Germano complain later.

I ask Dabondi to explain. She had warned me that I would become empty after the birth. This was the term she had used: empty. She had said the gods would extinguish my inner being.

*What is this emptiness? I've never felt so full*, I say.

*We'll talk about this some other time.*

*Tell me now, Dabondi. What was that curse?*

*Now that your son has been born*, she replies, *you will no longer know how to speak the white people's language.*

I smile, incredulous. That's impossible. That language is part of my body.

*Do you doubt it?* the queen asks. *Well then, try speaking Portuguese.*

I smile, shaking my head. Then I try to pronounce some words. And what I hear is different from what I say. I repeat it, and the mismatch occurs again: I think in Portuguese but the words are spoken in Txitxope. So the curse is real after all: From today onward, I will no longer know Portuguese. The queen was right. My roots are devouring me. I beseech, I implore. She must return the voice of my soul to me. *That was where you were always wrong*, the queen alleges.

*Your soul has other voices*, she declares. *From now on, you will no longer serve the Portuguese.*

She isn't punishing me, she says, putting the child back in my arms. On the contrary, she is merely giving me back a part of my being.

The next day, Germano's mother comes to visit me. She peers at the improvised crib and remarks, with relief: *He's light skinned!* I raise myself with difficulty, my hands barely able to support my belly. Delighted, I ask: *Isn't he beautiful, Dona Laura?*

*No intimacy, please, my girl! I may be a grandmother. But I'm not your mother-in-law.*

One of these days, she announces, she will come and fetch the boy. There's no ill intention, but rather a promise she made to Germano. She wouldn't proceed in this way, if I had the means to look after the child.

I hold my Sanga in my arms and swear to myself: To tear him away from me, they'll have to rip my body apart first. I weep, defenseless. I ask the visitor to leave, but as foreseen, the words disobey me: *Famba khaya, Dona Laura!* These are the words Laura hears. But the message produces the opposite effect. The Portuguese woman sits on my bed.

*I am entirely alone.* She sighs. *If only someone would come and look after me.*

She contemplates the baby, without going so far as to touch him. Her husband had never known how to be a father. And Germano, according to her, was following in the same footsteps.

Sensing he might die, her man confessed to her for the first time that he loved her. At that point, she burst into tears. *Why are you crying?* he asked. *I don't want to be loved*, she answered, sobbing. Far from a gift, that confession of love set her thinking about all the things life hadn't given her.

Years later, when her husband finally died, Laura started sleeping on top of his grave. It wasn't that she missed him. It was out of fear that the dead man might come back. Her body was a stone, a gravestone ensuring her old companion stayed where he was. The priest would come and fetch her in the early morning. He would forcibly drag her through the village while she screamed for her husband. But she got his name wrong: It was Germano she was calling for in her lamentations. She wasn't committed to a mental institution because, as she claimed, the whole village already was an asylum. She would pass through the cemetery and see the dried flowers on his grave. That little display of decadence did not trouble her. The detachment within her was proof that she was free from the need to mourn. She had already been widowed before her husband died.

A week later, Dona Laura returns to the fort. She has come to fetch the little boy. I do not let her come near me. Holding the child in my arms, I run off across the yard. The guards chase me. I remember all the mothers who, down the centuries, had to run in order to save their children. The strength and despair of those women now inhabit my body. And I fly over the courtyard until I am hemmed in between the troughs for washing clothes. Dona Laura shouts for me to be careful, for the ground is wet, and she doesn't want me falling over and hurting her grandson.

Suddenly, the ten queens emerge from the back of the laundry. They are all brandishing knives. They form a protective cordon around me. Then they threaten the soldiers. *This little boy is the son of all of us*, Muzamussi proclaims. The same knives that were given to them to civilize them now glimmer in their gesture of rebellion. They were cutlery, and are now weapons. Every time they did the washing up, an item disappeared. If they had been allowed to eat with their hands, the soldiers would not now have to confront them.

From the window of his room, the drunken king of Gaza watches and smiles. In times gone by, he had been struck by the idea of an African army composed solely of women. It wasn't a dream. It was a nightmare. Now there they were, women confronting white soldiers. It isn't the little knives that the soldiers fear most. What scares them is the mere fact of the confrontation. They learned how to face up to an army. But they have no idea how to overcome a group of ten women.

The battle, however, was decided before it even began. The women are dominated and my child is torn from my arms. Dona Laura wraps him in a blanket and makes off hurriedly. My baby's cry fades away in the distance. Until all I hear is the water trickling into the trough. From now on, that is how it will always be: The murmur of water will be my tiny son's only voice.

# 26

## BETWEEN EXILES AND DEPORTATIONS

*The great king is not the one who leads his people to war, but the one
who keeps war far away from his people.*

—ZIXAXA

In late afternoon on June 22, the soldiers burst into the prisoners'
cell. Shouting, they call for Ngungunyane, Zixaxa, Mulungo, and
Godido. They tell them to pack their bags. *Bags?* asks Godido, who
is the only one who understands what they are saying. They hastily
wrap their paltry possessions in a bundle. And they are not even
given time for that.

Ngungunyane sits on the floor in tears. Given the hurry and the
harshness with which they are pushed, he is now sure they are going to be shot. Their wives wail loudly in protest, while the soldiers
use force to separate them from the four prisoners. I look on with
indifference. They have taken my son away from me, anything else
has ceased to be important.

They tell me to accompany the prisoners as they don't trust Godido's translation. We travel in two carriages through the empty
city. The operation is carried out in secret. At the quay, the steamship *Zambeze* is waiting. Only then do they tell me: They are going
to transport the exiles to the Azores. On the quay, there is a short
wait. Ngungunyane calms down, for he realizes they are not going
to harm him. However, he looks as if he has gone to pieces: He is

barefoot, his shirttail is hanging out, his trousers torn, his hair disheveled.

*They're all dishonest, the whites,* the king of Gaza declares. *Would we ever do to them what they have done to us: capture us, bring us to another land and show us off like animals?*

*Did we never take any prisoners?* Zixaxa retorts.

*Why do you always take the side of the whites?*

*We are no better than them. That's all I'm saying.*

*You, Zixaxa, talk freely, because it's not you they want dead.*

*The problem, my Nkosi, isn't that. The problem is that they don't know what to do with you.*

Ngungunyane turns his back, saying he doesn't understand the language of the Tsongas. *That's the language we've always used to speak to each other,* Zixaxa maintains. Then he continues, challenging the king by following directly behind him: *It's not what I say that you don't understand, my king. You don't understand me because of what I am. Thank the Portuguese for having spared you,* Zixaxa shouts before they push him onto the ship. *Thank them, Ngungunyane, isn't that what you have always done?*

I watch the ship with its prisoners floating away into the mist. On my way back to the fort, I think to myself: Exile isn't enough to remove those rebels from Mozambique. It is crucial for there to be no land wherever they are deported.

The following day, I receive a visit from Captain António Sérgio de Sousa. He is surprised not to find the king there. The decision to take the prisoners to the Azores was so secret that the visitor was never made aware. He offers me a bouquet of flowers. He knows I have given birth, and wants to see the child.

*Where is this child of yours?* he asks.

I want to explain that they have taken my son away, but my tears deprive me of my voice. Concerned, the captain thinks the child has died. He doesn't understand what I am saying. He cannot fathom why I'm not speaking to him in Portuguese. I pretend I have a sore throat. I ask him for a pen and paper. I write brief messages which I give him to read. *They have taken my son away. Help me!*

*I'll see what I can do,* he answers.

I drop the pen and ink spreads over my legs. I speak, weep, gesticulate. *He's so tiny,* I blurt. *He almost fits in the palm of my hand.* And I hold up my hand as if I were still holding him.

*Men don't know, Captain, but it's when we hold a baby for the first time that our hands are born.*

I lean my head on the visitor's shoulder and stay like that, sobbing, while I pick off a rosary of sad, untranslatable laments, all uttered in Txitxope. The Portuguese pretends to understand me, perturbed by my unintelligible display of emotion. I've never met such a gentle person. *My name was once Ash,* I recall. *I was given that name to protect me. When we are ash, nothing hurts us. How I wish I had my mother's illness, for she never felt pain in her life! How I yearn for that curse!*

The captain clearly has no idea how to handle my sadness. He makes a clumsy attempt to console me. *Do you know how to read and write?* he asks. *You're lucky, my dear girl. My neighbors, who consider themselves cultured and well-off, prohibited their daughters from attending school in case they started writing love letters to the boys.*

António Sérgio de Sousa leads me onto the terrace, from where we can see the ocean on one side, and the city on the other. His hands on my shoulders take me back to more distant feelings of reassurance.

*There's a reason why I came here*, António de Sousa starts by saying.

I arch an eyebrow inquisitively. The captain rubs his elbows as if he suddenly feels cold. He woke up this morning and couldn't get up. For a moment, he thought his joints might have seized up during the night and his bones turned to iron. He woke up and said to himself: Today is the day when they will sell me for scrap along with my old ship. He sat on the bed and came to the conclusion that there were matters he didn't want to take with him to the grave.

*I brought you flowers, Imani*, he says. *But a flower isn't worth anything if it doesn't have a story.*

I wait for this story. But the captain remains silent, struggling with his ghosts. I allow some time to pass and then I ask about Álvaro Andrea. *Do you think he can help me?* I ask, scribbling down my question. *He needs people to help him*, Sousa replies. A newspaper published part of his report condemning Mouzinho. And now the man can't leave the barracks. Under the pretext of the need for a string of inquiries, he remains incommunicado. Most of those who criticized Andrea's report did not do so because he was condemning the national hero. What most irked them was the way Andrea treated the blacks as human beings, completely worthy of respect. The captain once again places his long arms on my shoulders and speaks:

*Now I'm going to get to the matter that brought me here. This is the doubt that has prevented me from sleeping: During the voyage, did Sergeant Araújo harm you?*

I do not answer. Even if I wanted, I wouldn't be able to. The captain heaves a deep sigh and says: *I always suspected it.* Then he adds: *It's my fault, because I was never able to command respect.* If he was a bird, he declares, ashamed, he would be a parrot. Never an eagle. He lacks a love of heights, he derives no pleasure from giving orders. That was why he always needed another soul to complement him. That soul was Sergeant Araújo.

This was his way of asking me for forgiveness. *A parrot, that's what I am*, he repeats as he withdraws. He is now at peace with himself, the old captain of the *África*. It wasn't he who visited me. I was the one who placated his ghosts. His generosity was what allowed me to do him some good.

# 27

## THE DRINKER OF HORIZONS

*I don't see with my eyes. I see with my dreams.*
—DABONDI

My dear Imani,

This letter must come as a surprise. It is I, Nwamatibjane Zixaxa, writing to you from the Azores. As you can see, it was a good thing I learned Portuguese. On the voyage, I learned to speak. Now here on the island, they are teaching me to write. For this first letter, I am still helped by a soldier who has become a companion of mine. I call him Munganu. And he laughs, not knowing that his name means "friend" in my language. I spend more time in his company than I do with any of those who came from Mozambique. The whites are mystified by my choice. I'm supposed to remain among "my people." As far as they are concerned, we are all blacks, without any distinction. They do not realize that I am an Mfumo. And that the other three prisoners are VaNguni, from Zulu royalty. They do not understand why I trust this white soldier far more than any of my fellow cellmates. The next letter, I have already arranged with Munganu, will be written by me alone.

We traveled to the Azores on a ship called the *Zambeze*. And that, after the ship that brought us from Mozambique was called the *África*. Ngungunyane is convinced these names were given the ships in his honor. The Lion of Gaza is certainly sick. The drunkenness of old is no longer enough for him. He now seeks his final refuge in madness. During the entire voyage, he slept hugging a bottle of wine. Early in the morning, he would hurl the empty bottles at the great seabirds flying over the ship.

On the island of Terceira, we were given a special welcome: There were no insults or threats as in Lisbon. They told us we were guests and not prisoners. They gave us a house within the grounds of the fort. We are allowed to circulate within the precinct of the fortress. On the whitewashed wall of one of the buildings, a sentence has been etched which can only cause laughter among us: It says: "Rather die free than in peaceful subjugation." Those words remind me of Pastor Machava's words upon disembarking in Cape Verde. António Sérgio de Sousa bade him farewell with a visibly guilty look. Justifying himself, he said: *There are things we would never do were it not for the war.* And the missionary replied: *No one wants peace more than my religious brethren, who have been imprisoned here. What is happening is that for us, living has now turned into a war.* Captain Sousa defended himself, arguing that the purpose behind everything he did was to bring the war to an end. Roberto Machava's last words were uttered in his own language. *So you want peace, boss? Well, we too want peace, and much more than that. We want another life.*

I heard it said that Machava was sent back to Mozambique. The English put so much pressure on the Portuguese authorities that they backed down and allowed him to return. But his fellow believers, his followers, remained in Cape Verde. They even hoped Machava would come back and fetch them. Or that God would ensure justice was done. They were sent to work in the salt pans. Most of them died, according to what I heard. The moment it was put in sacks, the salt turned as hard as stone. The problem was with the quality of the salt. But the bosses blamed the slaves from Mozambique. So they punished them, forcing them to sleep tied to the sacks. The men started to wither, losing body and substance. On the day they wept, they dissolved. It may be a lie. But that's what they say. Those who are absent are useful precisely for this reason: so that they can be turned into stories. These stories return to Mozambique. And like that, the absentees find their way back home.

I imagine you want to know how I spend my time here, surrounded by the ocean. Well, let me tell you: If this island is a prison, then I share this punishment with thousands of Azoreans. I am anything but a prisoner here. Behind the fortress, there is some woodland where we hunt rabbits. The trees here are different. We do not know what souls inhabit them. Ngungunyane does not take his shoes off to enter the forest. He walks among the trees that are unknown to him, without asking their permission. The insane are free from fear of the gods. To kill the rabbits, Ngungunyane uses a stick he brought from Mozambique. He throws this stick and never misses. Ngungunyane says the wood was ministered to by Dabondi. One day, he says, he will throw this stick into the sea. He will then benefit from the respect due to the hunters of the sea.

At night, the king wanders around the courtyard and we hear him crying out for the only woman he ever loved: *Vuiaƶe!* Godido goes out to fetch his father. He puts an arm around him and gives him a bottle of sweet wine. The king keeps the corks. He has hundreds of these corks, which he has been collecting in order to build a boat. On this boat, he says, he will one day return to Mozambique.

I confess, Imani, I feel sorry for Ngungunyane. The poor wretch has already been punished. He was castigated in the only possible manner: He is his own executioner. Now he does not even need to drink: The horizon fills his eyes, solitude floods his soul.

As for me, it no longer pains me to be surrounded by the ocean. In fact, it is not the first time I have been to an island. When I was twenty, the Portuguese sent me to Mozambique Island by way of punishment. Later on, they gave me a pardon. And they let me return to Lourenço Marques. That was a mistake. If they should hate anyone, it is me. It was I, and I alone, who attacked Lourenço Marques. I was almost victorious, I almost pushed the Portuguese back into the waters of the bay.

The understandings and misunderstandings of this world are curious. Yesterday, the soldier who is writing this letter brought with him a group of his white colleagues. They sat in a circle around me and, with great interest, asked me what my homeland was like. They want to escape from the island because they can't bear the poverty in which they live. Many of their age have left for Brazil. But these whites think Africa might prove to be a better destination, now that the war is over. They wanted to know what life is like in our homeland. This is the answer I gave them: *If you allow me, I'll take you to Moçambique, and if you don't change your race on the way, you will all end up rich.* And they fell about laughing. We all laughed. Laughing is like a warm hug.

So that, my dear girl, is how things are. Ngungunyane weaves baskets. I weave little episodes of joy. Being happy is my best way of reaping vengeance on Ngungunyane. The king of Gaza surrendered me to the Portuguese? Well, that's what I am now: a Portuguese, a dark-skinned Portuguese. A happy Portuguese who looks at the person who betrayed him and sees an unhappy drunkard. At the weekends, they take me to the whorehouses. I sleep with the women, and forget my wives who are so far away. Godido and I enjoy these nocturnal excursions. Mulungo is old, and never goes with us. Ngungunyane goes occasionally, when he is sober. But he leaves after one drink. After that, he is overcome by his fear of women. He goes home in the knowledge that, even worse than being dethroned, he has been demoted from his manhood. Our Ngungunyane hates the sea, women, and swallows for the same reason. He fears what he cannot govern.

I do not want to end this letter without mentioning that which I know torments you. The three prisoners who were shot during the voyage. Well, I want to tell you: Don't torture yourself, Imani. You are not to blame. It was I who disclosed Machava's plans on the boat. It was I who stopped my archrival from being assassinated. I did it out of fear of the reaction that the death of the Lion of Gaza would provoke. The Portuguese would have taken it out on me. I would also have been executed and thrown into the sea.

I shall take my leave of you by asking this friend of mine to lend me the pen he used to write this letter. For I now want to write, with my own hand, the following: *Ita vunana musuko, nkata Imane!* We shall see each other tomorrow, dearest Imani.

*Nwamatibjane Zixaxa*
*Terceira Island, July 1, 1896*

# 28

## THE FINAL LANGUAGE

*The Portuguese tore me away from my native soil. Now I have nowhere
to be buried. Those who pray for me will have to gaze at the sea.*
**—NGUNGUNYANE**

I get dressed when I should be dying. I put my shoes on and there's
no longer any ground. They push me along the fort's hallways, my
bundle of clothes brushing the path behind me. The soldiers yell,
tell us to hurry. They call us ugly names, which offend the queens
more because they don't understand them. Ever since Dabondi cast
her spell on me, I have not spoken Portuguese again. It is a pity that
her curse did not also stop me from understanding that other language which, though belonging to the others, is also part of my
flesh.

They are going to take us to a very remote island. It is an exile
within exile. The queens are resigned, no place has any hold over
them. That isn't the case with me. I have my son in this city. I beg
the commander of the fort to let me say goodbye to my boy. No one
heeds me. I was once the translator for a king. I was a spy in the
service of the Portuguese Crown. Now I am just the eleventh black
woman. Not long ago, I gave birth to my little Sanga, whom I shall
never see again. I shall never again find the father of that child, my
Germano, love of my life. I climb onto the cart, a total mess. Dabondi tidies my hair and buttons up my dress. My fingers seem to

have lost their use, my whole body was geared to showing love to my son who has been stolen from me.

We travel in silence to the quay. Four months ago, we arrived in a cold city, packed with people. Now we leave a Lisbon that is hot and deserted. Halfway to our destination, I go mad. I burst out shouting: *Dona Laura! Give me back my son, Dona Laura!* The queens weep, they put their arms around me, hide my head in their vast bosoms. The horses batter the silence, their hooves are stone scraping on stone.

The ship we shall be sailing on is now in sight. It is called the *São Tomé*, the name of the land we are being banished to. The queens step barefoot across the flagstones of the quay. They walk with their eyes closed; two of them have covered their faces with their shawls. It is four months since they threw us into a dark well, and two weeks since they deprived us of the company of the menfolk. They fear our sadness will turn into rage. Rage grows roots. That is why they are taking us on a long sea journey.

I still have one last ounce of strength. And I protest, even without any hope of success: If they are taking us away by boat, why don't they leave us in the Azores to be with our menfolk? But I forget that I can only speak my native tongue now. The soldiers laugh at my firm but impenetrable protests. At the same time, I know we cannot share the men's destination. António Sérgio de Sousa had already explained the situation to me: The Azores are a place where the power of religion is strong. They welcome suffering Africans with Christian piety. But they would not agree to harbor the sin of polygamy in their midst. Zixaxa's letters do not confirm such purity of customs. They even speak of whorehouses where the prisoners are taken at the weekends. Morality has its prohibitions as well as its concessions as far as women are concerned. Whores, yes. Lovers, perhaps. Polygamous wives, never.

So we are not going to the Azores. But nor do they send us back to Mozambique. And the reason is easy to understand: The arrival of the queens might kindle hostility toward Portugal. And there is even talk of a woman—Queen Zambili—who is leading a revolt at the gates of Lourenço Marques.

Twelve days of seasickness pass before we arrive in São Tomé. Dabondi, who is pregnant, is the one who suffers most. Her belly is now visible, her breasts are covered by a cloth that will remain there until the birth. In the end, the queen will be luckier than I was. On the island of São Tomé, there won't be a grandmother to steal her child from her. We shall be ten aunts helping to rear a child who, while being hers, will also belong to all of us.

I did not know there were so many Africas. A tiny island was all I needed to teach me the extent of African lands. São Tomé is a cross-roads for people, languages, and creeds from all over the continent. And that is why we are quiet and timid every time we pass another black person. We are of the same skin color, but not the same race. That is also why we hesitate before launching into friendly saluta-tions. And yet there is always the trace of a gesture, a contained smile, a hidden silence that we share at every encounter. As long as we stifle our instinct to hug one another, we hinder our kinship.

For the first week, we are accommodated in the buildings on a plantation, which they call a *roça* here. We sleep in a shed for storing coffee. Here we spend our time doing what we did before: abso-lutely nothing. Here, though, there are no prison bars or soldiers. A single guard—unarmed and in civilian clothing—keeps watch at the entrance. When it rains—and it rains constantly—we invite this watchman to shelter under our roof.

I do not know what would become of me without the company of the queens. The presence of these women is one more proof of

Dabondi's prophecy: The roots of my soul are now returning my whole being to me. It is not just a question of returning to the language of my native village. These women bring back my homeland and my folk. And they return me to myself.

The days of such familial conviviality were always numbered, though. On the second week, we are separated. Muzamussi, the matriarch, is sent away to a shipyard in the south of the island. She is the largest of the women, and is forced to heave rocks for building. Eight of the remaining wives are sent to work in the hospital. There they will be employed as cleaners. They will be lodged in an annex to the hospital. Dabondi and I are the only women who remain in the coffee warehouse. The reason for this is not exactly the best: They think we are the most attractive, and we are put to work in the army's brothel. They do not realize that Dabondi is pregnant. And she prefers not to say anything. She is scared that if she is considered to be of no use, she will be abandoned to the creatures of the wild. And so Bianca Vanzini's prediction comes true: I am finally a woman of easy virtue, selling myself at night like a piece of meat.

Every night, the queen and I walk along a sandy path lined with coconut trees. This shortcut leads us to the bar where the soldiers are waiting for us. In the early morning, we return exhausted and inebriated to the plantation warehouse. We fall asleep to the sound of carts and the workers loading sacks onto them. They are young, bare-backed black men, moving busily here and there. They carry the sacks like we women do: on their heads. Their bodies release a sweet smell, the same smell that emanates from the coffee beans. This smell dulls our senses. It must be strange to experience something that is as addictive as a drink: The load itself prevents them from feeling tired.

One morning, the queen wakes me up. She has blood running down her face because she was beaten up by a punter she refused to service. *Come with me*, she says. *We are going to see the administrator.*

Dabondi knows things I don't: The administrator is called Almada Negreiros, and his wife is a mulatto woman, native to the island, who is gravely ill. I get up with painfully summoned obedience: *So what are we going to do?* She doesn't wait to answer, instead hurrying me out of the building. As we walk quickly and breathlessly along, Dabondi explains. She is going to ask for work in the Negreiros household. *I'll take care of the children*, she says.

We climb slopes, cross streams and waterfalls, and walk through extensive plantations. The coffee bushes are in bloom, their lacy white flowers brushing against our arms. *I don't like this landscape*, she complains. *I've never seen such well-tended bush.* The queen keeps touching her stomach the whole way. Thin streaks of blood dribble down her legs. And she curses: *If that man hurt my baby, I'll kill him!*

The house of Negreiros, the administrator, is built on stilts, and is surrounded by caves from where rainwater drips. *You'll meet Dona Elvira, this white man's wife, and I bet you've never seen such large eyes*, Dabondi warns.

*She's heavily pregnant*, the queen adds, *she must be about to give birth, but if it doesn't happen soon, her eyes will jump out of their sockets.* She asks me to be her translator. At first, I resist: *You deprived me of my Portuguese, and now that you really need it, I'm afraid I've forgotten it.* Dabondi insists laconically: *You will speak!*

After a long wait, we surprise the administrator and his wife leaving for the hospital. Dabondi introduces herself. She tells them she is originally from the royal court of Gaza. The functionary looks at us suspiciously. *So you're queens, then?* he asks sarcastically. And he hurries his wife, who is holding a little boy by the hand: *Shall we go, Elvira? We haven't got time for this.*

Dabondi places herself firmly between the couple. And she defiantly confronts the Portuguese: *I know you, sir. Do you want me to say how we met?* Without my having to translate, António Almada Negreiros seems to understand. He leans silently against a wall.

The queen approaches Dona Elvira, places her hands on her belly and exclaims:

*Please, my lady. Look at me, I'm pregnant too. How can I be forced to go to bed with soldiers?*

Dona Elvira fixes her gaze on the black woman who dares block her way. She doesn't seem upset. On the contrary, she seems fascinated. She touches the bracelets on the queen's arm.

*Are you from Angola?* she asks. *I recognize your features, you're from Benguela . . .*

The queen doesn't understand, but she answers in the affirmative. The administrator reacts nervously. He is in a hurry and feels in an even greater hurry for having been troubled by these two strangers.

*Please, my lady, speak to your husband!* Dabondi insists.

All of a sudden, the queen jettisons her plaintive tone. She is barefoot, but she speaks from the throne of her dignity. *You, lady, have black blood in you, and must help me,* she declares. The administrator's family stands rooted, listening to the words that I translate in such an animated fashion. *My friend here,* Dabondi says, pointing at me, *had her baby taken away from her. And as for me . . .* She pauses for a minute before swallowing and resuming her speech . . . *As for me, they have harmed my baby.*

*So where is this child?* the administrator's wife asks.

*Here, inside me.*

The administrator tugs at his reluctant wife's arm. *Leave me!* She reacts firmly. Her husband persists, now with greater discretion: *Let's go, Elvira. They can come back again later.*

There was no later. The next day, Dabondi lost her baby in the hospital. In another room at the same health clinic, the wife of the administrator Negreiros died in childbirth. The moment she heard the news, Dabondi left her room and, with a determined step, crossed the lines that separated the races in that hospital. A nurse followed her the whole way, warning her of the consequences of her act of insubordination. In the dead Elvira's room, the queen burst through the crowd of concerned visitors, walked over to the crib and picked up the newly born infant. She nursed the baby and took it over to show to the little brother. The little boy stared at her with the huge eyes he had inherited from Elvira. Dabondi spoke in Zulu: *Your brother was born while my baby died. Two shadows touched each other, and you will find your mother in my arms . . .*

There was no point in translating her. I would never have had time: The other queens had met at the hospital in the meantime. And they took Dabondi back home.

*You will write to tell Ngungunyane*, Muzamussi ordered while we walked along. *When a child dies in the womb, we say it has "decided to return." And the mother is beset by deep pangs of guilt. We should tell Ngungunyane that wasn't the case here. The child was killed.* It was vitally important to inform the father, even with the knowledge that the news would take a long time to reach the Azores.

*It's Godido who must be told*, Dabondi responded, adding: *He's the only one who needs to know.*

I am on my knees in the place where Dabondi is resting. The porters bearing sacks of coffee leave their load outside the warehouse out of respect. Her eyes are fixed on the ceiling, and I pray in Zulu, the only language our gods understand. I recite an improvised prayer and Dabondi listens without interrupting me:

*The lady, my queen, wiped away the language I learned at school, and tore up one of my oldest roots. But she didn't wipe away my ability to read and write Portuguese. Well, I am now begging you to take these gifts away from me too. I don't want any more paper, I don't want any more ink, I don't want a pen anymore. Writing hurts me, and I want to clear my soul of its tattoos. The lady may not know this, but words, when written down, focus time. If I cannot see my son again, I don't want to have anything to do with time, I don't want any memory. This is why I beseech you: Tear up all the sheets of paper before they are written on and turn every drop of ink into water. I want to be empty. And when there is no more language inside me, I beg you to expunge the language of dreams from me. For all I need is the night of the creatures of the wild: a time to be born and to die, that's all.*

Then I fall silent again. Her eyes closed, Queen Dabondi raises her arm and feels for my face. Her fingers touch my eyes, slowly run down my cheeks, and then cross my mouth like two blades. She is exhausted, and doesn't want to listen to me anymore. But then I speak again:

*We are never going back home, Dabondi.*

*It is for the best, my girl, it's better that we die here,* the queen affirms. *We lost our children, we shall leave no seed in this world. We are no one. We have nowhere to go back to, Imani.*

# 29

## A NEW NAME FOR ZIXAXA

*Who suffers more? The person who is always waiting, or the person who
never waited for anyone?*
**—DABONDI**

Dearest Imani,

I am beginning this letter at the end. And I shall now sign it with
my most recent name: Roberto Frederico Zixaxa. As you can see, I
have been baptized. At my age and given my race, this is what it
means: They have washed my soul. And I can say that I was washed
with the waters of nobility. As they explained to me, Frederico is
the name given to people of distinction. In this way, the whites
wanted to show that they respect us as the kings of the lands from
which we came. The baptism was carried out in the largest church in
the city. They brought important people, *indunas* from Terceira and
the other islands. They went away satisfied in the belief that they had
changed our nature. But I imagine that, deep down, they know:
Names are emblems tattooed on the soul. No death will erase them.

This much I can confess to you: I wear this new name as if it
were a pair of shoes. They are useful for my feet, but they are not
part of my body. When we are born, our ancestors choose the name
we shall have. The bosses of the world decide the name we shall no
longer have. All this may be true in the case of Ngungunyane. But

in my case, I preserve my past in the name I have left. Any children or grandchildren I have on this island will not deny this African name: Zixaxa. I am happy with this little eternity of mine.

It wasn't just me whose name they changed. All four of us were baptized in the same ceremony. Ngungunyane is now called Reinaldo Frederico Gungunhana. In the register, they invented his age. They wrote that he was sixty years old. The poor man hasn't even reached fifty. One of these days, even though he may protest fiercely, they will declare him dead.

Last week, the Nkosi of Portugal, King D. Carlos, visited the Azores. To avoid such an illustrious visitor having to meet Ngungunyane, they told us we were going on a trip into the countryside. They say D. Carlos made a point of asking to come and greet us. They dissuaded him. Ngungunyane wasn't even worth the memory of what he once was.

That is why we were taken far away, to admire the Lagoa do Preto, or Black Man's Lake. The waters were created by the tears of a slave. The African fell in love with a great lady. Her husband discovered the affair and ordered him to be killed. The unfortunate man managed to escape from the house but was chased by dogs and soldiers. He sought refuge in a marsh. And there, he wept. He wept so much that by the time he realized it, he was in the middle of a lake. It was its waters that halted the dogs in their tracks. Surrounded by soldiers, the slave drowned in the lake.

Sitting on the shore of this patch of water, the king of Gaza was moved when he heard this legend. But then he immediately suggested that a man who wept so much over a woman could not have been of his ethnicity. *In our race*, he declared in a loud voice, *it's the women who cry out of love*. To which I asked: *What about Vuiaze?*

I was mischievous, I admit. I shouldn't have dredged up such a sad memory. For when the king heard his beloved's name, he staggered off aimlessly, barefoot like a ghost. The marsh is surrounded by great rocks, which they call "black mysteries." Our watchful guards followed the prisoner until he tripped over some bones. They weren't the remains of an animal. It was a partially buried human skeleton. Ngungunyane bent down and picked up a long piece of bone. Then he saw a name written on it. And he cursed the day he had learned to read. For he saw written on it his own name: "Reinaldo Frederico Gungunhana." He scratched it with his nails, trying to erase the letters. He scratched it frenetically until he felt blood running over his wrists. *I cut myself*, he thought. But his fingers were intact. And yet he saw blood dripping profusely onto the ground. Then he realized it was the bone that was bleeding. Ever weaker, he stood watching the ground grow red. And he dropped the bone that bore his name.

This episode left Ngungunyane upset. He returned to the fortress in silence. Then at a certain point, he held my arm and said: *They will come and fetch me, Zixaxa. My grandchildren will come and fetch me.*

It may be true, I admit, they may come and fetch him. As for me, they have already come to fetch me. And they didn't come from far. Whoever came, started right here. I have a sweetheart. Yes, it's true, a white fiancée, completely white. Her name is Maria Augusta, and she is the daughter of João de Sousa, an Azorean from Ribeirinha. Her mother, my future mother-in-law, is called Francisca Vila d'Amigo and was born in Spain. The world is small and vast, Imani. Here I am, an African on a Portuguese island, ready to marry an Azorean with Spanish ancestry.

I won't be able to pay a *lobolo*, a bride price for my intended. This island is like the land of the Zulus: An ox is worth more than a stranger like me. What can I offer her by way of a *lobolo*? For my consolation, I managed to secure invitations to a circus spectacle in honor of the African prisoners. In other words, in our honor. The family of my intended—the in-laws as we call them here—were very impressed by my importance. They were still more impressed when they discovered I have been promoted to the role of forest ranger. I have a job, I make my money, and I earn respect. Do you know what they gave me to look after? I guard an entire hillside, I guard a hill called Mount Brazil. From being the one supervised, I have become a supervisor. All this is happening, and Ngungunyane is a witness to it all from the great age to which he has been promoted. I confess, my dear girl: I am beginning to miss the hatred I once felt for Ngungunyane.

Early one morning, the king of Gaza woke up yelling: *Don't take him away, don't take him away!* As always, it was his son Godido who came to his aid. Only he is authorized to attend to the emperor in his delirium. Nowadays, Ngungunyane is increasingly unable to distinguish whether he is in the middle of a dream or a drunken bout. This time, he confessed to having seen the *isibaya*, the great sacred bull of the Zulus. The creature crossed two oceans to come and be with him. It emerged from the waters, crossed the beach, ascended the rocky dune, and climbed past the storm drain grilles protecting the fortress walls. When it found itself outside our cell, the bull bent its knees and made as if to be tethered. But it didn't manage to lie down because all of a sudden, a group of whites emerged, shouting and waving cloths and ropes. They wanted to take the sacred bull away to be used in the festival of the running of the bulls. One day, I shall explain what these festivals are. I have never seen such a sad but festive people.

Once again, Ngungunyane needed help to come out of his dream, and once again, Godido led his father along the narrow lanes surrounding the fort. The authorities allowed the king to be distracted by this little walkabout. Mulungo and I followed behind, wandering along the tracks between the rock-strewn hills. To Ngungunyane's joy, the island is full of oxen. Wherever the king goes he touches their horns, examines their size and the thickness of their horns. All these oxen are, he assures us, his property. That morning, the king decided he should teach the whites to speak Zulu. Only his language is rich enough to describe the bovine world. Cattle is gold for the VaNguni. They do not possess castles like the ones we saw in Lisbon. But they have a nation of cattle, kraals, and drovers. And their gods are invoked through the blood of the animals.

As we returned to the fort, morning had already broken, and we felt the earth shaking. The Azoreans are half lava and half ocean. That is why they are not afraid of the tremors. Perhaps they are unaware of the true cause of earthquakes. The earth trembles when the *nwamulambu*, the dragon that dwells in the mountains, leaves its cave to spawn in the sea. On that occasion, the dragon was angry: The earthquake was strong and long lasting. The rocks rolled along the road like maddened animals. The oxen jumped out of their enclosures and stampeded across the fields. The soldiers came to get us—each one of us had fled in a different direction—and took us back to the fort.

At the gate, we passed the commander of the fort, General Almeida Pinheiro. We call him *xipongo xa mahetche*, because of the beard that reaches down as far as his chest like an old billy goat. The Portuguese believed we were in a panic and invited us to his office. He served us some tea and opened a newspaper to show us a photograph of the visit of D. Carlos and Dona Amélia. Ngungunyane inspected the photograph with particular care. Then he remarked: *The queen is pretty but she beautifies herself like a man. The feathers she wears on top of her head are a male thing. The Portuguese queen is imitating us, our VaNguni warriors.* And he concluded: *You, General, are the one who should be wearing those feathers, sir!*

At first, the general reacted with cool formality. After all, the subject of conversation was the queen of Portugal. But then he let out a loud guffaw of hearty laughter. He stroked his long beard and challenged his colleagues to imagine him covered in ostrich feathers.

The king of Gaza once again bent over the photograph. His stubby finger gradually larded the image as he elucidated: *Permit me, General, but your queen is a little bit on the skinny side. My wives are bloated. They're not*, he said, *like other women who only eat meat on feast days. Tell the king that it doesn't look good for him to exhibit a wife who is so skinny and so full of feathers.*

Once again, everyone laughed. But suddenly, Ngungunyane became serious, almost solemn, when he implored the general: *Please, sir: Don't have me sent back!*

Almeida Pinheiro contemplated the king, surprised, and did not know what to say: *Back where? To Moçambique?* he asked in confusion. *You people didn't kill me, but my brothers would*, Ngungunyane affirmed. And he withdrew. The general's eyes were sad as he watched the black king dissolve into the darkness.

I am coming to the end. Let me confess, my dear girl: The person writing this letter is my father-in-law, João de Sousa. Only the first two lines were written by me. All the rest, the handwriting and arrangement are his. My father-in-law wants to know who you are, or rather, what you are like. I described you as the most beautiful of women. After Maria Augusta, of course. My Azorean sweetheart is without compare. I explained to my father-in-law that you live on an island, like we do. And he, with a mysterious air that is so typical of him, declared: *Everyone lives on an island.*

When I asked if I could dictate this letter to him, my father-in-law agreed wholeheartedly, but it would have to be somewhere of his choosing. *The girl is African, isn't she?* he asked. And so he took me to Praia da Vitória. There, he scampered around among the high rocks until he chose a stone pillar and said: We'll do it here. We sat down side by side. And we wrote this long letter, leaning on this white stone which stands in contrast to the great wall of dark rock that forms the backdrop to the beach.

*This stone pillar has a history*, he said. The person who had brought it to Terceira had been his grandfather, an old long-distance mariner. On a voyage down the African coast, the captain had decided to anchor off a beach. The intention was to visit a stone pillar that the Portuguese discoverers had erected there centuries before. They asked the natives how to get to the Cape of the Cross. No one had heard of the name. They asked about the stone pillar with the cross and five shields carved into it. No one had seen a stone like that. The sailors gave the exact description to the natives. Then the blacks showed them a huge hole. The stone pillar had sunk into it, as if the beach had been hungry for a piece of stone. The sailors dug it up and once again positioned it upright on the sand. The next day, the pillar had become submerged in the African soil once more. The blacks told the Portuguese: *Take this stone away. It's yours, take it with you. This ground of ours can't stand the weight of that stone.*

And so that's it, my dear girl. The stone listened to our story, and we listen to its story. It brought together my father-in-law's grandfather, you, me, and time. Please, Imani, do not read this letter to my wives. I do not want them to know that I got married. In the correspondence I exchange with them, they tell me news. Most of it consists of lies. I don't care. Isn't that what letters are for?

# 30

## THE SHADOW OF WORDS

*One hot day, a young hunter saw a cloud hovering over his house. The young man was taking care of his old grandfather. That unexpected shadow caused such wonder that the grandfather was rejuvenated. Fearing that the wind might blow this piece of happiness away, the young man decided to throw a rope over the cloud and secure it by its neck. No sooner had he thought about it than he went ahead and did it. Like a domestic animal, the cloud remained tethered to a post. The next morning, as he was leaving the house, the young man stumbled on the sky and tumbled headlong into the firmament. The same rope that had caught the cloud now held him in the infinite. And his grandfather now rested in an endless shadow.*

**—TALES FROM NKOKOLANI**

There is a knock at the door. I open it slightly and see a white hand.

*Germano?* I ask, startled.

I open the door wide with unexpected enthusiasm. I am ninety-five years old, I no longer even have the strength to remember who I am. For a long time now, my body has been a plow opening furrows with my feet. But suddenly, a strange vigor is born within me. I shade my eyes to try to distinguish the silhouette outlined against the light. And it no longer looks like my man waiting on the threshold.

*Sanga? My son?*

I hug him. It's my son. I am almost blind, I hug the darkness and allow my hands, which are feeling my visitor's face, to give me my sight. His shape seems to recoil in surprise as I embrace him.

*My son!*

My breast empties with a sigh. I have forgotten how to weep. My son must have had his fits of forgetfulness too. For he doesn't respond to my hug.

*Dona Imani?* he calls me.

That's what I seem to hear. I'm in Nkokolani, my native village. I returned from São Tomé sixty-three years ago. As time went by, what happened with voices began to resemble what happens with the hours: They all seemed the same.

No one knocks at my door anymore. The few who do are not looking for me. They are looking for my grandnieces, who pretend to look after me. This visitor is different: He smells of the sea, and he has a different voice and accent. And he asks for me. He can't be my son. He would be older, more hunched by time.

*I know now, you're my grandson! Call me Grandmother. Do you understand Txitxope?*

*No, Dona . . .*

*It's just that I stopped talking Portuguese long ago. Now I only speak Txitxope.*

*But . . . you are speaking Portuguese.*

*I can't hear you. You'll have to speak up.*

*I said you're speaking Portuguese. Very good Portuguese.*

I stick out my hand to touch his hair. My grandson shies away. The skin, eyes, lips, they can all falsify people's race. Only the hair never lies. And I'm in a hurry to feel the truth of that body.

*Do you understand all that I say?*

The boy nods and says: *Perfectly!* I invite him in. He hesitates, shakes his shoes, full of good manners. How I miss that courteous swerve of a body! The boy is carrying a rucksack on his back and walks with a slight stoop, not because of the weight, but out of consideration: He wants to talk closer to my face.

In the distance, we can hear explosions. *Are those shots?* I ask. *They are fireworks*, the boy answers. *They are preparing for the Independence celebrations.* And he rounds this off enthusiastically: *We are going to have a flag, Dona Imani! A flag of our own!*

*You're like Germano. You've got the same smile. What's your name?*

He cups his hands to make himself heard more easily. Then he abandons this strategy and takes a pen and notebook from a case. That's how it was, I remember. That's how it was the last time, when I communicated with Captain António Sérgio de Sousa. He scribbles short sentences, his fingers cause time to tremble. The handwriting is the same as mine! But the inevitable happens once more: The letters are visible up until the point someone writes them down. Then they become blurred. I pretend I can decipher his name, I don't want the boy to give up. I smile and invite him to come in.

I lead him down the hallway. I don't remember whether I'm ill. Age has transformed my whole body into an illness.

*I'm a writer*, my visitor declares.

The boy may be yelling at the top of his voice, but I listen to him as if he were expressing himself in the gentlest of tones. That's how the whites in the city talk, they're not like us, who communicate with each other by shouting. For the more educated Portuguese, talking loud is considered vulgar. For us, when the Portuguese talk quietly, it is proof they have something to hide.

We come to an inner courtyard where there are piles of pestles, saucepans, plates, and chickens. My grandson must be surprised. He has come from the city, maybe he even came from Portugal. He never imagined there would be a house made of concrete in such a remote village. *This is the house of the Nsambe*, I tell him, *what remains of your family.*

From the outside, you would never think that our dwelling would enclose such a spacious yard. In the shade of a mango tree, there are various women seated. They are my nieces. I call them my "umbrellas." Because they are all penumbra. There they are, draped out and still, as if anticipating their eventual fate in that living soil.

I hear these shadows suddenly shout: *Ubuyile, mulungo!* They warn me that a white man has arrived. As if I were completely blind. *My dear girls*, I tell them, *I'm not dead yet. My sight isn't so good, but I can still hear.*

They laugh, amused. *Wait*, I exclaim, my arm raised. *Let me explain: It's just that even when they're not talking, you can hear a white from afar.* And I know what I'm talking about: I spent decades with them, in their country. I speak, think, and live like they do. I'm black, that's true. But I enter and leave my race when I want.

*This fellow who has just arrived isn't a white*, I affirm. *It's my grandson. Do you understand?*

My grandson—how I long to call him by his name!—greets the shadows. The women, still seated, return his greeting. And they introduce themselves one by one. They are my distant daughters, they carry the blood of my father and Bibliana in them. They came from the Save valley, where they were born and to which they will never return. Now their only activity is waiting. They are waiting for me to die so that they can sell the family house. They wait like jackals: Their footsteps are silent, like those of an approaching killer. It is not so much a wait as an ambush. While they were waiting, these women had children. The boys ran away to the city. The daughters stayed behind and turned into new shadows. The most beautiful and seductive of these gets up to greet the visitor.

*My name is Moₓi.* She shimmies her words as if twirling her skirt. Then excusing herself, she addresses me: *I can help in the conversation, Grandma Imani.*

*I don't need anyone,* I assure her firmly. *I'm going inside because out here there are more mouths than there are ears.*

Mozi walks in front of us, leading us down a dark corridor that smells of the sea. I know what the writer is thinking. He must find it strange: With the sea so far away, where is that smell coming from? It can only come from Mozi's hair. The sound of seashells cascades over her shoulders. And her whole being is a wave that has been released by the ocean. Mozi's hips grip the stranger's eyes. And he looks down in order to save himself.

Eventually, we arrive at my room, the only part of the house where age forgets me. Although I find it hard to accept, the presence of this niece of mine is in fact opportune. For some mysterious reason, Mozi is the only person I can listen to without having to make an effort. Words uttered by her gain a strangely sonorous quality. In fact, she is like me in every way. Everyone says: Mozi is me, at another age. This comparison tickles my vanity but at the same time fills me with fury. We get old and what we least want is a mirror.

*That's a lovely name, Mozi,* my grandson remarks. *I guess it's a diminutive of the word "Mozambique."*

Mozi smiles. Her laughter is like a palm tree at an oasis: It wants to be seen, but at the same time, it wants to blind whoever sets eyes on it. She walks around my room, swirling her skirt. This whole exhibition tires me. I address my grandson peevishly:

*Have you come to stay here?*

*Stay here?* he asks.

*If you haven't come to stay with us, you can go.*

My grandniece exchanges confidentialities with the writer.

Then she turns to me, summarizing their conversation. *This man wants Grandma to tell her story.* She whispers into my ear: The writer thinks I was the emperor Ngungunyane's wife. I'm the only survivor of his more than three hundred wives.

*Do you want me to tell my story?* I ask.

*May I record you, Dona Imani?*

Excited, my grandson starts fiddling with cables and buttons. Then he starts recording even before I feel like speaking. The spool starts turning sleepily. My eyelids already feel heavy when Mozi nudges me and urges: *Tell him, Grandma, because I want to listen too!*

Here is what happened to me, dear grandson: When I was fifteen, I had a child. Days later, they stole the little boy from me and sent me to the island of São Tomé, in the middle of the Atlantic Ocean. I stayed on that island for fifteen years. After the proclamation of the Portuguese Republic in 1911, they sent for me and the queens who were accompanying me. They said they were going to transfer us back to Mozambique. Ten wives had arrived on that island, and now only seven returned. Queen Dabondi, my beloved Dabondi, was one of those who stayed behind, buried in the island. Whoever loses their life on an island does not know how to come back from death. Their spirit roams in the mists, without knowing whether it belongs to the land or the sea.

The ship that came to fetch us stopped in Lisbon. For fifteen years, I had dreamed of going back there. Or rather, that was the only destination in my dreams. I did the sums: five thousand four hundred nights, five thousand four hundred dreams. All of them identical: I rescuing my son, he nestling in my arms, as if returning in his entirety to my body.

During the few hours the ship was docked in Lisbon, I was

allowed to visit my mother-in-law's house. I was escorted there by a sergeant in the navy. My intention was to reclaim my son, my Sanga, and take him with me to Mozambique. My heart was throbbing when a boy opened the door to the Melo family home. I contained myself, my hands so tense that they even hurt my fingers. Germano's mother, Dona Laura, was in bed and it was my son who led me to her room. I followed him silently, looking at the silhouette of that boy who had once inhabited my flesh. Lying in her bed, her eyes closed, Germano's mother declared defiantly:

*Show that woman who your only true mother is.*

My son, without uttering a word, went and stood next to his grandmother's bed. I looked down, my eyes full of tears. I have died, I thought to myself. There's nothing left for me to do except to go. But how was I going to walk if I wasn't even alive? Clearing her throat, Dona Laura made a sign for me to approach her. Still prostrate, she held out her hand and fondled my shoulder. Then she murmured: *You've been away for fifteen years. Think of this boy, my dear. Think and then answer me: Is there another mother in this room apart from me?*

She opened her eyes and gazed at me for a while. She knew we would never see each other again. *No one is at fault in this story*, she said. *It was life that made its choice*, she added. I shook my head, suggesting that I didn't want to listen. But I let her keep her hand on my shoulder.

*So what name did you give him, Dona Laura?*

*The same one you gave him*, Laura answered. *He is our Sanga.*

And Germano? I wanted to ask. But I didn't have the voice for it. And it was as if Laura guessed my unsaid questions. For she murmured: *My Germano arrives next week, he is very sick. He doesn't even have the strength to write. But even so, he religiously sent an allowance for his son, every month without fail* . . . And then she corrected herself: . . . *for* your *son.*

As we returned to the ship, it wasn't just I who was weeping. The sergeant modestly shared my handkerchief. We walked along the Estrada das Laranjeiras and, at a certain point, the soldier paused in order to say: *It was here, right here that he killed himself!* And before I could question him, he explained: *Mouzinho de Albuquerque, it was here that he died.*

He brushed his fingers over the paving stones as if he could feel the blood. *These stones were his resting place*, the sergeant commented. *There were stories going around about how Mouzinho acted inhumanely in his African campaigns. The one who exposed him was my commanding officer, Captain Andrea, who was also out there . . .*

On the quayside, the sergeant said goodbye to me with an unexpected handshake. Maybe that marine was experiencing something new: respect for the sadness of a black woman. Incapable of expressing words of consolation, he attempted a distraction.

*And Gungunhana? Do you know what happened to him?* he asked. *Gungunhana, the king of the blacks . . .*

After all those years, I had long given up correcting the name Ngungunyane. But this time, out of respect for the person asking the question, I put the soldier right on his pronunciation. *They all died*, I said dryly. *The king of Gaza died, his son died, his uncle died. The only one who found happiness survived: Zixaxa. The last time I heard from him, he was about to have a son. A mulatto son, like my Sanga.*

The turning of the tape on the recorder makes me sleepy. I make to get to my feet so as to ward off this gentle feeling of indolence. But my body doesn't obey me. And I fall back into my seat. My eyes closed, I caress the arm of my chair as if I were returning a gesture of affection.

*How long have you been living in this house?*
*I don't live in it. I am this house.*

I repeat that I am this house, and these items of furniture are my sisters. I have wooden relatives who have never stopped keeping me company. *You should learn, my grandson,* I continue. *More than people, make sure you gain the affection of furniture. A bed and chairs,* I assure him, *are the things that remain the most faithful to us until the end of our days. Pray for the souls of things, my dear grandson.*

*Can we continue our recording, Dona Imani?*

I shake my head fiercely and firmly. I am tired. I see him take a camera out of his rucksack. I cover my face with my arms. Then I complain, mounting a determined resistance. My protest is a lengthy one, but my grandson listens without interrupting me. At the end, fascinated, he exclaims: *That's such a beautiful thing you've just said! Do you want to hear it?* he asks. *I just had to record it all,* he justifies himself. I feel embarrassed when I listen to my own voice with the volume turned up:

*You can record me but don't take photographs. Take a good look at me, my dear grandson. This creature you see in front of you isn't made of one body alone. There are a lot of bodies stuck together, each one fashioned in its own time, each one coming from a different land. The heart belongs to this village, the arms are from Mutimati, the legs have forgotten where they are from. Don't photograph me, grandson. This body is made of broken fragments. The people who are the most alive in me are those who have already died: the mothers who still give birth to me. The first, Chikaʒi Nsambe, and then the others, Bibliana, Bianca, Dabondi. Don't photograph me, grandson. Because I don't end in me. My body is now the whole world.*

The recording ends, the tapes keep turning in the emptiness. *And Gungunhana?* my grandson asks. *I don't know,* I reply. *I only know my story.*

The sound of the spools begins to fill the room. I ask Sanga if he ever met Germano. *Who?* he asks. *Your grandfather Germano,* I explain. He shakes his head, smiling. *And Bianca, have you ever heard of her?* I ask again. But I don't wait for an answer. I am suddenly assailed by an unusual feeling of anger: I attack the table in front of me with my feet. The tape recorder and camera crash to the floor. My grandson takes a step backward, between fear and astonishment.

*Don't turn up here again with those machines! Never again!* I yell.

I try to get up, but not even my fury is of any help. I remain sunken in my old leather armchair. I am imprisoned behind the grille of my body.

Mozi contemplates me in my chair, shakes her head impatiently, and asks the visitor to leave us alone. She tells him to wait in the yard. The writer gathers up his equipment and withdraws, with a deeper stoop than when he arrived. The moment the door closes, Mozi rushes at me. She is angry. I don't understand, she argues, that this is the chance of a lifetime. And I am just throwing it all away.

*Just pretend, Grandma. Is it so hard? Admit you were Ngungunyane's wife . . .*

She stubbornly tries to convince me. If I just put on a bit of a performance, we Nsambe would gain huge privileges. We would belong to the family of heroes, we would earn a fortune, travel to the capital, who knows, they might even take us to the Azores!

*Listen carefully, Grandma,* Mozi persists, now in a more mellifluous tone. *I'm going to tell you what to say to the writer . . .*

*He's not a writer, he's my grandson.*

*Grandson, great-grandson, great-great-grandson . . . You're going to tell all of them you were the king's wife. And you're going to tell them a story . . .*

*I'm not going to start lying at the age of ninety-five.*

*If you don't want to lie*, Mozi complains, *then stop calling that boy your grandson.*

She heads for the door, but hurls one final threat back at me: *Don't forget, Grandma: We are the ones who look after you!* And she furiously slams the door behind her. I sit there for a moment alone. I have never been so alone. And never has solitude felt so good.

I open the back door and slip out into the street. I leave the house for the first time in many years. And I follow the same path our mother took when she went to get firewood. I walk aimlessly, like children do when they take their first steps. I just want to get away from the house, get away from myself. On the corner, I almost stumble over a group of children sitting on the ground and playing a game. They are poor children, dirty and badly dressed. I remember the time when I was a little girl and think to myself: Even during the cruelest war, even among the ruins and the ashes, children never stop playing.

All of a sudden a fleeting shadow knocks me over. I'm so thin that I never seem to stop falling. And then I see a military truck full of guerrilla fighters passing by like a metal monster. I once again see the troubled times of my childhood. The difference is that there is more ground now, a ground that is calling my name.

I return home, supported by the young writer who has just saved me from being run over. *Come, Grandma!* he urges me. The boy is calling me "Grandma." He is calling me "Grandma" and the streets are once again mine. In the grounds of the house, we pass the old anthill. They cemented over the ground but left that sacred spot alive. They were afraid of lacking respect. The termite mound still survives there, sustaining the leafy mafura tree. They no longer tie white cloths to it. No one speaks to the ancestors anymore. I am the only one who does, and I am almost dead.

I ask the writer to wait for me. I return soon afterward, carrying a suitcase. *Is it heavy?* he asks, rushing to help me. At my age, everything is heavy, starting with my own arms. I empty the contents of the case. The ground is covered in papers. *They're yours, these notebooks,* I tell him. *All my bits of writing are here, the letters I kept, my whole life is here. Take these notebooks and publish them if you think they deserve to be known. You can claim authorship, I don't care. Just as long as you say you are my grandson, the grandson of Imani Nsambe.*

The writer steps forward, sits down, and starts to read the first notebook. As he reads, I nestle up to him as if I am seeking my final shadow in his body:

*Each morning, seven suns would rise over the plains of Inharrime. In those times, the firmament was much larger, and all the stars were contained within it, the living and the dead. Naked just as she had slept, our mother would leave the house, a sieve in her hand. She was going to choose the best of the suns. With her sieve, she would gather up the remaining six stars and bring them back to the village. She would bury them next to the anthill behind our house. That was our graveyard for heavenly creatures. One day, if we ever needed to, we would go and unearth the stars.*

# GLOSSARY

This book is a work of fiction. Many of the characters and stories are, however, based on real people and historical events. The following are terms from local vernaculars, place names and ethnic groups, and characters based on known historical figures.

ÁLVARO DE OLIVEIRA SOARES DE ANDREA (1864–1939): Portuguese naval captain who served in Mozambique during the 1890s. He was a republican, and played an active role in the overthrow of the monarchy in 1910.

ANTÓNIO ENES (1848–1901): Politician, writer, and diplomat, who was High Commissioner in Mozambique between 1891 and 1895.

ANTÓNIO SÉRGIO DE SOUSA (1842–1906): Captain of the steamship *África*. He was the son of a viscount who served as governor in various colonial territories.

CALDAS XAVIER (1852–1896): Portuguese military officer who participated in the campaigns against Ngungunyane.

*CAPULANA*: Dress worn mainly by women, akin to a sarong.

*CHILODJO*: Royal crown made of animal skin and worn by the rulers of Gaza.

GUNGUNHANA: The name given to Ngungunyane by the Portuguese throughout the colonial period until 1974, after which Portuguese reincorporated the final "e" into his name: Gungunhane. Nowadays, the Mozambican spelling of his name is used in most contexts: Ngungunyane.

*IHIMPI*: Elite Nguni army division.

*IKANYAMBA*: Legendary serpent of Zulu tradition said to live in a waterfall lake.

*IMPUNDU*: Mobola-plum tree (*Parinari curatellifolia*).

*INDUNA*: Local African administrator and tax collector.

JAIME DANIEL LEOTE DO REGO (1867–1923): Portuguese naval commander in Mozambique during the 1890s, and later a politician during the First Portuguese Republic.

# GLOSSARY

*LANDINS*: Generic Portuguese term for native peoples living in southern Mozambique, some of whom were recruited into the colonial army.

LIEUTENANT AYRES DE ORNELAS (1866–1930): Soldier and politician during the final decades of the Portuguese monarchy. Took part in the campaigns headed by António Enes against Ngungunyane, and was later a protégé of Mouzinho de Albuquerque.

MABUIENDJELA: Conquered and assimilated Tsonga into Nguni culture, and incorporated into the army of the kingdom of Gaza.

MFUMO: Small state at the headwaters of the River Nkomati, in southern Mozambique, or a person from that state.

MOUZINHO DE ALBUQUERQUE (1855–1902): Portuguese cavalry officer and leader of the expedition responsible for capturing Ngungunyane.

*MPACATXU*: Small necklace worn as a protective charm.

NKOSI, NKOSIKAZI: Terms of address directed at people of high social rank among the VaNguni. In Portuguese orthography, usually spelled "Nkossi."

NGUNI, VANGUNI: Ethnic group originating in South Africa, which migrated up into southern and central Mozambique, bringing many other ethnicities under its political control.

*NYAMOSORO*: Tsonga word for a traditional healer with telepathic powers.

*PSIKWEMBO*: Ancestor gods.

*RÉGULO*: Portuguese term to describe a local ruler, often imposed by the colonial authorities, and sometimes used in a derogatory way.

ROBERTO NDEVU MACHAVA (1854–1938): Protestant missionary and purported founder of the Methodist Wesleyan Church in Mozambique.

*TINGOMA*: From the word *ngoma*, a kind of drum.

*TINTXOLO*: Small bones used by traditional healers and soothsayers.

TSONGA, VATSONGA: Ethnic group originating mainly in South Africa, southern Mozambique, and Eswatini.

TXITXOPE: Language spoken by the VaChopi.

*UKANYU*: Alcoholic drink made from the fruit of the marula tree.

*UMPHAFA*: Buffalo horn (*Ziziphus mucronata*).

VACHOPI: Known in Portuguese as Chope, an ethnic group in southeastern Mozambique, here in uneasy alliance with the Portuguese.

VANGUNI: Literally, the people of the Nguni nation.

VÁTUA: Portuguese term for the VaNguni.

*XIDZEDZE*: Tsonga word for a hurricane or strong wind.

## A Note About the Author

Mia Couto, born in Mozambique in 1955, is among the most prominent Portuguese-language writers working today. After studying medicine and biology, he worked as a journalist and headed several national newspapers and magazines in Mozambique. Couto has been awarded the Camões Prize for Literature and the prestigious Neustadt International Prize for Literature, among other awards. He was also short-listed for the 2017 International DUBLIN Literary Award and was a finalist for the Man Booker International Prize in 2015. He lives in Maputo, Mozambique, where he works as a biologist.

## A Note About the Translator

David Brookshaw is an emeritus professor at the School of Modern Languages at the University of Bristol. He has translated several other books by Mia Couto, including *Woman of the Ashes*, *Confession of the Lioness*, *The Tuner of Silences*, *A River Called Time*, and *Sleepwalking Land*.